Monogamy Twist

by

Nancy Jardine

Monogamy Twist

Contact Information: info@thewildrosepress.com

Cover Art by *Kim Mendoza*

The Wild Rose Press
PO Box 706
Adams Basin, NY 14410-0706
Visit us at www.thewildrosepress.com

Publishing History
First Champagne Rose Edition, 2011
Print ISBN 1-60154-965-2

Published in the United States of America

"I don't expect *love*, Rhia, but I do expect *sex*." He closed the gap between them and positioned himself in front of her, straddling her chair, his long legs wide balanced as he looked down at her. "If you're honest, you'll agree we have enough chemistry going on between us to ignite a bonfire."

Rhia's face flamed at his candid assessment but couldn't deny what he was saying.

"I was thinking more of a mutually agreed arrangement where we share all aspects of our lives—including sex—till the year is up." He was a mere step away.

"That sounds like I'd be a long-term whore, or a mistress!" Rhia recoiled from him.

"We'd be living together legally as man and wife." Luke bent toward her.

"For a year?" She remained rooted in place, but her whole body sizzled.

"That's what it will take to fulfill the requirements of the will. Then the property will be mine."

Barely a hairsbreadth separated them now.

Rhia was still rattled by his cold propositions, her chin hitching up again as she faced him. "You would seem to be getting a lot more out of this arrangement than I would."

Dedication

Numerous people, family and professionals,
have given me help and encouragement
to keep the writing process going.
A huge thanks to all of you!

An even bigger thank you I send to my editor,
Cindy Davis, for too many reasons to mention here!

Chapter One

"Come on, Amelia!" Repetitive swearing amplified Luke Salieri's curled fist. "You reckon I'm a sucker? Even if I am talking to a friggin' ghost?"

A response wasn't remotely reasonable because he was talking to a damp wall covering that oozed around under his warm skin, definitely not replying—just like Amelia Greywood wasn't either, for she'd been dead the best part of two weeks.

"Your conditions, Amelia, are a blo…ody insult!"

Striding to yet another room he vented even more displeasure. The bedroom was brimful of contents, as though the room was still presently lived in, yet no one had inhabited it for a very long time. Sadly it appeared that Amelia's ghost wasn't residing in it either. The house wasn't the least bit spooky but if talking to her damned spirit would conjure her up, it would be worth it—to have his questions answered. What the absolute Dickens was he going to do about this property?

"Why me, Amelia?"

Luke loathed indecision, usually avoided anything that made him feel vulnerable; this was like playing some game with pieces missing, knowing his opponent had a full deck, and that only by resorting to some kind of dishonesty would he gain success. Yet honesty was almost Luke's middle name. Straight in business, candid to a fault in his personal life. Which often pissed off his current woman of the moment.

He could easily afford to renovate this dilapidated property, but the rest of her conditions were an antiquated, potentially deceitful, nightmare.

Temper barely leashed he confronted the elusive specter, wishing he could conjure up her image, but he'd never met the blasted woman. "So, Amelia, where did you dredge up my name from?" He swept open a Victorian monstrosity of an armoire, not surprised to find it still contained flouncy dresses—moth-eaten, moldy, and smelly. "Hmm? Was it a pin on a Trades Directory? I hardly think the internet was quite your style...unless you were a very astute silver surfer?"

That notion made him groan. Could Amelia have surfed the web to find the biggest dupe? Picked for his professional expertise was the only thing that made any sense: the only thing that gave the whole ridiculous scenario any credibility.

He strode to the nearest window to get the smell of camphor balls out of his nostrils. The tall sash casements were clad with seriously distressed claret brocade drapes, so distressed the color had sun-faded to a really pale blush wine. Pushing aside more cobwebs than material, Luke flicked the catch and yanked the window open, a shard of deteriorated wood slicing his index finger.

"Blo... ody *Dannazione!*" Curses grew garbled as he sucked off dripping blood and teased out the substantial splinter with his teeth. "How could you let a stately home like this decay so much, Amelia?" He tried to force the window down again, but it refused to budge, his frustrated grunts abruptly disturbed by some wildly frenetic barking.

Che diavolo? His question fogged the windowpane. The beast making the racket was a whirling dervish frolicking over the rough grass.

Luke grinned, the whimsical interruption lifting his tension.

"Thor! Get back here now."

The peremptory command came from a woman

who was exiting the woods bordering the lawn. Luke smiled again as the excited animal completely ignored its owner, instead bounding up to the dangerously dilapidated flagstones of what had once been an impressive terrace way down below him. He considered ignoring his dilemma as well; considered making a similar swift bounce-away. *Dio!*

From his third-level vantage point the young woman again snagged his attention as she plowed across the overgrown lawn grass, an even more welcome distraction than the dog. Definitely worth watching. Her husky voice was firm.

"You went off again far too quickly, you disobedient pup."

Pup? The beast was enormous. Luke's focus zoomed in on the woman's supple breasts as they bounced in rhythm inside a tight yellow T-shirt as she capered back from the animal's attentions. Very, very nice. His palms itched and curved by his sides, his eyes appreciative. Her glistening lava-black hair settled around her face as she halted and gathered the squirming beast to her. The dog's tongue licked her face revealing the ungainly quivering of body hair as the hugely long forelegs stretched up onto her shoulders. Luke imagined his own tongue snaking across her lips as she almost overbalanced under the onslaught of adoration from the dog. She was a tiny little woman and Thor was one very big canine.

"Get down, Thor!" The melodious chime of her laughter imprinted itself somewhere inside him as she thrust the hound down to ground level. "You're not a little pup any more."

Thor? A good name for a powerful beast, Luke thought, watching her rub the dog's underside. Unconsciously scratching his own belly he adjusted his stance at the window, the denim of his jeans a little too tight now as he enjoyed her pert backside.

Perfect for his hands to cradle. His imagination surged. The heat of the sun blasting through the window was more than a match for his spiking internal temperature.

"Who are you, a woodland fairy?" Luke's question misted the filthy pane. *Dio!*

The little pixie below made quite an impact on him. She had appeared suddenly out of the woods.

His harsh laugh echoed around him in the empty room. Was his fatigue so bad he was hallucinating? An ironic burst peeled out again, loud enough to perk up the dog's ears but not loud enough to betray his location. *Cristo!* He really did need a woman.

Warf! Warf! No quiet barking from this particular canine.

"Come on. Time to go, Thor."

Who was the woman? She ushered the animal back to the woods. What was she doing on the grounds of Greywood Hall?

Realizing he wanted answers to those questions, Luke erupted into the corridor taking the treads on the central staircase two at a time, trusting they'd not collapse under his pounding feet as he hurried outside.

Damnation! He'd missed her. There was no sign of her as he scanned the gardens.

Rhia was inside the tree cover when Thor's ears pricked up. "What is it?" She turned back to check. "What are you hearing, Thor?" It wasn't the first time she'd had to prevent him from chasing scuttling bunnies on the scraggy lawn.

Not this time. It was no animal Thor heard through the protective shadow of the trees. Someone stood beside the right hand staircase. Where the hell had he come from? Something akin to jealousy jolted through her. In all the months she and Thor had been coming into the garden she'd never seen anyone around. She'd become so used to using the deserted woods and garden for their walks that she'd come to think of this beautiful but very sadly neglected place as her own. It was outrageous to see someone else here—looking so furtive and obviously up to no good!

Bristling with righteous indignation she tracked the figure peering through every window as he rounded the front of the house and made his way along the side wall. Lurking behind a large oak near the edge of the woods her breath hitched, a feeling of alarm pricking her senses—yet curiosity overrode danger. She wasn't the bravest woman on the planet but she was no coward, and frankly, she was very interested in his stealthy intentions.

"Quiet, Thor!" She clutched both his collar and his long pelt, needing his absolute obedience. Sneaking along the fringes of the wood to the walled garden she approached the house without being visible on the front grass. She might want to know what the stranger was doing, but she wasn't prepared to alert him to her presence. Thor padded at her side as she crept along the cracked paving of the walled garden, quelling the mild flutter of dangerous exhilaration.

He was a big strapping guy. Dark hair, long enough to touch the neck of his shirt, curled appealingly at his nape, the hair above it very thick and inclined to naturally wave. Rhia's lips softened, fancying the idea of running her fingers through the tousled thickness.

"Take a look at him!" Rhia whispered as his soft polo shirt pulled across his powerful shoulders when he stretched up as high as he could reach, his brawny torso hiding most of each window. Her fertile imagination surged into overdrive, startling her for she didn't know she had a lust-driven imagination. Her focus shifted lower as he moved to the next window—the below waist back view just as appealing: neat jeans tapering over strong, long legs. "Sexy devil!" she whispered.

Just short of the kitchen door he placed his hands on the sill of a fairly narrow window. He disappeared, agilely vaulting inside. Why the heck was he trying all the other windows if he knew that particular one was already open?

"The bloody…" her voice hiked a fraction before she prudently amended her volume, "…cheek of him."

But what was she thinking of, drooling over some unknown intruder? The man was breaking and entering, for goodness sake. Possessiveness strummed her nerve ends again. What the hell did he think he was doing?

Rhia's heart skyrocketed as his head popped out the window again. She didn't want to believe what she'd fleetingly glimpsed. He couldn't possibly be that good-looking. Her pulse thumped with distress, so much that she thought she just might pass out or make some other stupid histrionic action like scream her lungs out: "Holy shit! He's seriously gorgeous." Squeezing her eyes shut, she blocked out his image. It was just her luck that she should find the man a stunner. Rhia faced her dilemma for she had to turn him in to the police.

Once in the safety of the woods she pulled out her cell phone hating what she had to do to such a gorgeous piece of manhood. She motioned Thor to heel and made the surreal and confusing call.

"Yes, I'm perfectly safe here in the woods," she reassured the dispatcher. "I'm pretty sure the intruder hasn't a clue I'm here." She winced when she was asked for her best description of the man, giving as practical a description as possible, inherently glad the dispatcher couldn't see the aroused blush that burned her cheeks, or the puckering of her perked nipples.

General questions about Greywood Hall were followed by probing inquiries about her own presence there, the implications of which were disturbing. “Well, yes we do...that is, my dog and I squeeze through a little gap in the boundary wall so he can exercise safely in the wood rather than on the busy lane.”

The dispatcher’s voice was disheartening. “Miss Ashton, are you confirming that without the owner’s permission you regularly exercise your dog on this property?”

Guilt crushed her as Rhia replied, “I’ve told you. I’m the nearest neighbor to Greywood Hall.” The line beeped furiously...then nothing. Something about those last questions made her feel really uncomfortable. “Well, that was just blo...ody dandy!” Her concern manifestly superfluous she ordered Thor back to heel. “Home time, Thor!”

A short while later, on approaching the main drive to Greywood Hall, Rhia was stunned to see someone had forced the ancient padlock open, leaving it dangling from the huge chain, and now the rusty gates were wide open. It was only when Thor nudged her onto the short embankment she realized a checkered police patrol car was coming to a halt beside her, the front passenger window partially open.

“Excuse me, miss? Would you be Rhia Ashton of Border Cottage?”

“Yes.” Rhia’s voice was strained as she bent toward the officer to reply. “I am.” Her knees wobbled: it was definitely far too late to wish the Neighborhood Watch Cap had not been donned!

“You recently made an emergency call?”

“I... Yes. I did.”

The torrent of irate Italian that blasted out from the back of the car froze Rhia to her very marrow. It sounded pretty fluent, but devastating, as the malice-ridden tirade was directed straight at her. She knew holiday phrases like please and thank you, and not much else, but was absolutely sure some of the words coming at her wouldn't be found in an ordinary dictionary.

"*Una sciocchezza!*"

Rhia reeled away from the thankfully still-closed back window as the intruder changed to just as loud English. "This is absolute nonsense. You're the one who informed the police?"

She was transfixed for the handsome face she'd glimpsed earlier wasn't quite so appealing now. What the hell made her think he was good looking? Thor growled alongside her baring his teeth as he propped his paws on the door, his bulk a defensive bulwark.

"I watched you down there on the lawn with that huge apology for a dog and you have the nerve to call the police about me!"

The man was really angry. Rhia had no doubt he was incensed that she'd had the effrontery to call the police about him.

"Be quiet please, sir!" The constable's peremptory tone was ignored as the intruder's mixture of mumbled Italian and English continued to berate her.

He crept forward in his seat forcing her to shrink back from the car. Tracking his sturdy fingers as they reached forward to grasp the sides of the headrest behind the uniformed officer Rhia fantasized them grasping themselves around her slender neck, stifling the life out of her.

"Sit back please, sir, and let us deal with this matter."

Rhia's manic vision shattered, the constable's stern voice jolting her back to the present as the intruder slinked back under the officer's unyielding glare.

"We'll need you to accompany us to the police station, Miss Ashton. We have a few matters to sort out about Greywood Hall, but please take the hound home first."

Belatedly aware the officer had raised the car window to almost the top the minute Thor's paws touched the side of the vehicle, Rhia managed a dumb nod. Grabbing Thor's long hair she stumbled off the verge on rickety legs, lurching along the short distance to her cottage on autopilot. How dare the burglar be so angry? With her!

The low grumble of the police vehicle slithered down her back as it tailed her back to her cottage. They were going to ask all sorts of questions about why she was on the premises. Guilt gripped her in a vice for breaking some kind of law was a dead cert. Securing Thor in the fenced off enclosure in her back garden she returned to the squad car.

"Thank you for that, Miss Ashton." The constable's tone was brisk but there was no anger in it as he got out of the vehicle to open the back door for her. "If you wouldn't mind getting in please, then we can be off."

Chapter Two

"You're expecting me to get in with...him?"

Luke's anger dissipated into a little quirk of satisfaction. It didn't take much effort to read into the little pixie's expression that she was completely appalled at the request.

"Come along, Miss Ashton." The constable was firm. "We need to talk to you both back at the police station but it will take a while before another vehicle can be put at our disposal for you to be transported separately."

Rhia Ashton was still not placated, her panic evident in the wide brown eyes that were too scared to look properly at anyone. The officer's tone lightened a little and grew more cajoling. Luke suppressed a snarl at the new strategy.

"So let's get on and sort out this little misunderstanding." The officer just about corralled her into the car. "We've already discussed this with Mr. Salieri and we know you'll be perfectly safe, so don't you worry now."

Right at that moment Rhia Ashton's horror indicated she didn't think much of his reasoning. Did she think he was any happier as she was poured in beside him?

He definitely was infuriated that she had informed the police about him. He fully understood the reticence of the officers to accept him at face value, grimly acknowledging that he didn't, at this moment, look in the least like the millionaire head of a very successful construction corporation. Though completely demeaning, being conducted to the local police station was the quickest and most expedient way they could verify the details about his potential ownership of Greywood Hall. But he didn't have to like it! Being escorted in a police car didn't sit at all well—with or without Miss Pixie Ashton right next to him.

Rhia Ashton scuttled like a mouse beside him, cowering into as tiny a space as possible on the far side of the bench seat. What the devil did she think he was going to do to her? "*Madre di Dio!*" His angry Italian muttering accompanied frustrated thrusts of his fingers through his thick dark hair, expecting the locks to stay off his forehead as he shook his head in disbelief.

He was in a police car with two police officers in the front! Did she think he was stupid enough to attack her or something equally dire? Presently he would quite happily wring her neck and ignore the fact that it was a very tasty little morsel. How could the woman look so good and be so dense at the same time? First she thought he was a burglar. And now some perverted attacker.

He actually did want to pounce on her but not quite the way she was most likely thinking from the scowls she was giving him. Up close like this, his body involuntarily reacted even more than the distant sight of her from the upstairs window had engendered. He'd been right about her face. It was utter perfection; just like the little pixie he'd thought her to be; flawless skin but now so pale. Her eyes were absolutely gorgeous, a death-by-chocolate brown with tiny little flecks of grey. The fact that she was so disturbed cheered him. Leisurely crossing his arms to keep temptation at bay his features relaxed. He smiled at her but it was a calculating, scheming smile because she really didn't know what she was in for, this little fairy of the woods.

"Soon be at the station, Mr. Salieri," the

constable up front briefly informed him, breaking into his train of thought. “We’ll have this little misunderstanding sorted out soon enough.”

Luke continued to stare at Rhia Ashton. A short little name. Rhia. It really suited her. It had a nice tinkling sound but admiring her name and super-tempting physical attributes was one thing; thinking about her damned interfering behavior was quite another. What had the infernal woman done? Poking her nose—albeit a dinky button of a nose—into his business?

“What a waste of damned time!” His reproach came through grated teeth as she nervously twitched next to him, her neck muscles straining to keep herself facing rigidly forward. “What the hell did you think you were doing?” He made his low pitch fiercely commanding, and he didn’t care one iota if he was upsetting her for she’d just caused him no end of hassle. “What the blazes were you thinking of? They thought I was a burglar. *Dio Santo*!” Luke ground out, moving another tiny bit closer to the quivering jelly beside him. “What made you think I was breaking and entering the property?”

He waited more than a trifle impatiently for a reply that didn’t come; his intent gaze focused on her still all-too-delicious face before eventually acknowledging his insistent pressure wasn’t working. The woman refused to even make eye contact with him, never mind tightly buttoning her still tempting little lips. It was time to change tack. He’d learned that technique early on in business. Bring on the personal! Biting back residual anger he opted for more subtle persuasion.

“Tell me, Rhia…” He softened his tone to a mesmerizing murmur, his aim this time to envelope her in his spell. “Tell me why, Rhia.” The change of pitch worked surprisingly well. Much to his delight, as her pixie face whipped toward him.

"But you are a burglar!" Eyes blazing with accusation she elaborated, "I saw you. You climbed in the window that you'd already forced open. And before that I watched you try all the downstairs windows."

Luke processed her words, flicking his eyes once, then drew his eyebrows together in a slight frown. "So that makes me a burglar?"

He moved back from her. He tightened his lips, a slight downturn appearing at the corners when all his remaining irritation turned to pure frustration. The prior softening leeched from his tone as he scolded, "You don't have a damned clue!" His determined whispers had hit the mark—her cheeks flushed. But his frustration deepened when she refused to speak again, regardless of his immense effort to sound more rational, her little pointed chin resolutely stuck up in the air.

Luke stopped whispering but kept staring, sexually cataloguing every one of her features and not even trying to be subtle about it, for he'd already given up attempting to control his responses to this woman. He didn't understand himself at all—what kind of moron got aroused, in a police car, *Madre di Dio*, by an interfering woman who'd just had him arrested. His bold stares paid off though when her eyes clashed with his for a fraction of a second before she dropped her gaze.

Wow! Luke couldn't prevent the grin that spread across his face when the little pixie's eyes momentarily fixed on his groin. Then she blushed like a lantern flare. He smiled in sheer satisfaction. So, the little minx was aware of him too. Useful to know. For later.

Sliding down slightly on the seat he lounged, deliberately outlining his bulge, his arms folded across his considerable chest. He rested his head on the seat back and closed his eyes, the lack of sleep catching up a trifle. He chuckled again; it had been a long time since he'd been near a woman who could color up like that. It made him want to get to know her.

Moments later the car swerved round an almost right-angled bend, hurtling him across the seat, his seatbelt stretching to its limit as he laid across her.

He could probably have avoided some of the contact, but it was just too tempting, too fortuitous, and much too appealing. So, he relaxed any instinct to halt his sideward lurch...and found her soft breast. Fantastic!

"Get off me you big oaf!"

From a very awkward, yet totally luscious, position Luke raised his eyes to her outraged face. He couldn't—didn't even want to—attempt to expunge the entertainment from his eyes, but her indignant command deserved some response. Right beside his cheek her nipples were almost poking holes in the cloth of her thin T-shirt. Her deliciously fresh-meadow smell might have been a laundry product, or her unique fragrance, Luke didn't care. It filled his nostrils and fired his loins. How could he not nuzzle a little as he slowly unfurled his crossed arms? The temptation was far too much to deny as he used her quivering leg muscle as a prop to push himself upright, her gasp of arousal at his effrontery the most entertaining thing he'd experienced in ages. He chuckled again as he attempted an apology. But before he could mouth it a laugh bellowed from the driver.

"Sorry Mr. Salieri! I should have warned you about that corner."

The pixie's body language indicated a near combustion.

He pulled his grin back into order. "Sorry about that."

His apology, it seemed, wasn't quite sincere

enough for her face was still flustered, her eyes furious but Luke was on a roll. He definitely wanted to get to know this creature much more intimately. His none-too-subtle wink was the icing on the cake.

"Stop that right now!"

Her husky command, uttered through clenched teeth amused him even more but he deduced it wasn't at all appreciated for Rhia Ashton turned her back on him, resolutely peering out of the window, hopefully to cool her fired-up senses.

Chuckling again, he settled back into his end of the seat, hoping the journey wouldn't last too much longer, yet wanting it to be contrarily long enough to quell his flaring desire for this strange woman.

A police car was not the best venue for a thorough exploration of her enchanting curves. He closed his eyes again and slid into a delicious daydream, drifting to horizontal surfaces and lots of bare skin, some of it still blushing rosily, and smelling delightfully. At first he didn't attempt to suppress the arousal that gained even more strength until with a few savage Italian curses he willed his thoughts elsewhere...Greywood Hall. What the hell was he going to do about that?

Christo! He really did need a woman, soon.

Some time later Rhia found herself the sole occupant of a tiny interview room where she'd been dumped after a brief identification process and even more brief questions about her call to the dispatcher. Why had they left her stewing? Was this part of normal procedure? She hadn't a clue since she'd never been in a police station before and didn't know what kind of crime they thought she had committed.

Dog fouling? Well hell! They could get her on that one. She'd allowed that repeatedly; how was she to stop Thor from doing a bit of business in the wood? Sometimes it happened on the lane—her pooper-scooper always at the ready, but in the wood?

That was a different matter entirely. Could they charge her for being on private property? Holy shit! That one was a definite yes.

Unfortunately the solitude gave her far too much time to reflect on the bizarre happenings of the afternoon. In a very opposing way it had been both the most exciting day, and the most perplexing one she'd had in years. Another shudder trickled down her spine, this time a physical re-creation of her earlier almost-out-of-control feelings. In the rear seat of the patrol car her responses to the gorgeous but crooked Mr. Salieri had been a volatile mixture of stimulation and dread.

He stopped his relentless questioning after she'd continued to ignore him; the embarrassing silence in the back seat continued the rest of the way to the police station, interspersed by the low murmurs of the officers and the incomprehensible crackle of the police radio. Silence the rest of the way, except when the burglar's face slammed into her chest.

Had she called him an oaf? Yep! But he deserved it. He hadn't even acknowledged her shocked outburst at the driver's apology. Mr. Salieri had merited it? She didn't think so! If she hadn't been so fired up the injustice of the constable's apology would have made her blood roil.

The physical contact made by the collision had been so annoyingly arousing. She'd felt the exhalation of Mr. Salieri's breath on the sensitive curve of her breast right through the cotton T-shirt, a little puff that had iced her nipple. His cheek had twitched against her. The little olive flecks in his grass-green eyes intensified as he glanced up at her face, so close she could see the new stubble on his cheeks and the soft skin of his lips. Close enough to smell the remnants of a woodsy fragrance, or maybe that had just been his naturally enticing male scent. It didn't matter. It had hit her senses like a sledgehammer even more powerfully than his cheek on her flesh.

"Sorry about that," he'd muttered but his apology hadn't sounded at all regretful. Besides, his lips curling up in an inscrutable smile said otherwise. The cheek-nudging had been followed by blatant nose-nuzzling. The nestling into her breast as he uncrossed his arms and righted himself, his strong fingers gripping her thigh as he regained balance and languorously pressed his way upright, had been impossible to ignore.

The memory warmed her all over again...right below her navel, and down to her very toenails. Her thigh muscles cramped with sensual reminiscence, her nipples tightened. He'd been playing her like a violin; she knew it but had been unable to stop it. She hadn't expected any of the capricious feelings that crowded her.

But neither did she expect the officer's words on his return to the interview room. "Miss Ashton. Thanks for your cooperation. I'm sorry we've kept you waiting so long, but it seems we don't need to talk to you any more about your presence at Greywood Hall. We've a patrol car waiting outside to take you home, so if you'll come this way please?"

"I'm not in the habit of thanking anyone for arresting me, but this time I will." Luke beamed as the officers dropped him off beside his own car back at Greywood Hall. "This time you've done me a big favor!"

He waved them off as he clicked his Ferrari open. His journey to the police station hadn't been a waste of time after all: in fact it was the catalyst needed to make him determined to keep Greywood Hall with all its ridiculous restrictions.

Once his status as prospective owner of the estate had been verified he'd initiated some official local notifications and had begun the processes for gaining authorized permits for a variety of transport requirements.

There were only a few minor details to organize. Well, more than a few, but Luke's grin was wide with no hint of possible failure tainting it. Climbing inside his car he whipped out his cell phone, powered it on, and placed a call.

"Hi, Jeremy!" Barely drawing breath Luke reeled off instructions. "Get Braydon Security. Request immediate details on a Miss Rhia Ashton of Border Cottage." Jeremy's quick question was fielded. "Yes. It's the same postal area as Greywood Hall. I want everything they can find within the hour." A quick update on his movements that day was followed by a long list of tasks, Luke's PA asking few questions. "No," Luke responded to the last one. "Nothing's wrong with my cell phone. I switched it off after our last call while I was assessing the property."

"You switched it off?"

Luke grinned at the total disbelief coming from Jeremy, unsurprised by his PA's next statement. "I've dealt with what's been forwarded, but you'll have some pile to deal with on your own voice-mail now!"

A little pause followed. Luke killed time, his smile widening, since he knew Jeremy wasn't quite done yet.

"Was the place so awful then?"

"Big updates on that later," Luke snorted. Jeremy, his PA of five years, always knew when to be diplomatic. "Let's just say some unplanned hitches held me up. I'll likely give a green light on it, but the decision's still a little undecided." Jeremy's professionalism was what he paid well for as the conversation switched straight back to business matters. "Sure, give me those details now."

He snatched a pen from the glove compartment

then lifted a file from the stack on the passenger seat and located the sheets he required. Noting the particulars given, he added the information and fielded numerous questions about other business matters. Then, satisfied with what had just been set up, he finished the call, "By the way Jeremy, don't have a heart attack if my cell phone is switched off again later this afternoon."

Luke clicked off his phone; his reply to Jeremy's last question had been evasive. Did something at Greywood Hall require more of his time and attention? Yes, something did, but nothing directly to do with the building itself, like Jeremy had implied.

Time spent having a little sexual dalliance with the delicious Miss Rhia Ashton was quite appealing. He didn't want to discount the possibility of getting to know Rhia Ashton carnally.

An hour and a half later, a bundle of other calls accomplished—some made and some received—he was ready to take up the challenge of Greywood Hall.

Turning his car he headed for Border Cottage. What he now knew about Rhia Ashton was ideal; in fact might have been tailor made for him. At the same time, the quandary regarding Greywood Hall might be solved—if he could coerce Miss Ashton to fit in with the plans he'd just made, precious time wouldn't be wasted finding another substitute.

Finding another substitute would be a breeze, but finding a suitable one could take quite a while! Time he didn't have. The women in his social sphere were generally unsuitable for the bizarre requirements imposed by the very-dead Amelia Greywood.

Bizarre requirements?

Had it only been a little more than a day since this farcical merry-go-round started? Luke's growl filled the car interior as he reviewed the recent events. The day before had in many ways ended up just as unpredictable as today's mistaken arrest. Yesterday had been going according to plan as he journeyed back to London, but once he reached his London office, the rest of the day hadn't quite panned out as he intended.

"You've been bequeathed the property in the Yorkshire Dales known as Greywood Hall," stated his lawyer, John McBride.

"You're friggin' joking!" he refuted the declaration, though John was a friend as well as a colleague. He wouldn't pull a joke of this magnitude. "I don't know anybody called Amelia Greywood."

"That may be the case Luke, but you are specified, listed as beneficiary of Miss Greywood's will. There's no doubt the property has been bequeathed to you. There are no further beneficiaries involved as the small monetary gifts to Beechlee Nursing Home staff have been dispensed with, all in accordance with the will."

"Surely there must have been some other relative or friend the property could have been left to?"

"No. Miss Greywood's instructions are unambiguous. You're the main and only remaining beneficiary."

John went on to spell out the terms of the will in detail so there would be no misunderstandings. After pacing his spacious office for a few stunned minutes, during which time John maintained a discreetly polite silence, Luke ceased his tramping. Some very necessary questions needed further clarification. Bracing his hands on his desk, his questions barked out, "Let me get this straight. The whole property is approximately ninety acres. Ninety acres?" John's nod encouraged him to continue. "Okay, 90 acres including the main house, and various outbuildings.

Some of the land is currently leased out." His mood had been skeptical. "It will be mine along with the small sum of six thousand, four hundred and twenty four pounds?"

John McBride's expression wavered from a frozen blank mask, the wince only just discernible. "You're being obtuse, Luke. I've made it clear that could be the case after one year."

"It could be? In one year!" Luke stomped a few more steps and continued, "You're also telling me that although my name is indisputably on that will, I can't dispose of it just now as I see fit?" He'd clumped around a bit more as he'd pondered the rest of the unwelcome revelations of the will.

John had cleared his throat. "That's correct, Luke. The property will be yours to deal with as you choose, but only if you use it for a period of one calendar year as a personal domicile in cohabitation with your spouse. And…if that period of residence is initiated within one month from today. That's thirty-one days from now."

"Bloody hell, John! You know I don't have a friggin' wife, and I've no intention of getting one any time soon, so I'm not likely to fulfill that little gem, am I?"

John again cleared his throat before adding, "We've tried to find a way around this term, but it's watertight and incontrovertible."

"Probably much more watertight than the property itself, I imagine?"

"As to that I couldn't say. My information states that Miss Greywood had been living in Beechlee Nursing Home for twelve years prior to her death and that the property has been locked up during that time."

"Twelve years! Has nobody been there at all?" The concept was incredulous.

"Twice yearly a representative from the local

lawyer's office ensured that the property was undisturbed."

"So to become owner of this estate I not only have to conjure up a wife, but fork out a fortune to restore this property to be able to use it as a main domicile living as a happy family with this, as yet fictitious woman," he thundered on. "And if I don't meet all of these terms—what happens to this property?"

"The property will revert to the crown after a period of fifty years. During that time no one at all will be allowed to do anything to repair, maintain, or even demolish the property, save what weather and age will do itself."

"By which time a substantial piece of land, not to mention a house of the size you're indicating, will be ruined. The waste is unthinkable!" Luke paced around his office like a growling cougar, knowing full well John was only the messenger and not the perpetrator of this profligate proposition. "Renovation costs I can handle. You, of all people know that." He spat the last out, thumping a fist on his desk then collapsing into his chair, thrusting his fingers through his thick dark hair, and forcing his voice level to reduce. "But the other terms are downright farcical, not to mention archaic. What the...was the woman thinking?" At that point he'd exhausted the vocabulary to vent his spleen.

At thirty-three, Luke's life was perfect; well on course for the way he wanted it to be. He handled large properties on a daily basis. He knew how marketable such a sizeable property could be, even in the wildest area of Britain—and the Yorkshire Dales wasn't that. He'd carved a niche for himself over the years buying up properties just like Greywood Hall, renovating and marketing them as corporate residential venues with multiple options for work and leisure pursuits on site. He had solid construction businesses in Australia, and more recently in the UK, and had earned a ruthless but respected reputation along the way. He could buy a property like this on the open market in a snap and do what the hell he wanted to it!

Dannazione! But he didn't need a total stranger to bequeath it to him in their will. And he didn't need anybody, alive or dead, to dictate his marital status.

John had again cleared his throat, merely an attention grabbing strategy. "I have to point out, Luke, that although the will terms might seem archaic to you, it would, I repeat, it would be perfectly legal for you to walk out onto the street right now and marry the first woman you bump into. So long as the woman in question has no legal impediments to the marriage and is in agreement, all you need is a signature on the marriage license."

"Just a signature?"

"I'll get Braydon Security to do a background check on Amelia Greywood, and see if we can find more about why you're the beneficiary, but I'm not promising anything. The local lawyer had no information for me when I asked him."

Now, as he drove to Border Cottage, Luke felt maybe he could do something about this ridiculous legacy. Rhia Ashton might possibly be the key—the immediate answer to his prickly little problem. Luke's mood enlivened for the first time in hours, as he drove along the sun-flashed leafy lanes. His energy levels perked up again—not due to the caffeine fix he'd had from the lousy coffee at the police station—but from the anticipation of speaking again with his little woodland fairy.

Rhia Ashton.

Chapter Three

Gawking at the document spread out in front of her, the words made no sense. Rhia's usual concentration was shot, the weird dismissal from the police station played out in her head like a repetitive refrain. She conceded that her regular forays into the woods at Greywood Hall had been trespassing, and her conscience niggled like a rotting mouth abscess. Man, she hated unresolved issues.

That didn't make it any easier to get on with her work.

A pair of incredibly angry green eyes kept intruding. They would not be banished, her vision rerunning his dark virility, her emotions still so tangled she'd already snapped three pencils—for wasn't it typical she was attracted to a sodding loser yet again!

Would she never learn about the attractions of the male sex? Fingering aside the document she headed back to her computer hopeful she'd have better focus with online researches. Her life story was repeating itself. Her last boyfriend—the serial-sex cheater of the century—had been cunning enough to conceal that little facet of his personality for months before a kind acquaintance of Rhia's spilled the beans on five other women she knew about. And what was it about the previous boyfriend? Rhia shuddered with the memory, cringing at her naivety. He at least, as far as she knew, hadn't been screwing loads of other women, but he owed money to half of London and hadn't a scooby to pay them back. Especially not all the hard earned cash he'd temporarily borrowed from Rhia—for a permanent job never seemed within his grasp.

Never again!

She would never again be suckered by good-looking, sweet-talking, walking disasters. That was why Rhia had removed herself to rural Yorkshire to get herself out of their orbit and away from the temptations of London society.

Thor's agitated barking permeated the fug she was in, and she realized someone was buzzing the doorbell.

"Who the…is that?"

The chosen vulgarity was one of her best. Rhia who had often been told she was a little woman with a big hair-trigger. To make nice to visitors right that moment held no appeal at all. What she wanted was to wallow in the bewilderment and guilt-driven anxiety that had settled on her like the Sword of Damocles. Unfortunately her sensitive gut warned her that those unresolved issues were now about to smack her in the face.

In this backwater area where she lived, any caller was a rarity, save Gus who was her only regular visitor. It couldn't be him though since Thor never made a racket when Gus arrived. Frustration screamed in her head. The only way to shut Thor up was to find out who was there. Yanking her heavy front door open, her inhospitable glare was meant to deter.

Good lord! What the hell was Mr. Salieri doing here on her doorstep? The last person she expected to confront stood right outside. Why wasn't he locked up in a police cell?

"What do you want?"

Knees buckling, Rhia shoved the door closed, but in a flash his foot blocked the space, the rest of his large body bending back from the entryway. Short of crushing his toes to bits—and she was very tempted to do that—she found herself unable to deny him access though she did her best to wedge him out.

"I'm not going to hurt you, I promise," he explained, his large hands held up in a gesture of surrender.

Those searching eyes—yes they were green—sought her compliance, but his conciliation was barely discernible over Thor's tumult in the back garden. Processing the dry chuckle that accompanied his next words, his gaze indicated a genuine amusement in the situation. Rhia winced. What a strange man! Who in their right mind would find the combination of Thor's rumpus and the spine-bending position at the door amusing?

"Look, I need to talk to you." His tone softened as he pleaded, "To explain about earlier."

Rhia fought the instinct to get rid of him. He did, after all, look sincere, and though he blocked the door he wasn't threatening her. With his strength it would be a doddle to push inside, and she'd not be able to prevent it. Her five feet three was no competition for his frame that was well over six feet, built like a tree trunk and likely twice as heavy.

"Would you please call off the demented watchdog and tell him I'm a friend?" his dark molasses voice cajoled, seeping around her frustration, melting it into a thing of the past.

Gone was the ferocious stranger in the car, gone the drawn brows and black frown, gone the harshly delineated lips. Now the twinkling lure of his gaze was persuasive, his attitude soothing. It irked that he looked dazzling again. Far better looking than any man had a right to be—especially a downright shady character like he was.

Oh God! Not again.

Rhia was disgusted at herself for any fleeting alarm had drifted off on the wind. It was replaced by a dull flutter of attraction she couldn't quell and a perverted curiosity—for she did want to know what the hell game this man had been playing at Greywood Hall.

"You're not my friend!" Her retort was accusing, her disbelief not even masked. "You can't possibly want me for a friend." Good heavens. She'd had the police arrest him.

"How can you know that? You don't have an inkling what I want from you." Those sparkling eyes teased her yet his words were candid.

"Who are you?" Rhia croaked, her grip on the door relaxing as tension seeped out of her taut arm muscles. He did look genuine. Her anger dissipated for now—she'd give him the benefit of the doubt.

"My name's Luke." He eased his foot free, tilting his head a little closer. "Officially Lucca Salieri, but I'm always called Luke."

"I know that." Rhia huffed at him. "But who are you really?"

His black lashes were remarkably long, his nose almost straight, and his chin was squared in a no nonsense way. The bristles that adorned his cheeks looked like way more than a day's growth and darkened his natural olive skin tone.

"I'm not here to hurt you, I promise."

Even so, her fingers remained glued to the still partially-open door. Thor continued his hullabaloo. Luke winced at the noise, endeavoring to prevent the creasing up of the flesh over his cheekbones, but he was failing as his irritation with Thor was difficult to stifle.

"I'd like to explain what I was doing at Greywood Hall—but can you tell your bloody hound to shut up first so you might hear me?"

Rhia gave a perfunctory nod, her mind made up. She puckered her lips together. "You'd better come in then."

All business, she opened the door wide and ushered him into the narrow hallway that stretched from front to back of the cottage. The man had put her through enough fluctuations of seesawing emotions already that day so she would let him explain himself, and she had to calm Thor anyway.

Relinquishing her hold on the door she closed it with her heel and made her way through the small hallway, beckoning him to follow.

"That's enough of that, Thor!" Her command barked out as she opened the back door. "Quit your yowling now!"

The dog, in full defense mode, bared his teeth, advancing toward Luke, who'd come outside behind her.

"Sit!" Rhia bent to reassure the dog, stroking his coat from head to tail and softening her voice. "Thor. I'm fine. It's all right, boy." Thor stopped his barking and shuffled around Rhia's legs, still excited but obeying her. "This is Luke," she instructed the dog. "Say hello to him."

Luke presented his hand for inspection; Thor sniffed around him for a few seconds, accepted the cautious stroking offered then obediently sank to the ground at Luke's feet. The surreptitious tug at his polo shirt collar maybe indicated a little bit of relief that Thor had accepted him? Rhia grinned.

"Good boy!" Her delight with Thor's perfect behavior was evident. "It'll be all right now. He's happy," she explained to Luke for she was the one now doing the reassuring. "Let's go back inside."

Making sure it didn't escape Luke's notice she purposely left the back door wide open. Luke's wry expression wasn't lost on her. He knew what was on her mind.

In the bright sitting room Luke sat in the wooden rocking chair she indicated. Stilling the movement of the rock he braced his feet on the wooden floor then hung his hands loosely over his knees, his strong fingers open and comfortable on the dark grey denim. The expression on his face was frankly appreciative.

She hadn't screamed blue murder and set her weird hound on him so he darned well should look suitably grateful! Rhia handled situations with caution, she was quick to rationalize, but this man was yet to learn that. Guilt kicked back in with a vengeance though, as she took the smaller seat opposite him on the other side of the fireplace. Maintaining eye contact with him was downright impossible so instead she fixed on the decorative logs and vase of dried grasses that filled the grate as she composed her words.

"I'm not sure why you're here."

His gaze settled on her profile, the tingling of her spine telling her it was so, but he didn't answer till she forced her attention back to him.

"I'd like to clear up this misunderstanding today." Her mute nod was all he needed to continue. "I'm not the burglar you suspected."

A hint of humor sneaked into those appealing eyes of his, no doubt a deliberate strategy on his part. His mouth twitched, and a tiny smile appeared to soften the contours of his strong jaw line, his gaze comfortingly earnest. "In addition I assure you I haven't escaped from police custody. They didn't need to keep me down at the station since I wasn't committing any offense."

Rhia let her lack of response refute his statement. At last she said, "But you were trying all the widows, and I saw you climb into one."

Her voice faltered as he grinned, a full-bodied grin that rocked her equilibrium yet again. The sexual fluster that followed annoyed her as much as the denial of culpability this man had just given her.

"You're right about that." Contrarily Luke's nod

confirmed her statement as truth as he further explained, "I was checking all the windows, and I did climb inside the one I'd purposely broken into."

"But you—"

Luke didn't let her finish. "The reason the police didn't book me is because I am the new owner of the property." Something between a grimace and a puzzled grin spread across his face, his deprecating gaze making a mockery of what he'd just said. "Well, I'm almost the new owner."

"You're buying it?" Rhia hazarded. He sounded so unsure, his comment baffling. At his minutest head shake she added, "It doesn't quite belong to you yet?"

"Wow! You're good." Luke Salieri chortled, the laugh lingering, his gaze ironic. "Those are excellent questions with no easy answer, Rhia." He again sought her confirmation as he continued, "May I call you Rhia?"

She gave a tiny nod of assent then noted his strong chin held a fascinating dent, not quite a full scale dimple but just enough to make her want to delicately place her tongue there and savor it. His curving lips invited hers to smile back, but she resisted. The earlier frisson of awareness elevated more than a few notches. Her observation was pretty blatant, but it seemed he found it amusing, that ironical look snagging her once more as his explanation continued. He pointed to a row of paperbacks nearby.

"My almost-ownership probably reads like one of those mystery novels on your shelves." Rhia's expressive eyebrows twitched a little, one more than the other as he went on. "You'll need some background to my story, but I'd appreciate it if you'd listen." His tone, now serious, encouraged her compliance.

Rhia nodded, still wary of his choice to confide in

her, yet resolved to hear him out. She rose to her feet. She was equally resolved though to put aside the ridiculous attraction she felt toward him for it could go nowhere. But she needed a prop, something to fiddle with as she listened, so pasting an almost-polite smile on her face, she inquired, "Is this a stiff drink story?"

Heartened by his automatic grin she was then thrown by the slight shake of his head as she burbled on, "No brandy I'm afraid, but I've got some white wine chilling in the fridge."

"The wine sounds excellent but not the answer for me right now." Luke beamed back at her. "Alcohol would probably knock me comatose since I've been traveling almost non-stop for three days." His smile widened, again with that cajoling twinkle winking back at her. "A cup of tea would be good though."

"You drink tea?" Rhia queried in disbelief, drawn to his affronted expression as his cheek muscles relaxed over strong jawbones.

"Hey, I'll have you know my mother brought me up like a good little English boy. Well, at least my nannies did."

Her slight frown and pursed lips must have amused him for he divulged a bit more.

"Tea at four p.m. in the drawing room was an afternoon requirement. I was summoned from the nursery to attend from quite a young age."

The nursery? Rhia's eyebrows almost hit the rafters as her breath jammed in her throat. She somehow didn't believe he was talking about a state nursery attached to a primary school like the one she'd attended with around thirty other kids. And the drawing room he was talking about didn't sound like her art classroom either!

Lurching up, Luke paced to the window, his amusement dwindling, his next words acidic as he studied the view outside before continuing, "Sadly the tea ceremony was in the nature of training the child, presided over by the current nanny, for neither my mother nor my father attended often, even at weekends. They were far too busy building up their respective business empires." His baffled expression as he turned back verified some regret at parting with that tiny bit of information.

Rhia decided it was way past time for her to move out of his mesmeric sphere. Action was called for. "Tea is coming up then! But don't look for any fancy ceremony from me, Mr. Salieri."

Rhia headed for the kitchen to rally her thoughts. Who the heck was this man? Could he be joking? As she filled the electric kettle with water and plugged it in, she thought not. But what she did know was that she wasn't in his financial league, nor would she be—not in a million years.

Rhia's pragmatic tone cheered Luke as she disappeared. She looked to be a frank woman—exactly what he needed. Sentimentality would be far too messy for what he sought for the next year.

His glance encompassed the sitting room. Though small it was cozy with bright accents in cushions and decorative elements, but for all that there was a definite practicality about it. The large oak dining table that was fully extended below the window was a work station of sorts. It held a pleasant mish-mash of tidy piles and messy areas, at first glance looking haphazard but on second, with some sort of order in mind—all at hand and ready for researching. Realistic!

Exactly the kind of woman he needed for the next year.

Luke followed, lounging his large body on the doorframe to the small kitchen. While she assembled mugs, milk, sugar, and cookies from a jar, he explained why he was at Greywood Hall.

"Think Dickensian novel, Rhia. Think unusual bequests and a strange benefactress, and you're part way there."

As Luke's tale continued he was conscious of her derision, sensing she was finding him a tad delusional. That wasn't wrong for he was feeling that way himself. On balance though, when he interpreted her reactions she was interested in a silent manner that amused him. Would he hear more questions from her?

As she listened she pulled out the fixings for sandwiches, which he was gratified to see she arranged with precision. Salad greens he could do without, but he was pretty partial to stacked layers of roast beef and mustard! His stomach growled in anticipation.

"Yesterday I was on the last stage of a very long flight back from Brisbane, having spent the last two frenetic weeks there on business," he said. "Not far out of London I picked up a message from my London legal team requesting an immediate meeting to discuss matters of a personal nature."

"You're Australian?" Rhia interrupted as the electric kettle clicked off after boiling. "Is that why you have an unusual accent?"

Luke chuckled, a deeply sensuous sound, appreciating her deft movements with the kettle. "It sure is. Australian with Italian inflections; my English boarding schools were supposed to knock that out of me. They didn't quite erase all traces, much to my father's atypical delight, and my mother's extreme annoyance."

Rhia swirled hot water around the teapot then dunked it in the sink before adding fresh tea to the pot, her glances in his direction alternating between being socially interested and sexually surreptitious. He was entertained enough already by her to look out for the sexual ones. What a pistol!

"Your father's Australian?" She turned away when he intercepted another assessing peek.

"He was Italian, hence the name Salieri. My mother was Australian, though for some reason, at times, she always wanted to push her distant English forebears."

Luke knew his scorn had her making a mental note of it as she set the filled teapot aside to brew. Did she think he was a bit Anglophobic? He hoped not, for he wasn't in the least—it was just that his mother had been such a snob, deriding anyone whose ancestry was in any way suspect.

Much to his surprise he was happy to fill in snippets of personal information in answer to Rhia's polite questions while she bustled about in the small space, working out how much he needed to tell her to ensure she'd acquiesce to his plans. He needed a level-headed woman. The fact that Rhia Ashton was also very easy on the eye was a definite bonus.

Her delicious little rear bent to get milk out of the fridge, the shorts riding up, delineating the shaped cheeks he was finding himself salivating to stroke. She was a lust-worthy little woman. Luke gulped, readjusted his denims, the cloth almost stretched into a new shape. Clearing his parched throat, he called his errant thoughts to order. A sexual dalliance wasn't the plan. Well, not in his main plan.

What he needed this woman for wasn't to nurture his libido, but he sure as hell wanted it to be! She wasn't anything like the tall, leggy women he usually gravitated to, but she had everything his current lust craved. He pulled himself together when he realized their tea tray was ready.

"So let's get back to yesterday." He straightened his six foot four frame, took the loaded tray from Rhia, and followed her back into the sitting room. Setting it on the small coffee table she had swept clear of magazines, he paced around the room like a penned up animal.

"Personal legalities are handled by my Australian lawyers so it was exceptional to be asked for a meeting in London."

Rhia's gaze widened. She was so transparent in her interest but he reckoned that could only work in his favor.

"My London lawyer gave me some astonishing information." Circumnavigating the room twice he positioned himself by the window. Luke half-sat on the edge of the cluttered dining table, placed under the window for best light, and gave the stacked historical papers a cursory glance.

As Rhia approached carrying a mug of tea, not a delicate cup and saucer, he was glad to note, her gaze flickered to the car parked outside: his gleaming black Ferrari, currently top of the range. She looked a little flustered as she relinquished the tea into his hands.

"Sorry," she said sweetly, brushing fingers with him. "I'm all out of lemon today."

Luke ignored the jolt of awareness that her brief contact made as Rhia retook her seat. "No problem," he replied, "I take tea with milk."

"Help yourself," she indicated the tray, "and to the food too." Amusement glowed in her liquid brown gaze as she added, "I'm not your servant. You'll get no ceremony here, Mr. Salieri."

Luke strode over to add milk to his mug. So she had a bit of spunk! What else would the little nymph reveal about her character? He was intrigued and more than a little aroused again. Or was it...still?

She sipped her tea, her slender fingers winding round the mug, making him wonder just how they would feel around his... *Christot all!* Everything about her was disturbing and disconcerting. He was very interested in her reaction to his story; in fact he was keen to see how greedy and grasping she would be, if the women of his previous acquaintance were anything to go by.

"Yesterday," he continued, "I was informed that I'd been named as the sole beneficiary of the will of Miss Amelia Greywood—a woman I've never heard of, by the way—and that I'd inherited her property called Greywood Hall." A good slug of his tea slipped down as he let that sink in.

"Earlier you said you were almost the owner," Rhia said. "Now you're saying she did leave it to you?"

The bewilderment was evident on her face, doe-eyes still suspicious as she bent forward and sipped from her mug, her lips cupping around the rim, lips he found himself wanting to trace with his tongue. *Madre di Dio!* The woman was unsettling! He turned away from her. He couldn't afford a sexual distraction. Well, at least...not till after he solved his problems.

"Both are true!" he shot back, his words staccato as he prowled the room.

"You're not pleased about it?" Rhia's tone indicated his snippy answer had startled her.

Contrary to her earlier statement about being a maid, Rhia reached for the plate and offered him a sandwich, which he devoured in almost one bite. Absently he reached for another, striding around while he chewed, then he picked up a third. He was starved. Food was one appetite he could quench.

"Not particularly," he answered when he'd finished chewing the third sandwich, appreciating them all for it had been hours since he'd eaten anything substantial.

"And you'd really never ever heard of Miss Greywood?"

Rhia's fascination about the unfolding story was evident as she nibbled a sandwich. Good thing too,

Luke thought, before they all disappeared off the plate, for he was still ravenous.

"Never!" he retorted, pacing around, while exploring the mini-office set up in the corner of the room. He stopped only long enough to drain his mug before re-filling it from the teapot. She seemed to encourage no formality, which greatly heartened him, though he knew his manners lacked some finesse. His gaze strayed to the bookcase groaning with history tomes.

"Did you know Amelia, by any chance?" Luke asked hopefully, though he very much doubted it.

"Sorry." She shook her head. The movement wrapped her lustrous dark hair about her chin; her cocoa-brown eyes reflected her regret. "I've heard a little about her from Gus but I only moved here about a year ago."

"Gus?" Luke's gaze narrowed on Rhia as he probed for an answer, though he realized he didn't want to know if it was a 'significant' other who might jinx his plans.

"Gus is a good friend of mine." Rhia's eyes remained downcast as she reached for a second sandwich.

Luke wasn't cheered by that—it wasn't enough information about this Gus person.

"Great sandwiches, by the way," he mumbled as he started on the plate of cookies after her heartening nod, knowing he'd have to do better to get her to open up a bit more about her life here in the environs of Greywood Hall. "So what does your good friend Gus know about Amelia Greywood?"

Rhia's answer followed after a miniscule hesitation. "Only that it's been years since the lady lived at Greywood Hall and that she was housebound for years before that."

Her reddened cheeks made Luke wonder what there was about this Gus that had her flushing so readily. Did she always get aroused when talking about this blasted Gus? Was he more than a good friend? *Dannazione*! That would put a spanner in his works. A 'Gus' person was something he could well do without!

Unfortunately, the dampening topic of Gus didn't have the effect he wanted. His libido wasn't listening to him at all—it wasn't weakened by the threat of competition. He paced about before continuing, again appreciating the bright and cozy colors around the room, in cushions, flowers and pictures on the walls, and in the scatter-rug beneath him, which was comfortably old and well flattened by years of treading feet.

"My lawyer tells me it's been nearly twelve years since Amelia went into Beechlee Nursing Home, and that the property has been unoccupied since then."

"That fits with what I heard," Rhia's gaze tracked his relentless movements, "although I don't know any more about her."

Luke was wondering how he could manipulate the conversation to find out how much this Gus meant to her. He needed to know that fast. Turning back he found her sitting patiently, waiting for him to continue, her expressive little face unable to mask her interest...in him!

Aha!

And she had been ogling him in the police car so Gus was in for a bad ride if this little sprite eyed-up every male she came in contact with. At that point Luke decided Gus was a total irrelevance. He switched his charm button on though he couldn't keep all irritation from his tone: in fact it increased as he switched subject.

"As you've indisputably observed during your visit today..." His censure was intentional as he trod the rug in front of Rhia, maintaining a penetrating eye contact. "Those dozen years haven't been kind to the property. It's a disgusting wreck!"

His empty mug plonked down on her small coffee table forcing Rhia to track his movements. The repugnance that mushroomed across his face, a disgust he couldn't mask, had shocked her. His lips narrowed, his hands clenched over the back of the rocking chair he'd vacated as he glowered at the fireplace.

"The condition of the property bothers you?"

Her question seemed cautious, possibly to minimize offending him. Luke detected that for she was not without manners, and…when all was said and done, he was a complete stranger who was telling her some weirdly personal information.

"Of course it bloody does, Rhia! It would disgust anyone with a grain of sense." He picked up the cushion from her rocking chair, punched it into submission, flopped down on the seat again, and placed the cushion across his lap. Strategically. He was having a hell of a time not pouncing on this gorgeous little sprite who was playing havoc with all his senses—body and mind.

"Well…" Rhia said.

The rocking of his chair was now a rhythmic background as he mulled over the fireplace arrangement.

Rhia doggedly continued, "I suppose some people wouldn't look at it that way."

"What?" Luke's feet firmed on the floor halting the rock.

"Well…" Her reply was again cautious, forcing back his focus. "I suppose some people would just value it for what it is."

"What that property is, is a bloody shame, woman!" His anger couldn't be concealed any more. "You've seen the friggin' place. It's decaying by the minute."

"Yes, I suppose it is," she whispered. "But it's a charming old place, Luke. I've grown to love it."

"You love it? Now isn't that interesting." Luke relaxed back into a steady rock his mood improving. His angry demeanor dissipated into one of collusion. "You made that conclusion based on your walk today?" he questioned as he processed the fact that she'd revealed more fodder for his scheme to snare her services.

"Well, er…not exactly." Her reply was hesitant. Luke suspected she was being vigilant in not incriminating herself further.

Chapter Four

"Not exactly what? Not today?" Luke asked, "But on another day?" The tone was ruthless as he tossed the cushion aside, no longer needing it, for he'd succeeded in quelling the fire in his blood. His gaze now rooted on her own…and nowhere near her delectable body.

"Yes I have been there before, I admit it," Rhia answered.

Again there was that profuse blush he was coming to admire, but was now wary of.

"The place grows on you. I know it's dilapidated, but it must have been lovely once."

"Yes, Rhia. That was a long, long time ago. And not just twelve years ago; it's been decaying for decades. It was left to rot!"

Relapsing again into a subdued mood he stared at the grate decoration as Rhia withheld any further inquiries. Luke didn't blame her, for his mood was murky. After a little while he turned back toward her, his gaze mocking, but not mocking her.

"Do you know by three a.m. this morning I was itching to come and view this decrepit pile?" His laugh was vigorous, but it was not a happy laugh. "My sleep patterns are always out of kilter when I return from Australia so I was awake. I couldn't wait till the rest of the UK woke up. My curiosity got the better of me—and that doesn't happen often I can assure you."

Relating how he'd jumped into his car rather than waking his pilot and ordering his helicopter, Rhia's tiny indrawn breath drew his focus back to her again. That derisive, doubtful expression had returned. What was it about his circumstances the darned woman didn't agree with? That disdainful glower, the raise of an eyebrow—they were getting to him.

"Of course that meant I arrived in the Yorkshire Dales around seven when I made an untimely check in to the Ruisdale Grange…"

Again her slight cough made him note both of her eyebrows rising up to almost meet her hairline.

It was a quality hotel, one of a small chain he frequented but nothing for her to get into such a snit about. The derision was irritating, but he determined to win her favor.

"I rested for a couple of hours and then made my way to Amelia Greywood's lawyer to discover he was on holiday for two weeks. Though the lawyer had left most of his pressing casework with a junior colleague the keys to Greywood Hall couldn't be located." Luke's laugh mocked. "They couldn't find the damn keys, Rhia! For a place like Greywood Hall? No keys? That should have warned me something was amiss, but I was determined to see what I'd bloody well been landed with."

Rhia's disapproving frown was in tandem with his reasoning. How many large estates would the lawyer's office have been dealing with? Realistically…very few.

"So you just came to look for yourself?" she ventured something still souring her expression that he couldn't quite read.

"Yes, after kicking my heels for a couple of hours to give the office time to find the damned keys." His tone was so sarcastic he felt Rhia's recoil. "Two hours. Do you realize how little there is to do there?" He named a local county town.

"Well I know it's not a throbbing metropolis, Luke, but I quite like that little market town!"

Her response was filled with sufficient outrage to make him chortle as she endorsed it. "I've found everything I could want there since I moved away from London, on purpose."

"Point taken, Rhia." She believed what she was saying though he didn't have to agree with her. "Well, suffice to say, it didn't occur to me I wouldn't be able to get the keys to inspect the place," Luke answered, scrubbing his fingers across his chin stubble, failure being a novelty to him.

"Why hadn't you phoned ahead?"

"Good question!" Luke laughed at himself as he disclosed his answer. "Perhaps the fact that I left London at three in the morning had something to do with that?"

Rhia's gleeful grin slayed him; she was finding his predicament funny now. Strange woman of mercurial moods! He plowed on, determined even more to get her on board.

"Anyway, I'm not known to be indolent so I decided to come to Greywood Hall and take a look around. I thought that even if I couldn't get into the house I'd be able to see the grounds." The rocking chair played a steady thump on the wooden floor as he switched from the earlier morosity to an agitated animation.

"But the main gates were locked when I first passed with Thor."

"Sure, the main gates were. I'd tried them first, but I didn't have cutters in my car, or anything to force the padlock, or break the chain with. It was the police who cut them open when they came to arrest me, Miss Ashton."

Luke let his gaze rest on Rhia's for long moments. Hoping she'd color up again…but she didn't. He waited, but she was ignoring his little jibe. Only after a long tense silence did she respond.

"So how did you get in?"

Luke wondered how Rhia regularly got in as he answered. “I found a back entrance to the stable block approachable from the far side of the property, also padlocked of course, so I left my car on the verge and nipped over the wall. From there, as you know already, I entered the house via that pantry window.” His smile was tight. “And the rest is history…except not quite!”

“I don’t understand why you were checking all the windows if you’d already broken into one. You have to know your movements were pretty furtive.”

Rhia wasn’t rising to his bait; her questioning was measured and purposeful. Needed the fine details tuned, did she? Well, he guessed she deserved to know since he needed her on board one hundred per cent.

“It’s my job,” he answered, perusing the photographs hanging in a montage on her wall, milking his statement for all it was worth.

“What? But you said you weren’t—”

“A burglar? Of course I’m not!” Encouraged by her naive responses sardonic laughter spilled from him. “I’m a Chartered Surveyor with a background in domestic and commercial construction. My current focus in the UK is renovation of old properties.”

“So you were checking the windows?”

She was so obvious Luke visualized her brain interpreting his earlier movements.

“As a professional?”

That rosy little blush again stained her cheeks. Now he contrarily wished it hadn’t happened, for it was far too alluring.

“I’m sorry about that.”

Brushing off her apology with a terse wave of his hand, Luke enjoyed telling her more of his story, but that cute little way she had of squirming up her button of a nose when she was working something out was too damned appealing. Distracting him from the main purpose.

"What did you mean, 'and that's history, but not quite'?"

"My being willed the Hall isn't quite as straightforward as it seems. That's where you can help me."

She was going to be perfect for what he needed. He just knew it.

"Me?"

Her bewilderment was exhilarating. For the same unknown reason he found her reactions to him fascinating. *Dannazione!* He soared up in front of her, uncomfortable again.

"We've established that I'm not a burglar, but you, it transpires Miss Rhia Ashton, are a multiple trespasser!" He let his index finger mock in front of her nose but didn't encourage her to join in quite yet. "You've been trespassing on that property for some time." He made sure his tone was chastising as his lids half-lowered speculatively. He'd been told before that his green eyes darkened in arousal, and he sure as shit wanted them to be doing that right now! A bit of seduction wouldn't come amiss.

"I-I didn't know it was your property. Honestly. Gus told me it would be fine to walk Thor there." Rhia's voice faded to nothing.

Creasing his dark eyebrows in doubt Luke determined that one of his first priorities would be to eliminate this Gus from her life.

"Ah," he exhaled, "but neither you, nor Gus had permission to be there. And unless you want to go back to the police station and be charged with quite a few offenses, I think you might at least listen to my proposal."

Rhia was flustered. "But, they said nothing at the police station about my trespassing. They brought me home."

Slanting his hands on the chair back, one on each side of her shoulders, he effectively trapped her, finding he rather liked being so close to her lips. She was an enticing sprite who was reeling him in, but he had to keep his mind out of his pants for he needed Rhia Ashton to scratch those other itches first.

She inched back from him, her head lolling on the cushion.

"Did you wonder about that, Rhia? Did you wonder why they let you go without a mention of the fact that you'd been wandering at will all over that property for ages? Doing who knows what damage?" He breathed his words on her flushed cheeks, his gaze not wavering a single blink, his body conspiratorially closer.

"Of course I wondered!" she cried. "But I never, ever damaged anything."

"Well now, you have me to thank for the lack of charges," he mocked, his gaze dipping down to track her moving lips, lips that quivered so close to his own. "I chose to tell them they didn't need to proceed with the trespassing charges, for the foreseeable future."

"The foreseeable future?"

He persisted, knowing his sexual sizing up was unnerving her! "Not forever you understand, just for the foreseeable future." His calculating stare locked onto her trembling lips; lips she'd just swiped her tongue over; lips that glistened like a honeyed target, making him want to trace their contours with his thumb…and his tongue.

"Are you blackmailing me?"

"Blackmail?" His contemptuous chortle and his raised eyebrows both indicated a twisted hilarity as he withdrew. Her siren song had to stop. "You and me both! Ha! This is where the old lady excels. She has the last laugh."

Again the startled bewilderment was undeniable, but by the way she leaned forward on the chair, he knew her interest was piqued. Rhia was too easy to entice, or maybe she was too enticing? It didn't matter. He needed to maintain a bit more distance, more control, over his lust.

After another circuit of the room Luke halted in front of her, one hand raking back his thick hair. She needed to be told all the facts. Well, maybe not about the tight deadline: he could leave that little snippet till he was sure she'd comply. He was feeling success was only a few words away.

"Okay," he said. "I told you it's a bloody Dickensian nightmare! Here's the real deal. I'm not the legal owner of the property unless I fulfill some very interesting terms, which you alone can help with."

"Me?"

Her horrified expression was like a rabbit snagged in a deadly snare. Luke was okay with that! He raised one massive fist in front of her while holding her spellbound gaze.

"One." Luke pointed one finger at her. "I must reside at Greywood Hall with my spouse, for the period of one calendar year, to eventually become the proud owner of this magnificently dilapidated property."

Her face blanched. Luke was almost sucked in by her disappointed indrawn breath and disenchanted eye-flare as he continued checking off his list. Now which word had bothered her? He was pretty sure it had been the 'spouse' word. Excellent! So easy to comprehend, she was a piece of cake.

"Two." Another finger joined his first. "I need to do extensive renovations to Greywood Hall to live in it."

Rhia mutely nodded back at him.

He was again pretty sure that even if she loved

the old building from the outside, like she'd declared, she wouldn't want to live inside it before some work was done.

"Three." All three fingers pointed at her. "I need to shell out a mountain of my own capital to do this, since the old lady left the princely sum of six thousand four hundred and twenty pounds, which will barely pay for a replacement door knocker!"

Luke waited while she digested that bit of information. A flicker of resentment flashed over her eyes. She looked fit to burst, but Luke admired the fact that she reined in her control. Her lips narrowed, but she remained silent...till he waggled his three fingers close to her nose.

"Can you afford the restorations?"

Wow! She was a snippy little cat!

"*Madre di Dio!*" Luke's free hand raked his hair back off his forehead as he scratched his scalp. "Of course I damned well can! I've got more than plenty of money to do that. Plenty even for the hugely exorbitant death taxes that will no doubt be involved," he shot back watching her lips indicate her extreme distaste.

"More than plenty?" Rhia's voice rose to a berating tirade, her expression sneering. "Some people would think six thousand four hundred and twenty pounds was a fortune!"

She was livid. A reaction he hadn't expected but...quite liked. Her anger boiled, her criticism was on a roll. Very entertaining, and not what he was used to—not at all.

"If you've got loads of money, then what's your problem?"

Her indignation bristled as she slipped forward, closer to him, body language challenging. Utter disgust flitted across her face as she attacked, her eyes molten fire. "You might well have to use your own money in the first instance, but you'll have a delightful property which will be worth its weight in gold. Then you can fob it off and make your millions if you want. So what the hell have you got to complain about?"

Wow! Her passion was impressive. Luke fired up again. He'd way-ruffled her earlier composure. He suppressed the grin trying to leak out. It was heartening to note that his confession over having a decent enough bank balance wasn't met with any indication of avaricious greed. No. Her reaction to his wealth seemed quite the opposite! Who was this novel sprite? If her ire was genuine, then she was unique...not the type of woman he had a history with.

"I don't have a money problem." He moved in on her again. "The problem is that right this minute, I don't have a wife. And if I don't have a wife I can't fulfill these ridiculous terms."

"Oh, I see."

Again Luke chuckled—he thought he could almost cook pancakes on her reddened cheeks. He could tell the exact moment when she willed herself to calm down, focus on the matters at hand and reply to his bald statement.

"But if you've no wife and it's going to cost you a lot of money anyway, why don't you just say 'no thank you' and walk away from the legacy?"

"Ha!" Luke strode away from her, needing a little space, but then whipped around trapping her focus once more as he stepped back into her sphere. "I knew you'd be smart and ask good questions!" His voice deepened as he leaned his whole body toward her. "You, with your knowledge of history, I'm sure, will appreciate this little snippet," he whispered as his strong arms banded her again, making a nice little prison.

All over again, he smiled. From her hitched breath, and the deepening desire flaring over her cocoa brown irises, she loved the captivity! Strangely enough...he did too. It took a moment for him to regain his thread—this particular little woman surely could distract him.

"As in all good Dickensian stories the old lady isn't finished yet. If I don't do anything with the property, after a period of fifty years it reverts to the crown."

"But if it does, it won't matter to you, will it?" Rhia reasoned, her gaze fixated on his lips.

He imagined their lip-locking would be devastating.

"Rhia!" he snorted instead. "Of course it will. How could I ignore such a valuable property?"

Rejection and then disappointment flashed across her lovely face before she answered, "You've lost me." Her gaze drew away. "Do you want it or not?"

"Rhia, please take heed," Luke sighed, his voice enticing her to turn back. He didn't dare touch her. And he did want it...but knew that wasn't what she meant. He didn't dare use his fingertips to turn her delectable little chin toward him, for he knew one fingering would never be enough. "It would be a crying shame to leave that house to rot for another fifty years. It's a valuable house and valuable land. It could be converted to multiple uses for corporate business, or as a hotel facility."

"Ah...future revenues?" Her eyes held that astutely impressive derision again.

His face crept closer, his lips only a pout away. "Rhia, you wouldn't want to be responsible for that house to fall into even more disrepair, that house you've already professed to love? Would you?"

She was floundering like a non-swimmer in a forest puddle, indecision hovering over her gorgeous eyes. He was confident she couldn't resist him. His libido kicked in triple time, but his resolve quadrupled.

"Would you want that on your conscience? Knowing it was your fault it happened?"

"My fault?"

He knew his propinquity was keeping her spellbound, but by her glower she wasn't taking the flack. Her disgusted expression informed him in no uncertain terms what she thought about his last words.

"Rhia..." He could tell his repetition of her name in that way was grating on her nerves. He intended it to: she was conscious that he was trying to wear her defenses down for that delightful little chin of hers rose up belligerently. He made sure his tone was back to cajoling. "Nobody can do anything at all to pull that property back to glory except me. I'm ready to take on the responsibility of restoring that so lovable property." One long finger tapped her nose once. "Almost your words by the way..." Then his hand returned to the back of her chair, trapping her again. "But I need your help to do it."

His comment had hit pay dirt! He'd realized how protective and almost possessive she was about Greywood Hall.

"But if you have to restore it...as a domestic domicile could you still use it afterwards?" Her antagonism was weakening in the face of his persistence. Just what he wanted to achieve. Her keen intelligence was overriding her reservations as she deliberated. "For business use without doing loads of further renovations," she burbled on, "which would cost you heaps of money again?"

"Well, that's another quandary, isn't it?" Luke lapsed into silence, his regard intense, and his eyes only inches from hers.

A little bead of perspiration dappled the dent below her nostrils. Rhia licked the lips as though they were extremely dry. Luke was mesmerized by it as she continued, "I appreciate what you are saying, but how does it affect me?"

She was killing him with her inadvertent come-ons. He savored her gestures before he resumed. "Well now, think about it. I have more than enough money to restore the property to its original grandeur, but what don't I have, Rhia?"

"No..."

"Rhia!"

His mouth was even closer than before. But instead of taking her lips his chuckle puffed on them.

"I don't have a wife, and I sure as hell hadn't been planning on having one anytime soon."

Rhia's lids fluttered. "So you can't inherit right now? But you could later. If..." Her voice faltered as though it was excruciating to utter the words. "You...er, got married?"

"Bang on," Luke chuckled.

His hands slipped from the back of the chair where they'd bracketed her in and snagged her fingers, encouraging her to her feet. A jolt of awareness channeled between their locked hands, rode up his arms and permeated his entire body making him quiver with anticipation. He'd never experienced anything so volatile before. It raised the triple-time libido even further—no doubt about that. He needed to bring his thoughts to order for he was losing it. Badly. He windshield-wiped his eyes and focused before continuing, his tone raspy for he couldn't quite get to grips with that yet.

"But not later," he growled. "I'm not a man to hang around and waste valuable time. It has to be as soon as possible—as early as can be arranged."

"What?" Her voice was a mere susurration into the stillness, her face a cameo of distrust.

"Why should we let the property deteriorate further?" His tone invited, his intensity luring her in again. He stroked her fingers. "You know you can't back away and let that lovely old estate you profess to love fall into complete ruin."

"What are you talking about?" Her irises widened at his words.

Luke tightened the pressure of his fingers willing the warmth of his grip to ensnare her. "I need someone to marry me, and I want that person to be you."

His tone was resolute. Right now coercing Rhia was all part of his grand action plan, but for some weird reason it didn't in the least alarm him. Till now, marriage had never entered into his head for he'd never yet met any woman he liked long enough to even remotely consider it. But his non-alarm wasn't due to Rhia per se. No. It was just reassuring to think now that this particular marriage would only last for the duration he needed it to. He was just using her as a woman in a different way from normal.

Rhia Ashton was a very, very different type of woman from his usual female acquaintances. She was mouthy and opinionated, but instinct told him he could handle her. Her attachment to the crumbling old estate could be a bargaining point.

He decided that the cottage she was renting could be transferred into her ownership as part of a payoff at the end of the year. He monitored the effect of his words, her expressive face denoting she'd never be an effective poker player—that was for sure.

A year. Not so long. But then again if the initial lust he felt right now for her sexy little body waned too soon, a year would be a tormenting prison sentence. He disengaged his fingers from their grasp.

Rhia wilted back into the chair and leaned against the cushions, her eyes clouded with confusion and definite desire. A question hovered as she contemplated.

"But why would you want me to marry you?" she croaked.

Luke moved away to look out the window, needing to create a little distance while he pulled his mind back onto the track.

"I've just told you I need a woman to marry me right away and live with me for a year so I can do something with the dilapidated pile of Greywood Hall—someone who knows this deal from the outset." He summoned his control. *Dio* knew from where! Removing all traces of doubt from his voice, he intoned, "And you're convenient."

Chapter Five

"I'm convenient?"

Rhia could barely answer; she was so offended by his glib remark after the devastation of his sexy seduction techniques. His attraction diminished to almost nothing for he was an asshole to say something like that after being so blatant about putting the moves on her!

He turned back to her. "You're not already married, are you?" Luke pointed to her empty ring finger.

"No, I'm not married."

Her teeth were almost glued together, resentment thick over his attitude, but even more with herself for being so stupid to be swayed by his little rich boy seduction techniques in the first place. What did he mean convenient? She let a mutinous look replace everything that had resembled her earlier lust. She was such an idiot to have been taken in by the slimy slug!

"You live next door and it just so happens you're also my tenant," he said.

He was so thick-skinned that he didn't even acknowledge her horrified gasp.

"That will be very handy for the first week or so."

Only good manners prevented Rhia from telling him to go to hell…or at the very least to sit still for a moment so that she could absorb everything as he meandered around the furniture. She tried to follow his train of thought, not sure of anything now but irritation that his crazy plans were still intriguing.

"I need to get me a wife right away so I can ensure that the property doesn't fall to bits any longer, and I know you don't want that to happen either since you profess already to love the moldering ruin."

Luke's urging was unremitting as he paced back and forth. Rhia wasn't thrilled by his outlining; he'd have to try much harder to persuade her. How did the blasted man dare think she'd just fall in with his incredibly implausible plans!

"And you know what, Rhia? You also just happen to have a very convenient profession."

Luke had changed tack a little. Had she missed something? When had her rational thinking and explosive emotions wandered?

"My profession?"

First she was convenient because she lived next door and now because of her job? What the hell did the pesky man think she did for a living?

Luke proceeded to astound her by his detailed knowledge of her work history. "You have the perfect historical research skills for finding out the history of Greywood Hall." His fervor was evident in his glittering eyes and in the huge smile splitting his face. "And you are perfect for sleuthing out why the hell I'm the one who's inheriting the dilapidated pile. For that's something I don't damned well know, and sure as shit I want to!"

Rhia couldn't suppress the interest at his mention of researching such a venerable old place as Greywood Hall. That would be an absolute heaven. But she would not be mesmerized by him again. Her lips thinned, and her resolution firmed.

"And let me tell you now," he ranted, "I don't for one minute think that unraveling why it was me will be an easy task for anyone. That house up there is like a bloody junkyard, Rhia. Every room is cluttered with hundreds of years of trivia...and *Madre de Dio* knows what!"

Rhia heard Luke's voice rise with exasperation and, she thought, almost unwillingly…passion. He was searching for the best words to describe the place as he stuttered through the next phrase. "And y-you know what else?"

It was meant as a rhetorical question for he lumbered on, not giving her any chance of response.

"I damned well can't get rid of a single piece of paper in case it happens to be the very one that says why I'm the beneficiary!"

Rhia's curiosity was now well-fired. "Junk yard?" She loved the sound of that! Every room full of historical artifacts just waiting to be exposed? Oh my!

Maybe Luke's proposal wasn't so bad after all? Her irritating conscience was kicking in at the all-too-wrong time! No, she couldn't compromise on that one, could she?

While she pondered her principles Luke continued to elaborate, still padding around. "You can even think of our marriage like one of your contracts. You'll just happen to be living at Greywood Hall as my wife while you're doing the research."

"Your wife? And also your researcher?" Rhia couldn't formulate any other questions; he had everything so well worked out, and pathetic though it seemed, for an historian the research was very tempting.

Luke halted his pacing and grinned at her, his convinced expression revealing his realization that the carrot he'd just dangled was something she wanted to nibble. He was enthused by the whole concept—but she wasn't too sure about it—or about him. Not yet. What she did know was that he wasn't finished, as his words tripped out like fine oil. "Living up at Greywood Hall while you research the place will be a marvelous experience for you. Just think about it. All those knickknack filled rooms…" His chuckle became a full bodied roll. "I'm not kidding about them, Rhia. Every single room, loads of them."

Rhia willed her features to remain impassive but it was hard to suppress the growing excitement. Being the first person to research all the prime sources at Greywood?

Unbelievable!

"The estate is a living history book," Luke explained, animated about it though Rhia was well aware that some of his enthusiasm was fabricated to sway her. "I mean, literally!" His sudden grin was compelling as he enthused, "The whole place is amazing. On the nursery floor I found original copies of children's classics, leather-bound versions like The Lost World by Conan Doyle." His eyes flashed fire and sheer incredulity at her. "That's exactly what the house is like!" He stopped right in front of her and clutched her shoulders, almost crushing her in his intensity. "It's a lost world that needs rediscovering by an expert. You, Rhia! You're the expert it needs so badly."

His fingers gentled, caressing her shoulders as he finished, his gaze locked on hers, willing her to imagine it all with him. "The only one who can help find that lost world again is you. You'll only have to be in it for five seconds to absorb its ancient pages and you'll want to read to the very end."

The bizarre idea tempted her, evident in the smile she couldn't quite smother and in the racing heartbeats caused by his recent touches.

"It's an astonishing place. You know you can't possibly miss such a fabulous opportunity."

His next deadpan, staccato phrases were another shocker.

"Of course the opposite to being my wife and

researcher Rhia, and living up at the Hall with me as your husband, is that you don't want me to evict you from this cottage. I might want it for another tenant—like myself or one of my workers."

Rhia gagged at his audacity. He was the most mercurial man she'd ever met. She equally loathed him and loved his cunning at the same time. The man was deranged yet she was entertaining his ideas? What a friggin' idiot she was!

Well, maybe not quite so duped.

"You'd evict me?" she gasped even though he was still smirking at her. "You wouldn't!" Surely not? Unfortunately his moods had already been so unpredictable that day she hadn't a clue what she could expect from him.

"As your landlord I guess I could do that." Luke's theatrical nod was emphatic. "Then again there's the little matter of prosecution."

Rhia couldn't help but ogle the forefinger tapping at her to emphasize his meaning. "You jerk!" Her own index finger waved back at him, her words clipped in tandem. "That's blackmail!"

"Only sort of." He was thoroughly enjoying her outrage. "On the other hand you'd get huge benefits if we married." He smiled that small calculating smile she was beginning to recognize, the one with its sexual overtones.

"You're mad! Stark raving bonkers! You can't want to marry me." Rhia sank back into the cushions of the chair.

"I do," he responded as though she knew the words were the simplest thing in the world to say.

"You don't even know me." Rhia had no idea her appalled expression was priceless to watch until Luke's grin widened even further. Then she spluttered, "You don't love me."

"Come on, Rhia! Who said anything about love?" His cynical tone was not lost on her. "I don't need to love you to have a bit of paper that says I'm married to you." Moving over to the window he peered out at her small front garden.

Whirling back to her, plans dripped off his tongue. "Think about it like this. We get married. You stay free of prosecution, and you can walk Thor all over the place every single day. I'll guarantee you employment as my researcher for a whole year, give you double your present salary. Then later on you can move back here to this cottage. A whole year's worth of double earnings. Doesn't that sound good Rhia?"

A year's worth of employment was persuasive. She was just building her Family History research business and, since she'd moved to the Yorkshire Dales, contracts had been hard to come by.

Luke had begun pacing again. He was quite the schemer. Rhia was impressed, in spite of the fact that he was a total dreamer, as he plowed on. "I can rearrange my current schedules to suit. We can stay here in your very well-located cottage for the first few days, as I renovate the property. That way I can be on hand, as it were."

She watched him rub his hands together as he strode his now well-worn route around the furniture.

"As soon as a few rooms in Greywood Hall are habitable, we can move in, live there for one year while the rest is being restored, and then when the property is mine to do with as I choose, you can move back to your life here in the cottage." His pragmatic tone matched his candid words.

"You're crazy! That's coercion." Rhia's hackles rose, against this man who now put forward such a cold businesslike proposal for his serious gaze told her he did mean business. "Why would I do that? Why would I marry you? I don't even know you." Her body, without doubt, had its own mysterious knowledge of this mesmerizing man, yet her mind rebelled at his hard-nosed tone.

"Rhia, you don't need to know me. You don't need to love me. You just have to sign the paper that says you're my wife." Luke catalogued the details as he stood in front of her.

"You can't make me do that!" Rhia retorted, wishing for time to think because part of her was aware that a lot of what he said was lucrative, both for potential earnings and for valuable experience. "I'd have to put my personal life on hold for a whole year." She wasn't going to tell him that her personal life wouldn't be much different from the last year and that by choice she'd had very little social life since moving to the isolated cottage.

"It's only a year." Luke's tone softened a hint, his dramatic sigh at her reactions spoiled by the sassy smile on his face.

Rhia squeezed her eyes shut on his cajoling green depths and sneaky lips so she could think her way through this bizarre proposal, or whatever the hell it was. She felt his breath on her cheeks again as he bent forward to whisper.

"It's not that long."

With his proximity lust roared right back in. Why did the infernal man have to smell so incredibly good? Just the right blend of masculine fragrance and...what? Arousal? Oh God! Rhia's womb clenched, and her nerve endings tingled.

If she started to live with this man she didn't think an eternity would be enough, not if the current attraction continued. And what if it was only to be a paper marriage? How could she be around him every day and not follow up on the attraction? Never.

"You can't expect me to do that!"

"Sure I can," Luke replied looking oddly pleased by her vehement rebuttals. Rhia didn't understand that at all! "Of course if you're not willing to follow those plans then I'll find another woman." His head cocked to the side, contemplating the idea. "To marry me, I mean."

He was more than aware of just how much he was yanking her chain, reading her like a book. Rhia wasn't sure at all how he managed to be so in sync with her emotions for she'd only just met the damned man. Her lips soured as she agreed with his egotistical statement for she knew he'd never be short of arm candy.

"I know lots of women who would be happy to help me fulfill the terms of the will as my wife, but none of them will be any good at all to help me unravel the history of the place."

Rhia was highly aware of him as his eyes flicked over her tight cycling shorts and cheap T-shirt, but was then gob smacked when hurtful mirth curled his lip. "Of course my previous girlfriends have all been very decorative, Rhia—not a bookworm like you!"

Her flush this time was not in the least sexually charged: she was infuriated. How dare he compare her to the airheads he most likely consorted with? She wasn't anything much to look at with her short legs and small bust, but how could he be so dismissive and cruel?

Luke strolled away. Rhia glared at his retreating back, pretty sure many of the women he'd known would leap at the chance to be married to him for a year, but she wasn't so naïve. His bubbly flirts would contrive to milk him for all they could get after that year was up. Well, Hell mend him! He deserved one of his 'Don't I look beautiful' empty vessels to rip him off.

She had to get rid of the bloody man before she totally combusted. Greywood Hall would just have to molder away, for there was no way she would marry an arrogant pig like him.

Greywood Hall?

How could she do that to the poor neglected

house?

She had to think. She wasn't an airhead...she did have a brain somewhere among the mess of emotions she was feeling right at that moment. She closed her eyes to regroup yet again.

"Rhia..." Luke's soft inquiry made her eyes flick open again. "It's a good offer."

Oh God, she was so fickle! Why was she unable to resist him?

"Of course, if I marry some other woman, I suppose you could do the research for me and still live up at Greywood Hall with myself and my wife."

As if she'd consider that. Rhia bristled even more and grew hotter under the collar. Her imaginative libido went spiraling out of control as he blundered on. "But I guess that might depend on what would happen after the marriage. Maybe three of us living there would become too..." He padded around again, leaving the end of his sentence hanging.

Rhia willed her heart to restart, firmed her resolution and pushed any thoughts of coercion onto the back burner. She couldn't allow any other woman to marry him. God, the man stirred her far too much for that. But she needed all the facts clarified and unambiguous.

She cleared her throat encouraging Luke to cease his pacing and turn back to face her. She leveled his stare, very guarded with her words.

"So, are you saying that since you don't need love for this marriage, it would be a business arrangement till you're the legal owner? Then we'd separate? It wouldn't be a real marriage?" Her limpid brown gaze searched his for the truth so that Luke could see she wanted no flannelling or prevarication.

"Your words, not mine, Rhia." Now Luke wasn't even attempting to hide his sexual appraisal of her.

"I wouldn't call what we'd do together just business. It would be more of an accommodation of needs."

"An accommodation?" Rhia wondered what the hell that meant, her expression matching her serious tone for she couldn't envision not wanting to jump his bones if they lived together for a day let alone a year. "We'd co-habit Greywood Hall as man and wife, without love but lead separate lives?"

"Not exactly." A small smile tweaked the side of his mouth, his twinkling eyes betraying his amusement. "I think the answer to that is dependent on your interpretation of love. I don't expect love, Rhia, but I do expect sex." He closed the gap between them and positioned himself in front of her, straddling her chair, his long legs wide balanced as he looked down at her. "If you're honest you'll agree we have enough chemistry going on here between us to ignite a bonfire."

Rhia's face flamed at his candid assessment but couldn't deny what he was saying.

"I was thinking more of a mutually agreed arrangement where we share all aspects of our lives, including sex, till the year is up. Then we'd stop the arrangement." He was a mere step away.

"That sounds like I'd be a long-term whore or a mistress!" Rhia recoiled from him.

"We'd be living together legally as man and wife." Luke bent toward her.

"For a year?" She remained rooted in place, but her whole body frizzled.

"That's what it will take to fulfill the requirements of the will. Then the property will be mine."

Barely a hairsbreadth separated them now.

Chapter Six

Rhia was still rattled by his cold propositions, her chin hitching up again as she faced him. "You would seem to be getting a lot more out of this arrangement than I would."

Luke stepped back from her and whirled away. His voice was softer, yet evaluating, as he walked to the window. "Well, apart from no criminal record and no slur on your character, when I sell the place I'd be prepared to make you a financial settlement when we get divorced as well as turning over the title deeds for the cottage to you. You will become owner of the cottage."

"What if I don't want your money?" Rhia was appalled at his attitude but stuck to her ground.

"We'd say goodbye amicably then." He launched back into pacing once more.

Rhia tracked his movements. Her brain whirred, trying to regain some equilibrium though her heart was hammering. "So let me clarify this again. We'd live together at Greywood Hall for a year? As man and wife? Then I'd say goodbye to the arrangement?"

He stopped. "Yes."

"During that year you expect to have intimate relations in this marriage?" She eyeballed him as close as one can do with a foot in height difference between them, seeing a heated spark darkening the lush green of his stunning irises.

"You mean sex? I don't like to go without sex for long; it's not in my nature. I'd expect over a year to have sex: lots of sex."

His absorbed gaze burned through to her core.

She had never in her life felt so vulnerable, but she was determined to have her say. “So it would be a normal marriage, sex included...” It was impossible to swallow the lump in her throat, but she still needed some answers for her own preservation.

“Yes.” His large body roved the distance from the door and back.

“So lots of sex,” Rhia sweated, aiming for the same businesslike tone. “And would you stay here at Greywood Hall all the time?”

Luke stopped, facing away from her probing eyes, his voice becoming muffled. “I don’t think so—it’s too far away from my main offices for that to be practical. I travel a lot.” He paused to glance out of the window as a heavy vehicle passed along the lane, one of the very few that passed since Luke entered the cottage. “The will stipulates that Greywood Hall has to be my main domicile so I imagine I’d need to be here quite a lot of the time.”

He’d be away from home...quite a lot? Able to forget about her and make love to other women? The mere thought horrified Rhia. She couldn’t and wouldn’t ever share a man with anyone else. She’d been there inadvertently and the lesions too many to contemplate again. She could only be in a sexual relationship with a man who was one hundred per cent hers and hers alone. She had to ensure what had happened in the past never ever occurred again. She looked at her feet as she mouthed her next words.

“So you’d expect me to be your researcher by day and your dutiful wife waiting for you at your stately home at night? Your woman in residence? Your sort of mistress-cum-wife, ready to have sex when you returned home?”

Luke cleared his throat, his answer a soft sigh. Rhia hoped he realized she was deadly serious about monogamy.

"That about sums it up!"

"When you're on your travels? What then?" Rhia sounded more confident than she felt as her words, and eyes, challenged him.

"What do you mean? What then?" He crept toward her, but Rhia shrank away, needing his answer first.

Belligerence screamed in her tight chin. "When you're away from home, to London or Australia, or wherever...would you expect to have sex with other women because we just have...an accommodation?" Her eye contact was unflinching, even though it cost her enormous effort to do so. It amazed her that she managed to keep her tone neutral when her insides were rebelling at the thought of him touching another woman.

Luke blinked, but she could tell he was wondering where her conversation was leading.

"I have in the past had sex in Australia, and other places..."

"So if you're away from home and having sex, in those other places, then I would have the same possibility for affairs here?" she prodded, her focus determined, for she wasn't giving way on this. "While you're away that is?"

Luke's face was wiped of expression. He turned his back on her and studied her bookshelves. She could almost feel the tension that radiated across his neck muscles as he ground out, "Are you talking about Gus? Or somebody else?"

"Maybe." Rhia's face reddened. The mere thought of having sex with Gus was ludicrous, but he was the only name that came to mind.

"I've not lived like a monk, but neither do I have multiple relationships going on at the same time."

"Would you please clarify that for me?"

He turned back to her, his gaze penetrating, his words dragged through gritted teeth. "I only have a sexual relationship with one woman at a time. Regardless of which continent I'm on."

"So if you were married to me, for a year, in this accommodation of ours, then I'd be the only woman you'd have sex with during that time?" Rhia knew she must sound like a dog worrying a very juicy bone.

"What are you asking?" An unexplained vitality lit his eyes.

Rhia couldn't stand still any longer. She too paced, though nowhere near Luke, unable to look him in the eye when she uttered her next tentative words. "You wouldn't be entering into a sexual relationship with me in the normal way, because of love or attraction or whatever. I would just be a convenience—sex on tap when you're home." She was now the one pacing the room for her sexual thread was pinging and fit to snap. "I want something which will clarify this temporary relationship of ours. Under the circumstances you are coercing me into I will marry you, but only if I have it in writing that I will be your only lover during the time we are married."

"You're asking for some kind of prenuptial agreement?" Luke looked amazed at her temerity.

Chapter Seven

"Prenuptial agreement? Don't be ridiculous!" Rhia scoffed, her distrustful eyes peering. "At least I don't think so. Not if that's some sort of way of extorting money from you." She flushed with embarrassment that he should think that of her. That she'd be so mercenary. "I don't want any of your money, Luke, but if you expect me to enter into this farce, then I do want some assurance that you won't be bringing diseases home to me."

Although the words were easy to say, Rhia knew she did, in her own way, have some mercenary reasons for agreeing. To be employed for a whole year was a very nice carrot, even at her normal rate never mind twice her earnings. The cottage belonging to her at the end of the year was too good to pass up on for she still had to clear debts incurred by the lazy, good-for-nothing boyfriend who had milked her of her savings. To research the house and the Greywood family, possibly even have some input in the restorations was a fabulous prospect and could lead to a lot of future business. But to get her teeth into solving the mystery of Amelia Greywood's choice of Luke as the inheritor was much more appealing than money since during her walks around the grounds she'd wondered plenty of times about its history.

"And if I don't meet this requirement of yours?" Luke probed.

Storming right up to him—stopping a hairsbreadth away—her answer was unequivocal. "If you're not prepared to meet that request then you can darned well take me to the police right now, for no marriage will take place." The words spat out like bullets, her arms were held out crossed at the wrists.

Dropping her tense fingers, cradling her hips Rhia continued, "Or…if you say you'll be monogamous, and you fail to keep to the requirement during the year, I'll start divorce proceedings and we will go our own way. Of course, if I go you won't meet the conditions of the will."

"But then I won't have Greywood Hall, and it won't be restored properly." Luke reached to gentle his fingers on her shoulders, the light touch setting a tingle reverberating up her forearms that shocked and aroused her in equal measures. "You don't want that to happen," he warned.

Shrugging out of his grasp, Rhia stepped back, hoping the passion couldn't be heard in her response, for his touch was electric. "No, you won't have Greywood Hall! And you won't have me either."

Turning her back on him, she didn't understand why that thought upset her so much. She'd only just met this man who was having such a profound effect on her. He overwhelmed her, consumed her.

"Now who's blackmailing whom?"

Luke's words whispered behind her, his huge body moving closer to somehow cradle her without making contact. Then he reached for her. Resting his hands on her shoulders, his thumbs kneaded the tension at the back of her neck, his lips feathering butterfly kisses behind her ear before turning her round.

"Rhia."

Rhia drowned in her own need. She reached up to him at the very instant he bent to her, lust no longer to be denied. She couldn't wait another second or she'd just die. She wanted his lips on hers. She needed him to touch her all over and stop the utter sexual torment.

"Kiss me?"

Rhia wasn't sure if the request came from her own lips, but it didn't matter since they were both on the same page. Luke's mouth plundered hers. His arms became a tight band around her. Their lips melded, gently to begin with, but she'd been waiting too long for finesse. He demanded she open her mouth to him allowing his tongue to savor; she complied. Their tongues shifted, sliding sinuously around, tasting and teasing each other, drawing a groaning response from her.

Through their mingled breaths she heard him murmur, "*Bella.* You taste so good," before he swooped in again for a thorough gorging.

When they surfaced Rhia couldn't draw a proper breath.

Luke touched his forehead to hers and held her tight. "*Cara*," he whispered. "You're entrancing." He captured her lips again with an urgency that wouldn't be halted.

Rhia thought just maybe her urgency was greater than his.

Luke's hand slipped down to cup a breast, forcing a gasp of sheer delight from her; the anticipation was altogether too much. She'd wanted his touch, and now it was happening. The backs of his fingers grazed her tingling nipple, arousing it to a hard peak before he took it in his clever fingertips, rolling and squeezing, the friction of the shirt causing even more stimulation. Maneuvering herself further into his tight embrace she locked his fingers in between their overheated bodies. Her fevered hands gripped his waist then she slid them around to lock them behind his back, enveloping his pulsating length between her aching thighs.

"I want…"

"I know what you want," Luke murmured against her cheek.

His tongue wrapped around hers, mimicking the thrust and parry they were both desperate for. Without breaking the kiss, his fingers found the edge of her T-shirt. “This has to come off!” His words muffled against her teeth as he eased up the material.

Rhia was unaware of her arms rising and the top being thrown off. Nimble fingers opened the front catch of her lacy bra, baring her to his touch, his thumbs strumming over her very ready nipples, the friction overwhelming. A floodtide of passion rippled through her at his practiced touch. Luke traced his hands up her slender arms to peel off the bra straps at her shoulders and allowed the filmy fabric to drop to the floor.

“Beautiful, absolutely *formidabile!*”

With no clothing to bar the way, his lips descended to her throbbing breasts where he laved, licked and suckled, inciting moans and pleas for more.

Rhia held his head tight to her breasts and grabbed his hair even tighter in her frenzy. Her pelvis shoved at his straining erection but it was impossible to get close enough. The connection went right down to her core as Luke drew a nipple into his mouth, suckling hard; setting the stage for a gargantuan orgasm.

A few deft touches of his clever fingers as they slid past her navel and under the waistband of her shorts was all Rhia needed. A few strokes only, her muscles stiffened then the pulsating tremors hit, tremors that reverberated on his fingers.

“*Magnifica!*” Luke mumbled in Italian, words she neither understood nor properly heard. Her pupils dilated, and her body went into meltdown. Luke continued to hold her till the pulses dissipated. She buried her head into his chest till her breathing evened out.

Rhia was staggered at what had just happened—and embarrassed. She didn't know this man yet she'd allowed him to be so intimate.

Luke's fingers lifted her chin, his lips seeking hers once more, stirring her passion again; wanting to finish what they'd started so spectacularly, but an insistent ringing penetrated their sexual haze. Latching onto it as an excuse Rhia backed away.

"The telephone." She struggled out of his arms.

"Ignore it!" Luke whispered.

"No, I-I'm sorry. I should never have let..." She wasn't coherent; she pulled back from him and tore out into the hallway to pick up the phone.

Through the miasma of his thwarted seduction Luke processed her response to the caller as he watched her out in the hallway. Bare-breasted. Beautiful.

"Gus! Hello."

Her cheery tone chilled him like an arctic breeze. He watched her turn toward him, the landline trembling in her hand. Her smile of welcome for Gus gutted him; she was so pleased to take the call. A knife twisted somewhere.

"No, I'm fine. It was all a dreadful mistake."

A mistake? What was a mistake? Making love to him? Rhia's answer was so soft it shot his temper to skyrocket proportions. He didn't like the way the conversation was going. The idea of Rhia sharing her body with Gus or anyone else while he was her lover was detestable. The way he was attracted that very moment meant he didn't think he'd have a problem with having only her as a sexual partner for quite a while—maybe not a whole year—but for a good while. She was already a delightful challenge, his hunger growing so much he wanted to start their partnership right that very minute.

"No, no Gus. Honestly!" Rhia's laugh echoed in the corridor, her breasts jiggling as she swung away.

"I don't need anything."

Luke scowled. Rhia couldn't be this genuine—she must want something, women always did. He'd wanted to see how grasping she'd be over his proposals, but she threw him a loop by issuing her own demands. A spitting little hind she'd been demanding he not be a rutting stag! He'd been thrilled that her words might be prompted by jealousy over him having sexual relations with another woman. Why that should be was a mystery for propriatorial attitudes usually turned him off, yet Rhia's demands intrigued him.

She was so soft, so fragile yet in many ways so strong, and now he was aching for her. But she'd blown him off for Gus. Luke's teeth grated.

"No!" Her laugh echoed again—the deep, husky reassurance becoming irritating. "No charges. No repercussions."

This Gus person had somehow heard she'd ended up at the police station. As Rhia nattered on Luke's fierce erection subsided. He wanted to punch something, preferably Gus, but as to repercussions? Rhia didn't know the half of it yet. But she would.

"Yes, okay…I'll catch up with you later." She chuckled. "Love you too."

Rhia replaced the handset before coming back in to the sitting room, her arms wrapped around her gorgeous breasts. Locating her T-shirt she whipped it on, her embarrassment obvious.

"Luke. I'm sorry," Rhia whispered unable to look him squarely in the eye now. "I don't know what to say. I didn't mean to be a tease. I guess I just couldn't stop myself."

She ran out of steam, waited for his response, and waited, squirming, till he couldn't stand her discomfiture any longer. Stepping in front of her he grasped her upper arms, his large hands slipping up to cup her shoulders, an instinctive caress he couldn't prevent. "We still have a deal, Rhia."

"We still have a deal?"

She was so confused. She'd just rejected his advances, left him high and dry, so it wasn't surprising she was baffled. He forced her to look at him. "We're getting married as soon as I can arrange it. We'll take up residence at Greywood Hall as soon as is feasible. We'll live as man and wife in the full sense of the word." He didn't add "as soon as possible" to the last words, but both knew without a doubt they were part of the subtext. Rhia shivered as Luke's hand cupped her chin and lifted her closer to his mouth again. He continued his litany. "You will be my only lover, and I will be your only lover." His lips a mere whisper from hers, he finished, "You'll have the satisfaction of seeing the property restored, and be able to roam with your dog, every single day, knowing you aren't trespassing."

Rhia's face turned pale at the word trespassing. In response his fingers soothed her cheek, the gentle handling at odds with the fierce glint in his eyes.

"But you can forget Gus or anybody else during that time!" Luke wanted no misinterpretation about his meaning. His thumb traced a gentle pathway across the contours of her bottom lip as he bent his head and sipped, just a tiny sip before he released her and stepped back. "I'll let you know about the arrangements as soon as possible."

He took off after a last whisper of a kiss.

Chapter Eight

An official contract arrived the next day before ten a.m., hand delivered by Luke's PA, Jeremy, whom Rhia guessed to be a little younger than his boss. Jeremy was maybe a few years older than her twenty-six, a likeable guy who, from first introduction, demonstrated he knew all the particulars of the outlandish deal.

He conducted their meeting with considerable aplomb. His curious gaze appraised her, but he never strayed from the professional, not asking personal questions as he worked their way through the simple but legal terms on the contract. Yet he did ask some puzzling questions. Questions which made Rhia wonder about their relevance.

"How long have you lived at Border Cottage?"

"Mmm? I guess just a little over a year. I relocated here last year on July the second."

"Have you made any recent trips in the last two weeks?" Jeremy scribbled on the pad lying on his knees.

"No." Rhia was bemused, her gaze quizzical, and her voice hesitant as she continued, "As long as you don't count my occasional trips to the supermarket in Hopton."

Jeremy chuckled. "No, I think we'll discount those trips. I was meaning some holiday perhaps?"

Rhia had not vacationed at all since moving to the cottage. A few more questions about recent days and her current work schedules were simple to answer, her mind drifting to wonder how the heck Luke had organized the contract, for he must have had his London lawyers work on it the minute he'd left her the previous late-afternoon.

Rhia realized what Luke indicated was true—he didn't ever like to watch the grass grow. If something needed doing, it was done with super expediency. Not only was she aware of the power of the man, she was becoming more aware of what he could achieve with the power of money.

Unable to find fault with it, she duly signed the simple but very explicit contract. It had been pre-signed by Luke who had indeed included an incontestable monogamy clause, and after penning her signature the paperwork was countersigned by Jeremy.

She was loathe to hand over her birth certificate when requested. It was necessary to prove her identity for the marriage license, but her fingers lingered on it, her whole hand shaking so much Jeremy had to ease it out of her grasp. At that point the bizarre undertaking became so real. She was signing away her identity—for a year!

Jeremy's voice was designed to soothe her frantic heartbeat, though her appreciation was vague at best. "Luke's a good employer, Miss Ashton. He's tough but fair and however weird this deal might seem, you can trust him. If he puts something on paper, he'll stick to the letter."

All done and dusted by 10:15 a.m.

The rest of the day passed; she longed to see Luke but dreaded it too. She still couldn't believe she almost had sex with a man she'd only known a couple of hours! She'd capitulated so readily to his accommodation, but she didn't see how she could have done otherwise. There was no way her body would have gone into resistance mode after his first lust-filled kiss. The dismay at her incomprehensible behavior had only come after that incredible orgasm. She'd never ever climaxed like that before, and never with only a few amazing touches.

Functioning on autopilot she mulled over what had happened the previous day, what hadn't quite happened, and above all what she had agreed to.

The day slipped away slowly with Rhia's nervous anticipation growing by the minute. It wasn't a quiet day though, not with the unusual sounds of a helicopter nearby, and the steady flow of vehicles that passed her door.

Out of sheer contrariness she walked Thor in the opposite direction from Greywood Hall twice that day, maintaining firm control over his movements. She needed to keep him close to heel to be safe with the increased traffic. After both sojourns she was frustrated. She wasn't at all sure what she'd been trying to prove by going that way, for she was nosey about what was happening in the other direction.

But of Luke, she heard not a peep. She'd expected him to at least call, but no—that didn't happen. She went to bed feeling out of sorts: the sexual frenzy of the previous day an implausible memory.

The landline phone rang the following morning at just after seven a.m. Rhia was awake and, by then, nursing her second cup of coffee. Her sleep had been fitful. And then the rumble of heavy trucks starting just after six a.m., ruined any further chance of dozing. For a quiet little backwater neighborhood, the vehicular activity could only be put down to one reason: Luke. The traffic must all be going to Greywood Hall.

She was grumpy when she lifted the receiver.

"Meet me here at the Ruisdale Grange for lunch, Rhia." Luke's brusque tone made it sound like an order rather than an invitation.

Frustrated with the speed at which events were taking place, and annoyed at being ignored the day before, Rhia listened without comment, only answering when he informed her that a driver would be along to pick her up.

"No." Her tone was resolute. "I'll drive myself, thank you." She knew how to get to the top class hotel though she'd never had the opportunity, or quite frankly the cash, to sample its exclusive grandeur.

On arrival, her breath hitched. Luke stood sentinel at the top of the short flight of stairs by the entryway. Her heart lurched. He was every bit as gorgeous as she'd thought two days before. The expensive dark suit was faultless, a collar and tie neatly in place—very formal. He stood as though he was master of all he surveyed. And wasn't that appropriate. This man was way out of her league!

Her composure deflated: she felt nervous and exposed. She'd had plenty of time that morning to consider what she'd agreed to. Unfortunately she wasn't convinced she could follow through on their agreement. The research part of the contract she'd have no issue with at all. Living in the same house she could probably manage. But being contract lovers? Then saying goodbye? Good heavens! Like the so-called sex buddies in novels, where partners only arranged to meet for recreational or stress-busting sex. That was an entirely different state of affairs.

She didn't think she could manage that. But then again how on earth could she have been so affected by him that she'd fallen into his arms the way she had done the last time they'd met? It was bewildering, and she hated feeling all at sea. She liked her life orderly and planned. She liked to know she was in control of what she was doing.

This situation was way out of her control.

His lifestyle was on another planet from hers. But Luke had seen her approach. She couldn't back out now, so swallowing her insecurity she straightened her spine and drew nearer, stemming the trembles that threatened to make her trip over the cobbles of the driveway.

Rhia was lovely. Perversely Luke didn't want her to be so attractive.

Personally, all he needed was her name on the dotted line on their marriage certificate. Professionally, he needed her considerable research skills, for he now knew she'd had a glowing career as a research assistant with great future possibilities at the Victoria and Albert Museum in London, where she'd gone after graduation from Oxford. He knew only the very best got such plum jobs, but something had made her resign from those great prospects to come and live in the Yorkshire Dales and set up her own internet business. Plenty of people did that kind of thing—of course they did—but what were her motivations for moving from the metropolis to the boondocks? Why? He didn't yet know but in the fullness of time he'd find out.

Pragmatically speaking if he needed to be married to someone for a year it would be better all round if he could get on with the woman on a daily basis. But to desire the person? That was something else entirely.

On leaving the police station two days previously, he'd geared himself up to go through with a paper marriage only—if that was the limit Rhia was prepared to go to. He'd planned to compensate her highly, if that's what she wanted. But to his surprise she didn't.

Porca miseria!

She was just as wildly attracted to him as he was to her. That would complicate things down the line. He lusted after her delicious body right now, but from experience, lust never lasted. Something always soured his relationships with women—ending them almost as soon as they had begun.

This time though, a whole calendar year was at stake. Whatever it was about him that made him restless with previous lovers, he'd have to suppress, manage it somehow...or sharing the same space for twelve months would become a huge problem.

Rhia walked toward him wearing a slinky suit of rich bronze, and sexily high ankle-strapped heels that emphasized her slim legs.

His physical reaction to her was the same as two days before. He didn't think it possible—even for him—that his blood could relocate around his body to create such a painfully hard erection in a blink.

The fitted skirt swept just above her knees leaving plenty of luscious leg to savor. The tight nipped-in jacket across her breasts accentuated the luxury of her curves, and her shining fall of inky dark hair bounced around her pixie face. Sexual awareness pulsed at the sight of her. The day before, he'd wanted to call her, but he'd quelled those urges for he needed her long-term cooperation more than her body, temporarily and fleetingly. Instead he'd turned to planning and plotting.

She wasn't smiling as she walked to him. She looked...unhappy? Maybe even angry, like she'd been on the phone earlier that morning. One thing was certain; she was not pleased to see him. Was she having second thoughts?

He was glad he hadn't welcomed her with the ardor that rippled through his taught, frustrated body. His instinct had been to pick her up and twirl her around before crushing her delightful body to his, melding his lips to hers in a leisurely kiss of welcome. But that wouldn't work. He wasn't sure what was wrong but something was. He wiped the smile from his face and forced himself to stifle the craving he felt for this enchanting sprite of a woman. He didn't kiss her or attempt to touch her in any way for he knew he'd not be able to stop at a simple touch.

"Hello, Rhia."

Perfunctorily welcoming her with a tight parody of a smile, he led her through the hotel foyer, escorting her to a table already awaiting them in the main restaurant, barely giving her time to draw breath. A hovering waiter performed services with napkins and menus, another waiter came for their drink order.

"Sparkling water for both of us please," Luke ordered, not waiting for a response from her before launching into his plans for the next few days.

She didn't look any more relaxed. The bristling porcupine of that first day had returned so he made his preparations as clear as possible. "I went to see the local Superintendent Registrar early on today, to make arrangements for a special license so that our marriage ceremony can be here at the Ruisdale Grange first thing tomorrow morning." He kept his tone level and businesslike.

Her little gasp of dismay wasn't as quiet as he thought she intended. Luke feared things might not go as smooth as he'd hoped.

"How can it possibly be tomorrow? You need three weeks for wedding banns to be read." She appeared dazed at the speed he was taking over her life. Nerves must be getting the better of her.

"Not so, Rhia."

Her face grew thunderous, but it got even worse as he elaborated. "You've been resident in this district for more than the required seven days. It only takes one of us to have done that, and it only took one of us to proffer the necessary certification and make the request for us to get married with a special license for tomorrow. As of this morning I gave the required one day's notice."

"What?" Rhia couldn't seem to absorb his words.

"This hotel is authorized to perform wedding

ceremonies and I've persuaded the Registrar to marry us here at seven forty-five tomorrow morning, giving her time to get back to the Registry for her next scheduled marriage ceremony at nine."

"What?" Diners around them turned interested ears at her pitch, but Rhia was oblivious to them. "Normal people don't get married after one day," she railed, her tone pretty bloody-minded about it all.

"I don't consider I need to do what normal people do, Rhia."

He tracked her agitation as she huffed, and looked everywhere but at him, "You've got that right. You're not normal!"

Unfortunately, he hadn't factored in the possibility she'd reject any of his preparations. What was getting her in such a fit of temper? She'd happily signed on the dotted line the day before, according to Jeremy, whom Luke sourly noted had been quite enthusiastic about Rhia's beauty—too enthusiastic.

A tense silence reigned till Rhia blurted, "What if I want to get married in a church?" Her tone was belligerent. Her agitated fingers twirled a fork around, tapping it against the table as though she was wondering what she was doing. She looked everywhere else but at him as she awaited his response.

"I suppose a church ceremony could be arranged, somehow—if it's what you want," Luke answered, wanting to soothe her, make her respond to him the way she had two days before. Though why he felt the need to do that quite baffled him. Not what he wanted or expected. He didn't know how to get back to the attraction they'd shared, but he did know his usual seduction techniques were not going to be in any way successful with Rhia.

She was too complex, too different from any woman he'd seduced before. Of course he wasn't seducing her. And the stakes were too high.

When had he ever interacted with a woman when sex wasn't what he had on the agenda? The answer to his question was probably never in recent years—not since his earliest forays into dating in his teens when he did have the mad idea he should get to know his dates before he bedded them.

Right now he'd already set the wheels rolling for claiming his inheritance so there was no way she could be allowed to back out. He needed to get Rhia back to the mood of two days ago, remind her somehow that they were in sexual tandem. If he could do that, everything else would follow.

He forced his tone to level, and softened his expression, made it appear more amenable. "I've looked into this and have taken the quickest route possible."

"Oh, anywhere will do!" Her answer was brusque, her fingers fidgeting with her napkin, twisting it around so much that had it been paper and not super quality linen it would already be shredded. "But not tomorrow!"

She was adamant, even more challenging now. "I need some more notice than that," she huffed again.

He heard panic in her voice now.

"You can't expect me to agree to tomorrow."

She was so stressed Luke decided maybe he had been a little precipitate in arranging for them to marry the next day. Information about the clause in the will stating his claim on the estate had to happen within thirty-one days he'd doggedly kept to himself. There was no need for Rhia to know that information…even if it did seem a bit duplicitous not to tell her. His usual fair-minded conscience only pricked a little.

"I need a little more time."

Chapter Nine

Luke's nod was reluctant. "Saturday then. We'll get married this Saturday." Already his mind had worked out the cancellations and rescheduling he'd need to do. Not to mention persuading the Registrar yet again.

There was a definite gulp. He couldn't help but hear it.

"No. We'll compromise," Rhia insisted, unwilling to back down. "Make it ten days from now. That's half of the time normal people wait."

"Ten days?" Luke repeated, amazed at her dead seriousness, yet impressed by her bargaining. Her jaw was antagonistic, but in a strange way her tenacity added to her allure. She was the most unpredictably arousing female he'd ever encountered.

He acquiesced, knowing the marriage certificate was legally necessary, but since the lawyer had granted the usual three weeks declaration of banns, her time scale still met that requirement. He'd wait ten days for the paperwork but not ten days to have sex with her. That was much too much to concede, but first he'd show her how he could compromise.

"Okay. We'll have the ceremony in two weeks." His answer was equable but gave her none of his reasoning.

Good manners prevailed as she nodded back. "Thank you. Well, what else have you sorted out?" she asked as though the earlier animosity was no longer needed.

"I'm taking you for a dress fitting at three-thirty

this afternoon to a recommended wedding shop in Derby. We'll leave after lunch, and you can choose your dress and other necessaries."

"No."

"What do you mean no?"

Luke was puzzled. Didn't women always want to go shopping for dresses on unlimited budgets? In the past he'd given girlfriends an authorized credit card or store account details in London or Brisbane, to buy something suitable for a special function. He didn't quite have a word for how he felt about Rhia's rebuff. Others might say he was peeved, but he'd scoff at that description. This was more than a random evening function, or charity ball; this was for their wedding; and although he acknowledged that the circumstances of the wedding were very unorthodox it still seemed to him to require some sort of effort.

He'd geared himself up to accompany Rhia, to select a dress with her. He'd been daydreaming of her constantly for the last day, imagining her in a vision of white, the dress redolent of a fairy princess, a woodland sprite. He'd been looking forward to selecting wispy lingerie that he'd remove once they got back to the hotel room after the ceremony. He'd thought a lot about the sexy strapped heels he'd remove with infinite care, sliding down the silk stockings, paying lots of attention to her dinky little feet…the garter belt, as he laid her bare. The insistent thoughts had interrupted lots of his rescheduling and reorganizing of his work the previous day.

He was well aware it wasn't the traditional thing for the groom to accompany the bride to choose those garments—but darn it—he wanted to select them with her. He wanted to see her in lots of possibilities and then choose the perfect ones.

"No."

Rhia's tone brooked no argument. In fact she sounded so much like the peremptory matron at his old boarding school he almost gagged.

"I'll organize my own dress, thank you," Rhia persisted, "and you'll not pay for it or any other accoutrement for our so-called wedding. I'm not your paid whore, though I'm beginning to wonder about that now. I told you I don't want your money. I'll enter into this marriage because I said I would, for the refurbishment of Greywood Hall, but I'll do it in my own way." Her chin was firm, and her tone brooked no adaptations to her dictates. "And anyway it would take forever to get to Derby."

"My helicopter will pick us up in about an hour," Luke smoothly added.

"Helicopter?" Rhia mocked, "Now why didn't I think of that."

Luke was exasperated with her sarcasm. He realized in an instant that he'd need to concede a little, compromise a little more to get his own way. Things with Rhia weren't going according to plan.

Hadn't he made a concession with their monogamy clause too? He didn't normally do concessions. His voice was terse. "I'll cancel the appointment then...if you'll excuse me just a moment?" From her flashing eyes and tight-lipped expression he realized there was no way she was backing down on the dress fitting. He held up his cell.

The merest nod was her assent.

Luke gave Jeremy brief instructions to cancel all afternoon plans and the registrar for the following day. Then he told Jeremy the wedding was still on, just not the following day but to reschedule the registrar for two weeks hence. That was it. A few words were all it took to cancel a wedding, a helicopter and a specialist dress fitting.

Luke continued outlining his plans after repocketing his phone. “I’ve already asked Jeremy to be a witness to our marriage. Is there someone you’d like to ask to be the second witness?”

“No. Of course not. This isn’t a real marriage so I’m not asking any of my friends to attend such an absurd situation,” Rhia answered, her tone flat. “And I’ve no immediate relatives that I need bother about.”

Her fingers smoothed the pristine white tablecloth, needing something to do to quell her panic over the trap she was getting into. But that wasn’t true either. Her own actions had instigated it. She didn’t need to go through with this so-called deal. She could face up to the consequences of her trespassing—she could do that—but then she’d never see Luke again. Never know what it would be like to make love to this man who drove her insane, for even though she was angry and confused by his cold manner she was still drawn to him more than to any man ever in her previous acquaintance. How could she go through life wondering what it would have been like to be his lover… and not ever find any substitute?

But how could she do it so soon? It terrified her!

“Well then, would you prefer me to arrange the second witness too?” Luke persisted, his annoyance not a surprise to Rhia.

“Yes, although I don’t imagine you’ll want to be asking your parents or relatives to this charade either.”

“My parents are both dead, so I won’t be inviting them, Rhia.” Cynicism and impatience loaded his tone. “Roger—he’s my London butler—will be happy to do the job.”

“Your butler?” Rhia couldn’t stop her tone from turning sarcastic, patronizing, maybe both: she knew she wasn’t being complimentary or mannerly but couldn’t prevent her nerves from getting the better of her. "Of course, I'm sure your butler would be delighted to perform such services for you."

She was unnerved by the concept that this man had a London butler. He probably had another in Australia. She reeled at the opulence of his life. Butler. Helicopter. Ferrari. This rich man lived an existence nothing like hers. She couldn't measure up to his standards.

What was she doing entering into this travesty of a marriage?

But it was just supposed to be a business arrangement after all so that he could, in time, get his hands on Greywood Hall. She gulped again. Looking at his tight-lipped yet calculating expression she thought about the concessions he'd already made and the contract she'd already signed. She wasn't sure why any victory won seemed so hollow.

"Roger does what he's asked to do." Luke's confirmation was cool.

"So what else have you already arranged?" Rhia was irritable, not sure if she wanted to know but was striving to be at least a little polite as they awaited their meal.

"Tomorrow I've arranged for a delivery of necessary equipment from my London Office. I take it you have a bedroom or somewhere I could use?" His manner was abrupt.

"In my cottage?" Rhia bellowed, flustered that he was going to rearrange everything in her humble abode. It was already bad enough picturing him in her small sitting room and kitchen from his earlier visit. She couldn't sit now without reliving his lips on hers, his oh-so-expert hands exciting her body to orgasm, and his hands bracketing her on the chair, almost stealing kisses. But she couldn't let him know how that affected her. "What do you think you're going to do in my cottage?"

"Tonight I'm booked here but tomorrow I plan to move in with you, although I know it's going to be a challenge because it's so cramped."

"This is my cottage, my home, you're talking about. You've no right to talk about it in such a condescending way. It may not be a huge mansion, but it's where I live!" Rhia was both appalled and contrarily thrilled by the idea that he'd move in, but she wasn't letting him know that! He was taking over her life in a big, big way, and she wasn't going to have that happen without him knowing she was under some stress about it.

The waiter arrived with their superbly presented entrees. Rhia was too edgy to even taste hers; Luke proceeded to clear his plate as he picked up the conversation. "That's not what I meant. I run a huge operation, and I have several computers running concurrently, hence the need for space. I'll limit as much as possible while we're in your cottage since it will be only for a few days. You do have somewhere I can use?"

Rhia's answer was obstinate. "But if we aren't getting married for two weeks why do you need to move in to my cottage tomorrow? Why not wait till we can move into Greywood Hall, then you'd have all the space you could ever need?"

With precision Luke placed his cutlery at the edge of his plate and explained that he'd contacted Miss Greywood's lawyer, and that under the unusual circumstances it wasn't a problem to begin the co-habiting count of one calendar year from the following day, acknowledging the intention to officiate their marriage, and a complete renovation to Greywood Hall could be initiated without delay.

Oh God! He'd still be moving in tomorrow? Even if they didn't marry for ten days? Rhia's body was quivering, but she was proud of the businesslike tone she employed. "You're desperate to start tomorrow so that the year will be completed sooner?"

"Not precisely how I was thinking, Rhia."

"And the residence qualification—did the lawyer clarify how often you'd need to be home?"

"He did." His answer was brusque as he scanned the dining room.

"And?"

His gaze slid back to lock onto hers. He wanted no misinterpretation as he parroted. "It would seem I must be in residence with you for the whole duration, initially in your cottage and soon at Greywood Hall. You must accompany me if I have to be away from Greywood Hall for more than one night for any business or pleasure visits abroad, or elsewhere in the UK. If the two of us are away for longer, except with prior authorization, the visits can be for no longer than one week."

"In other words we're literally joined at the hip?" Rhia's jaw dropped, unable to prevent her noisy gasp. A waiter hovering to collect their plates perked up his ears at her comment. He had heard it, and she was embarrassed.

"A nice way of putting it," Luke murmured not in the least put out. In fact he seemed amused by her reactions.

"What if you have to be away and it isn't convenient for my work schedule?" she asked, going off on a tangent.

"Rhia, I know what you do for a living." Luke's tone was frustrated. "You're an historian, currently a researcher of family history. I know perfectly well that you can work almost anywhere if you've got internet access and courier services. You'll manage."

"That's very kind of you." She didn't try to stop her words from sounding waspish. "For your information, sometimes I do have to be away from home looking at original sources which can't be sent as copies. What happens then? Do you have to follow me around the country?"

"No." Luke's admission was reluctant as though not happy to be put on the spot. "I'm the one who has to be in residence most of the time."

"So I could be away without you and still meet the legal requirements?" Rhia's eyes were beginning to lose the bile and were now sparkling with something more like devilment.

"I'd have to clarify that again with the lawyer, but I imagine it could only be for the same short periods of time as stipulated for me."

Going off gallivanting was beginning to sound quite appealing, though Luke's scowl indicated he didn't care much for the idea. "Maybe this won't be so bad then if I needn't have to be shackled to your company all the time." She brightened for the first time that day. "I do like to get away from time to time."

Luke was riled. "But remember we do have our signed contract. I am your only lover and you are my only lover!"

"I wasn't necessarily meaning I'd go off somewhere and have mindless sex with some one-night stand, or some passing acquaintance. I merely meant we'd not have to be quite so much in each other's pockets."

She acknowledged she'd quite like Luke being in her pockets—or panties—anywhere on her at all, but his fixed glare didn't mean he wanted that too. He was proving to be the most frustrating man she'd ever met. The waiter happened to place their main courses down just at that moment. His mouth twitched, his eyes hard put not to show his amusement at the interesting statements being made by them. Rhia stuttered a little to clarify for Luke, her answer blithe.

"Except, it just so happens, I like living in this part of the world. I moved here by choice a year ago so I don't suppose I'll be away from home too much."

An edgy silence followed till Rhia felt she'd scream with the agony of it. Doggedly she picked up the threads of her conversation. "What else?"

"What do you mean what else?"

"I mean what else have you organized already?" She grabbed up her knife and fork and stabbed the first thing she could find on her plate.

Luke exhaled as though any conversation was a trial for him now. "You may already have heard some activity at Greywood?"

She nodded her tone still challenging. "You're right about that. They woke me up far too early this morning."

"Sorry about that," Luke continued not sounding contrite. "We start early to maximize the daylight hours."

"Of course, never waste a minute!"

"You're right; I don't like wasted time." He sounded very irritated by her censure but resumed the conversation. "Teams of craftsmen are starting roof and stonework repairs at Greywood Hall at first light tomorrow. Other teams are going inside to finalize the assessment of internal damage so that work on internal renovations can begin as soon as possible, once I evaluate their findings."

He forked a bit of salmon into his mouth. Five minutes later he was still outlining the long-term plans he'd instigated for Greywood Hall.

"You arranged all this in one day?" Rhia was astonished. She'd moped around for the past twenty-four hours daydreaming, wondering what the hell she'd got herself into, and he'd been organizing goodness knows what. Not lusting after her as she'd been lusting after him!

"Rhia, it's my job." Luke smiled, for the first time a natural smile.

"But it's impossible to get craftsmen to do even

small repairs unless it's a major catastrophe. How did you manage it?" She was impressed by his information, her gaze incredulous, unable to maintain the stiff attitude for she was by nature a generous person.

Luke grinned. Her tension eased a little more. They continued to eat, their food interspersed with sips of the delicious crisp white wine he'd ordered.

"One advantage of having a lot of money, Rhia, is to pay people to do what you want, when you want. I have an army of highly skilled workers at my beck and call. If they have to be away from their home base for short durations, they know their pay will be generous, covering any inconvenience caused."

"But Greywood Hall is a large property. It's going to take lots of people forever to restore it if you do it properly." Her face was a mask of doubt.

"Properly? What do you mean?"

"Well, I mean renovations need to be thoroughly planned and not rushed and... You mustn't spoil the character of it, Luke," she had the audacity to insist.

Not in the least put out by her doubtful tone Luke smiled as he answered, "Rhia, for the last five years I've been doing major renovations on English properties: most of them sites of some historical significance. I assure you I won't be rushing in and wrecking the character or the ambience of the place."

"It's got a lot of dignity, even if it is run down." Her tone was wistful her eyes emotional.

"Have you ever been inside?" Luke looked pleased that they'd lost the earlier snapping tension.

"No, of course I haven't."

His hand reached across the table and clasped her fingers. "Would you like to?"

His light touch was a balm. Rhia hadn't quite realized that his touch would matter so much as she agreed she'd love to see inside.

"Well, since we're not going for a wedding dress we'll look over Greywood Hall this afternoon."

Luke's fingers played with hers, his thumb idly caressing her palm.

Whether it was the wine or something else that mellowed her, Rhia wasn't questioning: she felt much better than earlier. Those undeniable physical charges were flowing again. She listened to Luke explain that locating the keys the day before had been a tedious priority.

Rhia sank back from the table, removed his hand from hers and stretched her legs underneath, her toe inadvertently nudging his in the process. A shudder of awareness arced up her leg. When Luke shifted his foot closer to her, the anticipation notched up even further, a flush spreading over her cheeks that she couldn't do a damned thing about.

He went on to detail other processes he'd already put in place, arrangements for him to move his main operations from London to Greywood Hall, telling her briefly about things he'd delegated to his capable teams of employees.

"But how can you just up and leave your work base, and still maintain your business?" Rhia asked, amazed at how easy he made it all sound.

Luke explained how he always had support teams at a new project venue, so setting up at Greywood Hall was not so different from other situations, and about the delegation processes he put in place when he traveled.

They finished their meal, Rhia realizing that her earlier fears about being with an impressive millionaire like Luke had been largely unfounded. When all was said and done, he was just a man. Well, maybe not just a man. She'd never met anyone quite like him before.

The sexual tension that had been an undercurrent bubbled to the surface as they finished their coffee. For all they'd been at loggerheads, that undeniable something drew them closer again. By the time they left the restaurant, Rhia had a much better understanding of what great wealth could achieve in a short time, and she was seriously impressed by the plans he'd already put into place for Greywood Hall.

"I'll follow you back in my own car, Rhia."

Chapter Ten

A short while later Luke's Ferrari drove through the main gates of Greywood Hall. Thor panted in the small rear seat, his tail swished, and his muzzle was squashed against the now drool washed windowpane. The hound's breathing was the labored type of wheezing that dogs exhibit when they can't wait any longer for something to happen.

However, Thor wasn't the only excitable one in the car. The accord at the end of their meal was still in force, the now no longer subtle sexual attraction increasing in strength and threatening to dissolve Rhia into a little mound of mush on the skin-soft leather. All it took was Luke's close proximity in the low-slung car that was seemingly built for intimacy. What Rhia felt though, wasn't the comfort it was designed for—she in fact felt the opposite. Tense with desire, her awareness of Luke was overwhelming. Her breathing was no steadier than Thor's: she prayed it wasn't so ragged sounding.

She forced herself to engage in conversation that would take her mind off things. Things like Luke's strong sensual fingers caressing the small driving wheel, his thumbs worrying the inner edge of the leather-made her imagine the fingers caressing her inner edges. Things like his strong thigh set next to hers that just one slight movement of her hand would allow her to stroke the muscles beneath his suit trousers and stop his slight tremor. Things like the woodsy shaving product she was coming to associate with him. Things like the musk that was purely him.

Her nerve endings flared and frizzled in expectation. Of something. Something that would stop the sexual torment engulfing her. He didn't even have to be conversing with her. His very nearness magnified the yearnings that had started in the restaurant—once she'd put aside her misgivings and had suppressed her nerve-driven attitude.

Heavens above! What could she talk about to end the intense silence in the car—the passionate silence that ruled, with the exception of Thor's boisterous exhalations?

"Where are all those noisy vehicles that woke me this morning?" she asked, for there was now no evidence of them on the driveway. Some had to have been delivery trucks.

"They'll not be back till tomorrow morning," Luke said. "My team completed the initial assessments before noon today. They'll be dashing out their proposals right now so that they've got some down time tonight before another early start tomorrow."

"Ah! I'll set my alarm for five thirty then?" Rhia laughed at Luke's marginal apology as she teased.

"Five. Depending on how long it takes you to shower."

He wasn't joking about the time scale. The sensual promise in his sparkling green gaze told her he was able to talk about one thing but was thinking about something entirely different. Her mirth vanished in mock dismay. "Are you telling me those trucks really will be there before six o'clock?"

Luke chuckled at her pretended indignation. "It's summertime. Dawn is hours before six, and some of the haulage companies work a 24-hour day. I'm expecting deliveries throughout the night—"

"Overnight?"

Luke resumed as though she hadn't interrupted

at all, his smile wide, his expression intended to placate. "...but those trucks shouldn't bother you tonight. They'll be going through the back entrance. They'll approach Greywood from the opposite direction, and use that access to unload roofing materials in the stable courtyard. My technical team, however, won't arrive till after six, at the earliest."

"But where are they going to arrive from if they're getting here so early?" She already knew from his update at lunchtime many of the team had been flown up north the day before from locations scattered across the south of England.

Luke named a hotel in the nearest town.

"Why there?"

The heat he bestowed on her fried her to a crisp, his answer a deep whisper that did amazing things to her insides before the words fully registered. "I didn't think you'd appreciate waking up the day after our wedding knowing my team was roomed all along the same corridor."

"Oh!"

What more could she say? Absolutely nothing. Mortification glowed as the implications of what he'd just told her sank in. She'd wrecked all his careful plans with her confrontational attitude, refusing to have the ceremony the next day. He'd planned it so that the two of them could be more private, staying away from his team regardless of the inconvenience it would cause to his business requirements.

Although quite chagrined by it all, there was no way Rhia would back down on agreements they'd already reached. She latched onto a different topic as the powerful car growled up to the house. "This avenue of shrubs won't take too much to restore to full splendor."

They swept up toward the now overgrown turning circle to the side of the main house—a wide loop that would have originally been for a coach and horses. The travelers would have spilled out of the coaches beside the archway that led round the back to the stable block. From the archway the honored guests would have walked up the few steps to the main terrace and the imposing front porch.

"Are you a gardener?" Luke avoided the worst of the potholes and debris that littered the long disused turning area. Though focused on the terrain he kept the conversation going. "Are you personally responsible for that riot of color in your back garden?" He flicked a swift glance her way. "I hadn't considered that you might do all the garden maintenance yourself."

"When I was little I learned a lot from my grandfather. He had a large garden." Her captivating grin bounced back at him. "As a young child I'd plant seeds during my Easter vacation visits to my grandparents. Then I'd always be delighted with what had magically grown when I returned for my school summer holidays. Naturally I had no inkling of how much work went into the growing in between times."

"But over the years you learned that magic has to be worked at and encouraged, didn't you?" He brought the car to a halt and killed the engine.

"Oh yes! I was taught to do the hard graft as well. My fingers got very dirty."

"Would you recognize other plants in this garden?"

"Yes to that too!"

"You're very confident." He grabbed a small backpack from the rear seat and slung it across his shoulder. "Wait till I open the door," he cautioned. "I'll check what the surface is like for those devastating heels. I don't want you to break an ankle just getting out of the car."

Rhia accepted his hand out, mindful of where to

place her feet, relinquishing his touch with regret when he let go to release Thor from the rear. The huge dog bounded out and made off down the stretch of lawn, as usual treating it as his own playground.

"I should admit at this point, I've had a lot more opportunities than you to find out what's in this garden. When I've walked Thor here I've identified a lot of the plantings; others I've looked up when I've gone home just because it annoys me not to be able to name them."

"Well now, there's another advantage to you having been here before. You can find out why I was willed Greywood, you can research the house, and you can also get yourself involved in the garden restoration."

Luke seemed increasingly satisfied with the idea she should get some pleasure out of helping to restore the whole property, not just the house itself during their contracted year. The appeal was mounting for Rhia.

"I'd love to." She looked around at the overgrown wilderness that was meant to be formal borders and edging for the wide sweep of unkempt lawn. "It's been easy to imagine what this garden was like about thirty years ago, and well before that too, though many parts of the estate are strangled with serious weeds and would need lots of effort. Too much for one person."

Rhia caught Luke's gleam of amusement in his eyes and his soft chuckle. "Ah. Silly me." She giggled at his humor. "I guess you're planning on an army of gardeners?"

"Whatever it will take to get it in shape. And if that's a huge team—so be it."

His arm snaked around her shoulders, holding her in a light sensuous grasp, as he turned her and pointed alongside to the walled garden. She was so close to him, an involuntary shiver of anticipation rippled through her.

"So what would you do with that?"

"From the contours that are still discernible, the walled kitchen garden over there I believe was replanted in Victorian times." She flushed recalling that was the precise place where she'd first spied on him a few days before. The memories were magnified by virtue of the fact he now stood with those powerful biceps around her. Embarrassed she might be, but no way would she move out of the heaven that was his arms! Swallowing a little, she got her act together and concentrated on answering his enquiry. "It's a total nightmare, but it would be a magnificent project to undertake its restoration. The scale of it could comfortably feed and flower the whole house, which was what it was designed for, of course."

"What would you do with this terrace?" Luke turned her around a little and embraced her from behind, his arms loose over her shoulders yet imprisoning her tight to his body. Rhia was in no doubt about his seduction now. Again a delicious little shiver rippled. Sometimes anticipation was all it was cracked up to be.

She felt the ridge of his penis behind her, not sure how to cope with her own raging emotions, not knowing how to be assertive or aggressive in taking a sexual lead. She'd never done that in her life and hadn't a clue how to up the tempo. Her voice sounded strained as she said, "It needs complete repaving but that needs to be solicitous and as close to the original stone as possible."

"Why do you say that?" Luke's chin was perched on the top of her head, his breathing irregular.

"It's obvious!" she answered thinking he was serious till she felt the twitch of his lips as he grinned, his chin muscles widening across her crown. "The paving matches the stonework of the walls so it's natural that it needs replacing as close to the original as possible—though the original quarry is unlikely to be still active."

"I couldn't agree more," he chuckled, tucking her even closer to his body, sliding his arms around her rib cage and clasping them tight at the front. Her quiver of sexual awareness seemed to be the assent Luke needed to continue. Her temperature spiked; she could swear she felt the same hike in Luke even though layers of clothing separated his fingers from her skin.

His hands slid up to whisper the lightest caress across her aching breasts making her gasp with longing, her body shuddering at his ministrations. But his touch was fleeting before his hands returned to her shoulders. His lips descended to sigh at her ear before he stepped back from her.

Why was he backing off? Rhia hadn't a clue, but it seemed he'd changed his mind about seduction. Rhia stood paralyzed for an aching second. Oh God! Didn't he like her body after all? Why the hint of touch and not the full-scale onslaught she craved? Confusion left her bereft and hellishly disappointed. He didn't want her after all.

But she knew someone who did.

"Thor!" she bellowed. "Here boy! Come here now!" The huge dog halted his gallop across the lawn and bounded back to her.

Disconsolate, Rhia started off toward the central pillared entrance-porch nestled between the bases of the curved staircases, desperate to put space between them till she got her senses back into shape.

Luke grasped her hand before she'd taken two steps. "We're not using those doors."

Wrenching her fingers from his light grasp her voice was wobbly, the glistening dampness in her eyes a testament to her tattered emotions as was the slight quiver of her lips that she couldn't quite handle.

"Why not?" Her attempt to sound normal was anything but. "Don't you have a key?"

"Oh yes! I've got the key," Luke's chuckle was forced, attempting to lighten the sudden agonizing tension between them. "Rhia? Please look at me."

Hard though it was to look unaffected, she tried. She didn't think she'd succeeded.

"I didn't back off there because I don't want you. It's because I want you far too much." His eyes strayed to the straining in his trousers. "From the state of me, you know how much I want you...but not out here." He raked his hands through his thick hair. "We're not having sex today." His blunt words shocked, but his plea for her understanding was unmistakable. "Not yet."

"Not yet?"

Her question was muffled, her eyes downcast and unable to maintain focus on him, hearing what he said but not understanding his reasoning. Was he backing off till the day of their actual marriage? Even though they'd almost made love a few days ago? And even though his erection flared so blatantly? Now she was doubly distressed for she was the one who had delayed the day of the marriage ceremony for two more weeks! What the hell was she going to do about this infernal craving? God forbid! She'd never survive two weeks.

"Trust me, please," Luke persuaded, clutching her hands and bringing her closer to him again, though not close enough for their bodies to make contact. "Tomorrow will be different."

"Tomorrow?" she echoed, regretting tomorrow would not be their wedding day. What was he talking about now? She had lost the thread of logic to this whole confusing scenario.

"Tomorrow, I promise."

The trusting smile, and the sensual green heat he bestowed on her, went a little way to reassure her. The tiny peck at her cheek helped even more for she felt the tense self-control in his fingers. He did want her.

She had herself almost under control but waited for him to continue as he rummaged in his backpack and brandished the biggest iron key she'd ever seen. As he rubbed it against the cloth of his trousers to dislodge some of the flaking rust the material tightened across Luke's still-evident bulge.

"It's huge!"

Her naive outburst broke the absurd tension between them as they both realized how easy it was for her words to be misinterpreted. Amusement zapped across her cheeks as he rearranged his trousers before holding up the cleaned key with a triumphant flourish.

"It is huge, isn't it." He grinned, his kissable lips bracketing his even white teeth.

"I went into that with two huge feet, didn't I?" Rhia chortled, able to laugh at her artlessness

Genuine smiles of rapport wafted between them, chuckles unrestrained, their eyes dancing with mirth at the double entendre. In total harmony it seemed they could now laugh a little at their sexual predicament.

Thor galloped around mystified by their behavior but excited by their exuberance.

"This is the key, but that's not the problem," Luke explained. "On the other side of those doors is the rudimentary security that Amelia Greywood must have ordered." His grin deepened, his eyes flashing more than one message to her. "She was a resourceful woman...or she had somebody else acting for her."

"Well, come on!" Rhia urged affected by his humor. "You're bursting to tell me."

"There are three or four layers of the heaviest vestibule furniture blocking the doors—a basic barring of the door—to keep unwanted burglars out."

"Didn't keep you out though." She grinned.

Luke grabbed her hand and towed her to one of the outside staircases. "Be careful with those heels. The stairs are passable—but only just." He grasped her hand as they climbed up to the balcony and along to the centrally situated first level doors, Thor sniffling at their heels, unwilling to miss anything during this exciting adventure.

At the substantially glazed double-doors Luke produced an immense chain of keys from the backpack. Each key had little color-coded sticky labels indicating their use. Selecting one, he turned the key in the ornate metal lock. To her amazement it made almost no sound at all, and the door glided open.

"How impressive!"

"A little oil yesterday." Luke cleared his throat. He bowed in front of her. "Would you care for a guided tour of this magnificently elegant property Miss Ashton?"

"I'd be delighted, Mr. Salieri."

Rhia curtsied back, failing miserably in her attempt to hold out her tight straight skirt, accidentally making the hem ride up higher on her thighs.

Luke's gaze flickered, the green deepened as he focused on her momentarily exposed legs. "*Porca miseria!*" The moan that escaped from him reverberated right through Rhia as well.

She was taken by surprise when he slid one arm around her shoulders, reached down with the other and tucked it under her legs, swinging her up as though she was marshmallow-light, and then stepped into the upper hallway. He cuddled her tight to his chest savoring her floral scent with a noisy sniff.

"Gorgeous!"

"What are you doing? Put me down."

She was both delighted and embarrassed by the gesture. It was so much like a bride being lifted over the threshold. But that wasn't how they were. Yet.

Rhia tracked Luke's gaze as it locked onto her lips his words so quiet she scarcely heard them. "This is how you make a grand entrance into a magnificent property like this one will be." He snatched a quick kiss before continuing, "In the arms of your lover." He swooped back again magically drawn for a longer taste. "Your only lover!"

Life stopped. Without halting his hungry exploration Luke released her to the floor, allowing her to slide down his body, slowly enough for her to feel him all the way. He cupped her head and deepened the kiss, holding her in a gentle embrace. After a long and thorough searching he lifted his head his forehead making touchdown with hers as they gasped for breath.

"*Madre di Dio!* I needed that Rhia," he whispered his mouth a heartbeat away from her own, their noses doing a sensuous nudging. "And if you're honest, you needed it too. Tell me. You want it too."

"You know I did." Again she was confused by his mercurial sexual behavior, but no way was she stopping him now.

She reached up to snag his lips, telling him without a doubt she welcomed his lovemaking. Their tongues searched and learned all the soft ridges and inner layers. Rhia was dazed when Luke abruptly halted their over-heated kisses. "We can't do this here," he mumbled releasing her enough to hold her in a light grasp. "There's too much debris. I do want to make sweet love to you, I'd love to lay you down and—But it's not going to happen. We have to put this on the back burner till later." He punctuated the words with arousing little kisses. "I promise. Later."

"Don't do this to me, Luke," Rhia pleaded her eyes closed as she seized him. "I'm never going to survive if later is tomorrow."

His deeply amused chuckle lightened the tension again. "Open your eyes and look around us." His words were literally mouthed against her lips as his hands held her head still, and he waited till she turned around. He gentled his answer. The sincerity of his words in no doubt. "It's not safe. One wrong step and you'll have a broken ankle."

Rhia disengaged herself with extreme reluctance. He wasn't joking. The hallway was littered with potential hazards from the considerable damage caused by the leaking roof and ingress of rainwater close to the now badly-fitting doors.

"Okay!" she sighed, "You win…again."

Her capitulation won her a tight but brief cuddle before he led her further into the grand entrance hall.

Rhia forced her mind out of Luke's pants.

Back to business—the business of being a tourist in this grand but dilapidated house.

The first level entrance hall was a room of magnificent proportions, with a two-story high ceiling dominated by a huge chandelier of dull metal and even duller dusty crystal.

"That will be marvelous after a good cleaning, Luke. It's beautifully fashioned."

His wry expression told her he wasn't as sure as she was of the hidden beauty beneath the grime.

"Heel, Thor!" Rhia called the dog to join them as they went exploring.

The first floor level, above the ground floor, was a maze of formerly splendid reception rooms. Luke said he was delighted to find they were not in quite as bad shape as originally suspected. The water damage was largely confined to the attics and one side of the third floor. The large formal drawing room was in reasonable shape but furnishings were sparse. The smaller, informal sitting room was the opposite—it was crammed with well-worn mismatched pieces.

"Wow! This is a very grand dining room." Rhia's enthusiasm bubbled over as she entered the impressive rectangular room. The elegantly decorated room had a huge mahogany table set with more than a dozen matching chairs. The table had been swept clean the previous day, and was now being used by Luke as a temporary operations centre.

An enormous painting dominated the fireplace wall: an equestrian scene with a handsome young woman seated regally on a beautiful chestnut horse.

Rhia commented that though beautifully done it was disproportionate. Luke said he thought it looked quite pleasant but explained he was no expert of paintings, especially Victorian or Edwardian ones.

"The woman and horse have been added to an original landscape, and their proportions are wrong," Rhia pointed out. "See here? These brush strokes have been over-painted by an amateur. The bucolic background, which has been done by a much more skilled artist, is probably an image of what the estate looked like in former times. That practice of over-painting isn't all that uncommon."

"Why would someone do that?" Luke was intrigued as he inspected the areas she'd pointed out.

"Often it was because there was no new canvas to use. A prepared canvas of this size would have been pretty expensive for an amateur to have bought."

As she demonstrated historical knowledge, they

wandered around. He took her hand, as though unable to leave her alone. Rhia was more than happy to comply.

The sizeable library, an unusually bright room for the purpose, was well preserved. It had escaped most of the dampness and water damage some of the other rooms had suffered from.

"This room has been well used," Rhia exclaimed, delighted with her findings behind glazed cabinets and on the open shelving. "Oh, my God! Look at these, Luke! These dog-eared books have been read, unlike some country homes where the books were only showpieces."

"I know what you mean," he answered, her enthusiasm mirrored in his smiles. "Some of the properties I've renovated came with rooms partially furnished, and in a few cases the stock in the library wasn't wanted at all by the departing owners. Like you say, never valued and rarely read."

Faded wallpaper with outline marks where paintings and wall hangings had been were evidence that treasures had been removed for sale many years before. Some rooms were minimally furnished, indicating the furniture that had been left had been spread around leaving an eclectic but mismatched décor, the condition fairly poor—not water damaged—but suffering mainly from continuous use and sheer age.

Rhia's fervor bubbled over when she discovered something ancient or beautiful. The value of each individual piece was minimal yet they were period pieces nonetheless. She shared her knowledge of the antiques with Luke as they wandered.

"How come you recognize these so well?" he asked as she elaborated over small marquetry card tables in the main salon.

"Antiques and old memorabilia are a hobby of mine. I factored in some specific furniture and architecture classes into my degree work at university. My grandmother had a few interesting bits and pieces. As a child, I was fascinated—not by their value but their anecdotal history. All these pieces have a story behind them, whether a personal family history regarding the people who used them on a daily basis, or the history of the craftsmen who created them."

Luke was silent.

"Sorry. I didn't mean to bore you."

"Not in the least. This is the part I always leave to other experts. When I renovate a property I call in the best people to restock with suitable period artifacts. I never ever entertained the thought that they might have an actual personal history. It's a fascinating thought." His grin widened even more, his expression quite delighted. "Now I know your expertise will be a godsend in interpreting and sorting through all this guff."

"Guff?" His particular vocabulary offended the historian in her, yet she knew he was teasing.

"Guff!" He laughed again. "Plenty of guff, and I can't get rid of one single bit till it's all investigated and you reveal the mystery."

"Luke Salieri." Rhia's mock severity made them both chuckle even more. "You're a total Philistine! Do you know that?"

The large family and superior guest bedrooms on the second floor, some with adjoining bathrooms and sitting rooms, were in reasonable condition, structurally speaking, though very dated. Luke explained he was very glad the furnishings on the first and second floors would be able to be renovated, not because they would be worth more money but because they could be used in the future.

Thor's sudden lively barking made them descend to the ground floor. They investigated the kitchen area, Rhia hoping against hope the dog wasn't ferreting after some small livestock—like mice. They found him sniffing around the back door, which led out to the stable yard.

Rhia realized he wanted to get outside, giving them notice of his needs. "Sorry boy!" Rhia gurgled into his coat as she hugged him. "Too well toilet-trained now, aren't we?"

Luke's answer was to unlock the door with a grin and let the hound flash outside. "I'm very glad to hear he's trained. Think of the places he could leave a little parcel inside this enormous house."

The kitchen cupboards were full of items from varying time periods, from pre-Victorian through to the 1950s and '60s. It was a treasure trove of historical artifacts, which together made a wonderful collection.

"These ground floor rooms are almost perfect for opening to the public," Rhia laughed in delight. "The house is stuck in a time warp."

"You're saying that and you haven't seen the third floor or the attics yet," Luke warned, "Next place on our tour, Miss Ashton."

Finding a suitable enamel bowl Rhia filled it with water for Thor, who was gamboling outside the kitchen door, overheated from the warm house and his enthusiastic bouncing around. Setting the bowl in the shade of an outhouse, she tethered Thor's leash and ordered him to stay there for their return as they went back up to investigate the third floor and the attics.

"I first saw you from this bedroom window," Luke explained, his voice whisper soft. "You and Thor came out of the woods. You looked like a little woodland sprite!"

"What?" Rhia gurgled. "Me a sprite? Some folks I know would call me more of a bad-tempered imp!" The fact that he was exposing his feelings warmed her up in a delicious way. She was happy to listen to his mesmerizing voice a lot more, especially if it was so complimentary.

"That autumn colored suit you're wearing today makes you look even more like a woodland nymph."

Luke's arms snaked around her waist, his chin resting on her shoulder. He hugged her as they looked at the scene below.

After a few delicious moments of almost-torture where Rhia wanted more than a gentle hug, Luke turned her in his arms and kissed her. Devastatingly. The kiss deepened into more and...more. And again, each one segued into an even more heated version as their mouths, and tongues, mimicked other sexual gestures.

"Mmm... *Squisito*," he murmured. More Italian endearments followed that Rhia interpreted as good from Luke's honeyed tones. "Tell me to stop, Rhia! You've got to be the one..."

"No, I don't want you to stop."

Luke was making her feel needy, desperate, ravenous, and out of control. She'd read all those words and more in passionate novels but had never before experienced the hunger for fulfillment that Luke so easily stoked. Her ardor evenly matched his. Nothing else mattered. He just had to continue his lovemaking, or she'd cease to exist—it was so overwhelming.

In tandem he moved their still tongue-tangling bodies back from the window, step by retreating step, toward the inviting bed where they sank as one body. Laying her full on her back he opened the buttons on the jacket of her suit.

Chapter Eleven

“Stuff the lawyers!” His muffled words wove their way into her neck as he nuzzled her ear. “I have to have you, Rhia.”

Sliding the jacket open he spread his fingers across her pale orange camisole. His groan held a keening sound that shocked Rhia with its intensity.

“The lawyers?” Rhia’s question was automatic but she couldn’t care less about his answer if it stopped him from continuing to remove her clothes.

“You’re not wearing a bra?”

Before she could form any kind of reply his lips locked onto an aroused nipple, suckling through the silky material, a contraction of sheer pleasure darting from her breast to her womb. She gasped, clutching him closer as he sucked harder and plucked at her other breast with his free hand. Her fingers clutched at his hair as she rode the sensations.

“More. Oh god, oh please…more!” She was almost incoherent. The sensations were fantastic, so fantastic she couldn’t stop the whimpers from escaping as his tongue licked a pathway back to her mouth.

“Rhia? You okay?”

Her words were stifled against her teeth. “Oh yes! Don’t dare stop what you were doing.”

As his clever mouth returned to her pebbled nipple under the now very soaked silk, he reached for one of her hands and thrust it against his aching erection, squeezing it between them, producing such a heart felt groan from him that Rhia absorbed into her own moans.

"Touch me!" he ordered.

Hands and lips squeezed and kissed in a tumult of fiery passion as they rolled around the bed creating an incredible dust cloud as they spun. Eventually breaking free, Luke leapt off the bed to remove his jacket, which he dropped onto the dusty floor. Rhia watched in a daze as his shirt followed, pulled straight up over his head. Before she could blink he was down to boxer shorts that strained with his impressive erection. He reached for her just as sanity was seeping in. They were going to make love!

Rhia was unable to hide her haste as he lifted her up to remove her jacket and peel off her camisole.

"I want you so much, Rhia." Luke skimmed his knuckles back and forth over her nipples, making her shriek before he reached for the zipper of her skirt. "But maybe we should cool it a little."

"Don't you dare!" she cried.

Luke pulled her off the bed to remove the last of her clothing—her wispy lace panties, his lips touching every possible part of her body on the way. His boxers followed till there were no clothes between them at all.

With a quick flick of his wrist the whole dusty brocade bedcover was yanked into the air, landing on the floor behind him in a crumpled heap. The state of the mattress cover underneath wasn't important—getting rid of the dusty top layer was.

"*Incantevole*! You are breathtakingly beautiful, Rhia!" He pulled her into his arms and sank back down with her. His lips sought hers once again as his questing fingers roamed across her responsive flesh, teasing her nipples, rolling them between experienced fingers.

Rhia groaned her approval at the sensations he produced. His tongue invaded her mouth, teasing and sucking as he thrust himself against her soft stomach whispering, "*Madre di Dio*! I have to have you now."

Rhia's legs squirmed, seeking a way to stop the absolute ache between them. Luke's skilled fingers made their way down past her navel to find the tiny bit of throbbing flesh that demanded to be stroked and satisfied. His stroking was mirrored by the thrusts of his tongue in her accepting mouth till he tore his lips away to gasp, "Are you protected?"

"What?" She was too overwhelmed to think and answer properly.

"Contraceptive pills?" His question was muted by his seeking lips, pressed so hard against hers.

Rhia shot back to reality! Just enough to make her conscious of their situation but not enough to guard what she was replying. She was so far gone she hadn't even considered the issue of pregnancy.

"No. Why would I be on the pill?" she mumbled, her lips still eagerly seeking his, not wanting the experience to stop in any way, unaware of how disappointing her statement might be to him. "You don't have a condom?" Her words whispered against his clean-shaven cheeks. "Maybe in your wallet?"

What blasted her ear was possibly a very polite Italian endearment...but she doubted it. "Purposely emptied it out this morning!" He swore again.

"You did what?" Rhia backed away, her heart hammering even more with crushing disappointment.

"Never mind," his words soothed as he imprisoned her again. "I know lots of ways to take the edge off."

The erection that prodded her stomach was so rigid he must be aching. Sliding his body down a little he latched onto her nipple and suckled as his fingers made her squirm with abandon. She groaned her delight for the arousal was so... good.

“Do you like that?” he asked his voice muffled and raspy with passion.

“Love it,” Rhia whispered. “Just…yes, there.”

Luke surged against the mattress as his mouth and fingers worked their magic on her. She was so aroused, she pushed and thrust at his fingers and lips and then that tense moment before orgasm came on in a flash. The beats of her climax burst through his fingers, her heartbeats drummed and her breathing became almost non-existent.

“Luke!” she screamed.

Luke’s heartbeat wasn’t much better; it too was racing as he slid up alongside her after her tremors ceased. He brought them both to their sides facing each other, clutched his arms around her and locked onto her lips. Then he pushed his throbbing penis between her labia and thrust hard, again and again, between her legs but not inside her. Her soft fleshy nether lips pulsated again; another orgasm built and flooded her as his tongue mimicked the sex below. In the midst of her trembling, Luke lost it. One last long thrust and his orgasm gushed from him, spilling between her legs and onto the mattress. He held her till his breathing stilled.

“Wow,” Rhia gasped, “I haven’t had a real orgasm for years and now I’ve had three, in two days.” She lay smiling at him, so pleased with herself and with him.

Luke couldn’t be anything but amused with the situation, for she knew he’d also had a gusher of a climax. He rested his chin on her head. “Do you realize that wasn’t the best I can do?” he grinned.

“Of course, you dolt.” She smacked him on the arm. Her humor sobered though as her little fingers stroked a pathway over his chest, stopping to arouse his nipples, feathering across his flesh. Passion again erupted and wouldn’t be denied. His erection, which had not completely subsided, surged again and prodded at her soft stomach. She reached down with tentative strokes and Luke moaned, somewhere between an agonized gasp and a groan.

"Don't you like that?" Rhia innocently asked him.

"You can tell I do, you little nymph." He nibbled at her lips again. "But my control just isn't that good. We need to call a halt. I have to be inside you next time."

Grabbing her arousing hands Luke broke their embrace and slid off the bed. "I want everything you're willing to do with me, Rhia. But the next time we have sex I want to be inside you when we both come, and I'll make sure we're protected."

Rhia's serious voice stopped him. "Thanks for stopping, Luke. You have to know I wouldn't have been able to."

"Getting you pregnant isn't part of the plan."

He struggled to shove himself back into his trousers and close the straining zipper before he leaned over her to capture her lips in a fierce kiss. "Tomorrow, I promise."

"You said that before. I get the message."

Her tone was playful, not in the least annoyed. She didn't need to add an unplanned pregnancy into the mix of their year's arrangement.

Long-term birth control had never ever been an issue for her, for she'd never been in a live-in situation. It was something she'd seriously need to consider, immediately, if their current ardor was anything to go by. No man had ever made her so reckless before or made her disregard her own health.

"You sure you don't want to get married tomorrow?" Luke asked casually as she pulled on her camisole and slipped on the wispy, almost-not-there at all, lacy briefs.

As soon as the words left his mouth she

wondered what magic genie had put them there. It was obvious they were going to have sex with or without the document signed. Her answer reflected none of her thinking, or her easy capitulation though. She'd got him to make compromises, and she was sticking to what she'd achieved—but only regarding the actual ceremony—not any pre-wedding sex.

"I'm sure!" Any smiles of earlier sexual satisfaction were wiped from her face as she repeated, buttoning her neat little jacket, "I'm sure Luke, we'll get married in two weeks as planned."

No way was she backing down on their bargain. She wasn't certain why she continued to answer in such a negative fashion, but she did know she would have the best of both worlds. The marriage would take place, but more importantly she was going to use Luke to scratch her sexual itch just as much as he was going to use her.

She zipped her skirt with a flick not needing to slide into her strappy shoes for they'd never been off her feet. Her words that followed were just as efficient as her unhurried movements. "As you very carefully pointed out two days ago Luke, we don't have to love each other to marry. In the same way we can have proper sex tomorrow but not be married for two weeks."

Luke didn't react as she expected. He looked a bit offended.

Grasping an end of the bedcover they flipped it back in place, grinning a little at the multitude of dust motes that flew into the sunlit air around them.

"Yuck!" Rhia exclaimed, chuckling and coughing at the same time. "Think how much of that we must have coating us already!"

"Angling for a shared shower, Rhia?" The green deepened once more in Luke's gaze as he purposely came round the bed towards her. "I'm sure we could arrange that somehow…"

"Whoa! Down boy." Rhia skipped toward the door to avoid any more of his advances, though it was really the last thing she wanted. "Keep your pants zipped till tomorrow." Her deep laugh gusted out as she dashed into the corridor. "Tomorrow! Tomorrow!" she sang tunelessly, "Is only a day away…"

Luke trailed after her as Rhia wandered around the children's bedrooms; he watched her examine the Victorian crib and listened as she described some of the more obvious decorative artifacts that still littered the rooms.

He appreciated her chuckles of merriment as she squeezed herself onto the built-in seat of the desk in the schoolroom and lifted the angled wooden lid, something he'd not thought to do a few days before. Her eyes twinkled with enthusiasm. She rummaged around the still-cluttered inside and pulled out a small book. He was coming to the conclusion he'd like to do an awful lot more watching of this captivating woman.

"Oh my goodness, Luke!" she squeaked, "Look at this. It's beautiful. Maybe even one of the first editions."

Luke leaned closer to read the title of the gold-tooled burgundy leather bound volume. "A Child's Garden of Verses. R. L. Stevenson 23rd May 1896. To Jo-Jo on your eighth birthday from Aunt Maria."

Rhia's voice hitched as she read out the inscription written in flowery copperplate writing on the inside front cover. "Get well poppet, the world needs your cheerful smile."

Rhia twisted around to look up at him. She shot him a gleeful smile. "Look at the postscript!" Her laughter bubbled over as she shared the book with him, pointing to the area of the page.

Luke's arms bracketed around her as he

finished the oral read. "And don't climb any more trees. Young ladies do not ever have broken legs—it's not dignified."

There was a further post-postscript that they read together. "Check page 83."

They flipped the pages till they came to the relevant one. The poem was titled Good and Bad Children. Again they read the verse together, enjoying the closeness and shared camaraderie.

"Children, you are very little,
And your bones are very brittle;
If you would grow great and stately,
You must try to walk sedately."

The rest of the poem didn't seem relevant to Jo-Jo's predicament, but the message from Aunt Maria was very clear.

"Maybe you can find out who Jo-Jo was." Luke's words were muffled into her hair as his arms snuggled around her. The hug was automatic, his arms binding around as they found weird enjoyment in the typical censorious attitude of the Victorian era.

"I'm sure I can." Rhia's response was confident. "Eventually. There's a museum full of stuff here, Luke."

"Are you telling me you're already angling for an assistant?" he chided.

"No bloody way!" The denial was vehement her husky laugh reaching parts inside him he didn't know existed. "This is my project, Sonny Boy. You've given it to me, and you'd better believe I can manage."

Luke didn't doubt she'd manage it for one minute. He already knew his little sprite of the woods had a tenacious streak a mile wide. But it was time to call a halt on the bedrooms floor for he was powerless to prevent the sexual tension from again bubbling up. Luke's control was ready to twang, a catapult primed to fire.

As one, they disengaged themselves and left the temptations of the third floor behind, ascending a narrow staircase in the center of the house, which led to the attic level. Luke forced himself to refrain from touching her, from even holding her hand. Rhia, on the other hand, seemed to manage to switch off her sexual button, their constrained love making no longer an issue for her, her blithe attitude indicating she could deal with it.

Rhia could take it? Or leave it?

Luke wasn't too enamored at that last thought; women usually couldn't get enough of him. She was a puzzle indeed, a contrary piece of work. But he had plenty of time to find out what made Rhia Ashton tick...

He'd never been with a woman before who could defuse the sexual tension with humor in quite the same way Rhia could manage. He reckoned he'd be able to live with that for a year.

Maybe he wouldn't get bored of her after a few weeks, like he usually did?

Rhia was nothing like any of his previous lovers. Perhaps he could string out the sexual thrall for two or three months? That would be a real achievement given his past record. And after all, Greywood Hall would keep her actively employed...long after their sexual ardor waned. He quite liked the thought that Rhia would still have that to look forward to.

"Oh my goodness, Luke!" Rhia exclaimed when they reached the attic floor. "It's so gloomy up here. And this is what it's like on a sunny summer day. Can you imagine how awful this must have been during a freezing dark winter?"

He didn't want to contemplate any concept at all for he was aroused yet again from following Rhia's rear end up the steep narrow staircase. It was just as well she was excited by their explorations of the dusty and smelly attics for the leaks in the roof were all too evident on one side of the house. The deteriorated wood was fetid in places, to be avoided in others as it looked unsafe, but it gave Luke something concrete to focus on.

The attic staircase led onto a narrow paneled corridor that ran the length of the whole house at the back. Although it had walls, it didn't have a ceiling. A few tiny windows provided a little natural light—but not much. It must have been a dismal prospect for the army of servants who would have been housed up there. Luke didn't need Rhia's input to tell him that in Georgian and Victorian times the female servants were likely to have been quartered here, well away from the horny male servants who were more than likely housed on the ground floor, if they ranked senior enough and lucky to be inside. The other males would have been quartered out in the outhouses, the abode of the lower ranks.

At each end of the long corridor, alongside the cold exterior side walls of the house, lay six small domestic servants' bedrooms accessed from another little corridor that lay across the breadth of the house. So twelve in all, tiny cubicles barely bigger than cupboards, that were minimally and poorly furnished. Each held only a narrow wooden cot, a very small wooden dresser, and a series of iron hooks on one wall.

There were no bathrooms on the attic floor, not even a privy of any kind. In former times the chamber pot ruled.

"After a hard day's work—fourteen or sixteen hours of sheer toil, what did the servant have to look forward to?" Rhia asked as they wandered along the seriously damaged end. "How heavenly to be up here, at the top of the house, nearer to her God and the sight of the rafters." She sighed dramatically. "Imagine the parlor maid just dying for her thin mattress of straw with a tick cover, a scratchy woolen blanket, and these simple wood-paneled walls."

Luke laughed at the description as she covered empathy with sarcastic humor. "Yes, and I'm sure some of them did die up here, of illness, loneliness and old age."

Both of them had been around old mansion houses long enough to know some of the sad parts of their history.

The four main storage rooms were huge in comparison. Taking up the rest of the attic space they were open to the wooden joists and roof trusses. They were stuffed with discarded furniture, trunks and cases, earliest bicycles, toys and other memorabilia.

"There's weeks of work just in this attic storage alone. It goes back centuries!" Rhia almost danced a jig in excitement. "Although some of it is damaged beyond repair there's still plenty that can be restored.

The Greywoods had been a family of natural hoarders. By the time Rhia and Luke descended to the ground floor kitchen door they were surprised to find they'd spent over three hours investigating the premises. Thor was pacing, growling with hunger. Luke knew how Thor was feeling; his hunger to fully and properly have Rhia was astounding. They had to separate till the next day or he'd go bananas. He'd lusted after women before but had rarely had to exercise the same degree of restraint.

And for the last long while, witnessing her professional enthusiasm, he'd had to keep reminding himself she wasn't a potential girlfriend or even a mistress—he was using her in a different category—for a whole year. So what was she?

He had no words to describe the situation he'd got them both into.

They returned to the confines of his car and drove the short stretch to her cottage.

He climbed out to open her door and pulled her into a tight clutch, his body still thrumming for her. After he kissed her soundly, he informed her, “I’ll be here at your doorstep just before nine o’clock tomorrow morning.” His autocratic and commanding tone was back in full force. “My office materials are being delivered around then.”

Chapter Twelve

Luke was moving in!

Rhia spent the evening hours in a frenzy of sorting out the only spare room she had. Upstairs in her little cottage there were three bedrooms and one bathroom. Her own bedroom wasn't the largest, but it had the best view over the countryside. The fully furnished guest bedroom was the biggest of the three; the third she used as a storage room for her historical paperwork, packed away in stacking plastic crates. Deciding she'd be best to have the largest room empty she moved all the furnishings from the guest bedroom into the smallest room. By the time she'd done that, and had scarfed down a light meal, exhaustion had descended. At ten o'clock she flopped into bed and fell fast asleep, to awaken at around three o'clock, restless till after six when the traffic making its way to Greywood Hall started up again.

By then there was no point pretending to sleep. Feeling both groggy and hyper with nervous energy she got up.

Luke was moving into her little cottage! It was insane. It was gloriously excitingly and recklessly insane. She hardly knew the man.

She spent far longer in the shower than normal, pampering herself just a bit more thoroughly.

Luke arrived and took over Rhia's life.

Unfortunately he was in a bad mood.

"Come up and see if what I've cleared will be enough space," she urged, her diffident tone indicative of her increasing irritation as he rejected the need to check it out. “Although if it’s not good enough there’s not much I can do about it!”

She wasn’t quite sure how to handle his mood. It was as though he regretted what happened the previous day. He’d simply said good morning and was avoiding eye contact—but he was the one invading her life, so why should she be doing all the accommodating?

What the hell had happened to their frantic lovemaking of the day before? Had that just been for show to ensure she’d acquiesce, and the sexual thrall wasn’t needed any more? Did he now think she wasn’t worth making love to?

By the time he agreed to check out the room Rhia had decided to play it cool. She could do it for she’d be getting a whole year’s worth of mega-interesting work out of it—if he stood by their contract. He didn’t need to be friendly or even like her at all for that. She’d done without his sexual advances before yesterday so she could do so again.

Upstairs Luke bypassed her bedroom without even looking in then went into the room she’d cleared. “It’s fine, Rhia. My crew might need to do a little rewiring, but they won’t make any mess.”

His answer was abrupt. Adding a brief appreciation of her efforts for clearing the place he then high-tailed it back downstairs and went straight outside, barely acknowledging her trailing presence behind him. Spending time in the garden getting acquainted with Thor was obviously his plan, so Rhia left him to it.

She was still miffed when the doorbell pealed, heralding the delivery van. Rhia left it to Luke. She focused on the work in front of her, ignoring the footfalls overhead, and his terse instructions to the men, only acknowledging a disturbance when Luke’s head and shoulders popped in the sitting room door. The smile on his face was forced.

A fact not in the least missed by an irritable Rhia.

"Rhia! I'm taking a quick nip along to Greywood to check on the roofing materials. I'll be back in an hour or so when the guys here should be through."

"Do what you like!"

She let her mutinous face show how she felt about his offhand attitude.

"Rhia." Grasping her hands from her keyboard Luke pulled her to her feet and into his arms. "Believe me. I'm not pissed off at you. Just frustrated."

Her scoff belied his words. "Could have fooled me!"

One of his crew loped noisily down the stairs calling Luke's name.

"See you later, gorgeous!" Luke swiped a fast kiss before she even realized his intentions, then he was gone like a will o' the wisp.

Rhia could make neither head nor tail of this man that she'd agreed to marry. God help her! What the heck had she done?

A while later the efficient crew had installed everything: the furnishings, the complex telephone answering machine. Computers and peripherals were up and functioning where Luke had ordered them. He had been back for more than thirty minutes and was chomping at the bit. His agitation rolled off him in waves. He'd been up and down the stairs so often—popping his head into the sitting room to give her unnecessary updates and disturbing her pathetic concentration yet again—she thought he must have worn out his shoe leather by now.

Perfunctorily thanking the men, Luke closed the front door then he hurried into the sitting room. Barely drawing breath he fireman-lifted her over his shoulder before taking the stairs two at a time to hurry them into her bedroom.

"Luke!" she griped. "Put me down!" Her muffled command was lost in the cotton of his T-shirt.

"Can't wait!"

The heaving reply accompanied an unceremonious dumping on her bed. Any objection Rhia made was squashed by the excitement he produced.

"I must have you now!" His passionate declaration was blatant as he ground his lips down on her.

In seconds, he divested her of the tight little white shorts, panties, and the loose top, frantically kissing her all over. At the same time, he was removing his own jeans. Rhia was nonplussed by his haste and by the demanding kisses that accompanied their disrobement. She was confused but was as desperate as he, since simply being in the same room with Luke was sufficient to arouse her to an incredible degree.

"Rhia, it's got to be now," he gasped into her mouth as he peeled off his boxer shorts and reached for the hem of his polo shirt. Breaking contact only long enough to get rid of it he clutched her to him for the longest and most passionate kiss ever, his large hands roaming her body, learning all her curves and places of arousal. His rock hard length poked relentlessly into her softness, twitching like mad in his desperation.

"I want you too, Luke," Rhia groaned, aroused beyond measure by his desperate need for her...and hers for him.

"I need to make you ready for me... Okay?" he whispered, kissing and fondling one breast with arousing fingertips, then sucking the other nipple into his eager mouth. His teeth nipped, and his tongue swirled, making her squirm and push against him, desperate to have the ache between her legs satisfied.

Luke's finger slid down to part her folds, starting up a stroking rhythm that made her call out with need. His clever fingers spread her moisture around. She was getting close to orgasm when he darted off to grab a condom from the pocket of his denims then slipped it in place.

Chilled at his departure, Rhia blindly reached for him. He placed her back down on the bed, laid on top of her, braced his body with strong forearms and kissed her soundly. Nudging her legs apart with his knee he moved in between and probed her core with the tip of his so-very-ready penis. His lips locked onto hers, their tongues mating in a surging rhythm that was soon echoed below as he slid himself home.

Rhia gasped at the first feel of him inside her: he absorbed her incredulous catch of breath with his kiss and probed further. She smiled beneath their locked lips, knowing that she was accepting him into her special place. His lips remained fastened onto hers, demanding her response as he surged into her.

He set up a gentle rhythm, then a faster and more exhilarating speed. Rhia was soon rigid with impending release. "Luke!"

When the orgasm tremored through her, Luke joined her with an almighty roar then collapsed on top of her until he regained his breath.

He shifted his weight to rearrange their bodies, their fronts still fully aligned as he slid out of her and lay beside her, holding her tight.

"I've never had it like that," Rhia chuckled.

"It's not always like that," he answered, idly stroking her hair. "For me, and no doubt most men, I'm not always so aware of the woman beneath me." His voice slid into silence, his head bending to capture her lips. "Back in a moment," he informed her, his withdrawal leaving her cold.

In seconds he was back. Rhia closed her eyes,

not quite sure of the protocol. What would a mistress do now? She wasn't quite sure whether she was one.

Lying alongside her he cuddled her close, their combined breathing becoming even and relaxed.

For a short time.

They were both too aware of each other for that to last for long. Soon his lips were stealing tiny kisses around her face, his tongue sliding into and around her earlobes, finding erogenous zones that made her gasp and squirm, eager for more...and more...and more.

His hands slipped down, caressing her breasts, his penis jerking against her leg as blood surged back into it. His lips reached down to supplant his hands as he moved around to gently suck her nipples, tweaking, and plucking with his teeth, arousing her all over again. His mouth and lips traced a pathway from her aching breasts past her navel, his tongue and lips worshipping and sipping from her soft and delicate skin.

Rhia nearly shouted with delight when his middle finger found and rubbed her. His lips kissed their way down through her curls to the area below. Gasping with surprise and total abandonment as his tongue slid in to replace the digit, to lave and suck, she squealed, "Oh my God, Luke! I never knew how good that would be..." Moans replaced her words as she panted and writhed.

His mouth worked magic as two fingers slipped inside her, tweaking and finding her most erogenous places, his pace demanding the highest response. Rhia was lost to reality as Luke brought forth another orgasm with his tongue and those magic, thrusting fingers.

"Luke, I want you inside me again," she pleaded, greedy for everything. "I need to feel you inside, please?" She felt his lips nibble against her tender skin but those sensations still weren't enough for she craved his length filling her to the hilt. "More, Luke. I need more."

"*Dio*! Rhia! You're making me insane!"

"Please, please." Her hands pulling his head away as she attempted to drag him up her body accompanied her cry. He needed no more invitation as he surged into her, setting up a slow and steady rhythm. Rhia was too into the moment to wait. She was desperate for fulfillment again and was soon pounding against him, forcing him to thrust back-bringing more delight for both of them. They collapsed in a tangle of limbs. After a minute, Rhia's hand unconsciously traced a pathway across his backside as they surfaced to a more normal heart rhythm.

"You're insatiable, Miss Ashton," Luke chuckled tickling her earlobe with his tongue, "I've unleashed a tigress."

Rhia pulled her hand away from his buttock. "Sorry, I wasn't aware I was doing that." Her voice was sleepy, her eyes drifted closed.

The sound of the shower running stirred Rhia, who snuggled under the covers. It was the proverbial morning after: except it was almost afternoon. She wasn't his girlfriend, she wasn't his wife yet—but she was his lover!

Luke strode back into her room as naked as the day he was born. "Hello, gorgeous!" His greeting was cheery as he reached down to give her a sound and thorough kiss but didn't quite meet her eyes. After stirring her libido once more he deflated it with his next statement. "I have got to stay away from you, my lovely…at least for a few hours. I'm going along to Greywood to check on progress."

Luke reached for his clothes and pulled them on. His tone was so matter of fact, Rhia was disappointed. She couldn't lay claim to all his waking hours to continue the fabulous sex they'd just shared, but how could he switch off like that? To stay in bed and make love all day long sounded like heaven. Now that she knew what sex was like with him, she wanted more...a whole lot more.

He finished pulling on his polo shirt and zipped his jeans, the window holding his fascination instead of her.

"I've ordered catered lunch for the crew up at the house. I'm already late for an arranged meeting, but if you want to come up and eat there will be plenty. Otherwise I'll call later in the evening and let you know when I'm finished with the initial assessments of Greywood."

He strode over to the bed, grasped her shoulders lightly, bent down and snatched a tiny peck, almost a duty contact before leaving her, abandoned and somehow bereft.

Rhia lay stunned by the events of the morning. She was not the same woman any more. Not only had she given herself to him totally, and gladly—twice—but she had metamorphosed into some needy creature that she understood, but didn't want to. When he held her close it was the best feeling she'd ever had. She was selfish enough to want that to continue...but it couldn't have been so catastrophically good for him. His aloofness was all too plain to see. So it was all down to sex...amazing and powerful sex between them. That he could switch off in an instant.

Of course!

She was convenient.

The thought made her wretch. Lurching out of the bed she rushed to the bathroom: not physically sick but sickened by how easy she must seem.

During the course of the afternoon the sounds of Luke's helicopter flying in and out a number of times disturbed her. It was ferrying men and materials back and forth Luke having established one of the backfields as a suitable landing space. She wanted to be in the thick of things at Greywood, making a start to her investigations, but Luke hadn't invited her. He hadn't even hinted she should start that afternoon.

By eight that evening she hadn't heard a peep from him. Peeved by the lack of contact, and very nosy about how things had progressed, walking Thor gave her the perfect excuse to head to Greywood. It was too tempting not to use the main entrance and front drive to enter the property. The gates now permanently open, she walked up the long rhododendron sweep with no thoughts of trespassing or guilt. Well, maybe a little guilt still remained, but Thor pranced about enjoying what he had come to think of as his territory.

Up in the dining room Luke heard Thor barking. If Thor was down there then so was Rhia. His body reacted. Lust. Pure lust. It was the newness of their relationship. He told himself lots of things to justify why he was inordinately pleased she'd come to him.

Earlier he'd walked purposely out of the cottage, even though he wanted to hole himself up with Rhia and not surface for days. She was so responsive to his ministrations she stole his very breath away. When he left her bedroom he'd been unable to look at her without feeling guilty. How to broach the subject that he'd climaxed inside her that second time? He hadn't known how to say it. He always used condoms, even when his lovers were using their own form of contraception. He always controlled that, but he hadn't with Rhia. He was furious with himself. In the future he'd have to carry more than one condom in his pocket.

But his craving probably wouldn't last. He'd had her twice already. He'd get bored with her soon.

Moving up from the long mahogany table he couldn't resist looking out into the garden to watch her approach. She was wearing a short skirt; her top shimmered around her breasts as she jogged across the grass, and Thor bounded around her. A surge of recognition flooded him; the tiny spark of libido he'd tamped down for the afternoon flared up again. She was just a woman and Thor was just a dog, so why was he so happy to have them disturb him?

Usually he was so focused that very little would break his concentration, but he was honest enough with himself to acknowledge it had been shot to hell that afternoon. The tension that still beset him had nothing to do with the complexities of the new project of restoring Greywood Hall, and everything to do with concentrating on blocking out the thoughts of Rhia's delightful body. She was right down below the window now, playing the fetching games Thor loved.

Luke had again lost track of what the assembled group were discussing. "We've done enough for today guys," he declared as he turned back to the table. "It's already well past eight o'clock. We'll resume our findings tomorrow morning." For all of them it had been a long day, a very early start. They were all more than happy to wind up their discussions. "Meet at nine tomorrow, here in the dining room."

A hasty shuffling of paper accompanied happy mutters of where the guys intended to eat that night as they filed out of the room.

On the fringes of the lawn, Rhia held tight to Thor and calmed him as the long file of people exited the upper doors and picked their way down the crumbling staircases. Luke stood motionless at the top, watching her. Only after the last person had disappeared into the parked vehicles did Rhia climb up to meet him.

Luke waited and watched. As she reached him he gathered her into his arms and crushed her to him, dropping his lips to meet hers in a hungry kiss.

Rhia clutched at his shirt showing him just how much she'd missed him.

"It's been hours since I tasted you." His hands slid up and down her back rumpling the fine camisole she was wearing. He smiled down at her. "Missed me?"

"Now why do you think that?" she teased, her hands sliding round his back and burrowing in even closer.

"Maybe because you almost devoured me?" Luke replied, his mouth returning to hers. Eager for more, he could tell from her response just how eager she was too. "Much as I don't want to stop, we've found this isn't the most comfortable place. But soon it will be different."

"I didn't come here to disturb you," Rhia hastened to explain, "I just wanted to..." Her embarrassment was evident. "You didn't need to call a halt to your meeting because I arrived."

"We were winding up for the day anyway. I do work long hours, but sometimes forget my team needs breaks too."

That hadn't quite been true for if she hadn't appeared he would have made the meeting last longer...perversely so that he stayed away from her for longer...to test his restraint. But she was here now, and testing his self-discipline no longer appealed. Reaching for her hand he drew her into the hallway. Thor bounded in beside them, his paws skittering on the tile floor, surprising himself so much he dropped to his haunches, whining. Luke laughed.

"Thor!" As he bent to the dog his tone was mock serious. "Serves you right, you silly hound. No gamboling inside the house!" He could have sworn Thor nodded and for the rest of their short visit Thor remained glued to his side.

"You've got a conquest there," Rhia informed

him. “You don’t realize how wary he is of most people.”

“My only conquest?”

“I’m not going to even think of answering that one,” Rhia laughed up at him, poking him with a sharp little fingertip, boldly pecking at his lips.

Luke deepened the kiss then lifted his head. “I need to tidy up some of the paperwork on the dining table. Then we can go.” His arms were still securely locked around Rhia’s, unwilling to break contact for a second. He hugged her to his inflamed body and propped his chin on her head. “I don’t want to move, but we need to get out of here.”

He extricated himself from her clutches, grasped her hand, and tugged her into the dining room where he strode over to the enormous table that when extended sat at least thirty people. He closed down his laptop, gathered up papers and blueprints and placed them into various containers and wallets. Within minutes he held onto his laptop case with one hand and gave Rhia another filled document case, expecting her to take it without any fuss. She did. He grabbed her free hand with his and led them back out the main door and locked it.

They skipped down the staircase like nimble kids followed by a doting Thor who had tagged Luke’s every movement. At the bottom he paused and held Rhia’s gaze. “Give me time to have a quick shower when we get back to your cottage, then we can go out somewhere for dinner?”

His question fell on deaf ears. She didn’t reply as her eyes twinkled back at him. She didn’t want to share him with anybody, not even a waiter in a restaurant, not for a single second? “You’d rather be at home?” he asked relieved by her decision.

“Mmm...” she muttered, nodding, shining cocoa brown gaze fixed on his lips, smiling a smile of sheer seduction. She was not just a fairy of the woods, she was a spell-maker personified.

They made it back to the cottage in record time, Thor delighted at the spanking pace they'd set, alternating between jogging and full-out running. He was a little put out when he was popped into his outside enclosure, given food and water, and then left alone. He whined and fussed, but neither his mistress, nor his new master, was inclined to do anything about it.

Upstairs Luke slowly removed Rhia's limited clothing, marveling that her silky top was again great to suck through, and that it emphasized her aroused nipples much more than a lacy bra. In minutes the slow pace he'd forced on himself was a thing of the past. He was as hard as he'd ever been. He slipped on a condom; he couldn't risk another mistake for he was sure Rhia hadn't even realized they'd made love without protection that morning. They tumbled onto the bed in a tangle of appendages, desperate for connection, rolling around in their haste.

"Now Luke!" she gasped. "I can't wait!"

Rhia was a wanton woman in his arms. Already he knew where to touch with his capable fingers and hands, and where to nip and suckle and kiss. It was astonishing how rapidly he'd become tuned into her needs. And, she to his, he was also overjoyed to find.

He rose above her and pulled her to the edge of the bed, her bottom tucked right on the edge. Opening her legs he took centre position, his erection bobbing against her thigh. Bending over her, he caught up her lips in a searing kiss that rocked his very soul, his tongue mimicking the loving that was to come. Rhia rose up toward him in desperation for fulfillment.

"Slow down, woman," he groaned, "you're going to kill me."

His lips made a trail to her breasts where he

spent eons laving and sucking them to hard points, making Rhia squirm and pant. From there his hands replaced his mouth; his lips caressed their way down to her core, lavishing attention that drew breathy gasps from her till her muscles clenched tight around his lips.

"I can't believe…how good…that…aah…"

Luke held tight to her tensed buttocks till the pulses stopped, his mouth absorbing them all. She was the most amazing woman, the most responsive he'd ever made love to, and he couldn't wait to be inside her. Sliding up he entered her, holding her legs to her chest to achieve better penetration, then surging into her, he let her grow accustomed to his thrusts. When he was sure she was building a new orgasm he quickened the pace and soon felt her inner muscles tight and throbbing.

"Now, Rhia! Now…" No longer able to hold back, he gushed his own climax. His leg muscles still trembling, he pulled her up properly onto the bed and curled against her back, where they rested till the rumbling in Luke's stomach drove them down to the kitchen.

Chapter Thirteen

"This stir-fry is amazing, Rhia!"

Luke complimented her cooking skills around a mouthful of delicious Japanese noodles. They'd been discussing the first stages of repairs to Greywood Hall as she'd whipped up the meal like a professional chef.

In a lull in the conversation he found her studying him intently. This was not unusual since he was also constantly watching her.

"You don't need to answer, but I'm more than curious." He spoke into the silence, his inquisitive eyes willing her to respond. "You're so beautiful, so how come you're inexperienced at sex?"

A red tide flushed over her cheeks. Rhia was struggling with embarrassment; but he was pleased to find she forced eye contact with him. The smile of pleasure curving her lips he presumed was in reaction to his well-meant compliment.

"There must have been scores of men who were just as desperate to bed you as I was," he persisted. "You must have had loads of boyfriends in the past."

Her eyelids flickered as Luke waited for her hesitant answer. "I've dated a lot but most of the men never got closer than kisses and mild foreplay."

"They never had sex with you?" His question was incredulous for he truly couldn't imagine it.

"Oh they wanted more, but I wouldn't let them," she chuckled.

"I'm sure they did. You're the most responsive woman I've ever had sex with." He slid around the table and locked his arms around her, crushing her to his body. “But you weren’t a virgin this morning.” He was pretty sure of that, but he wanted it clarified.

“For goodness sake, Luke. I’m twenty-six. My virginity went a long time ago—it was over in a blink, you could say!”

The sarcastic words said it all. Her earlier sexual encounters hadn’t been spectacular.

“Have you never had a long-term lover?”

“Just one, in the long term, but we didn’t live together and we had such busy work and social lives we’d only date a handful of times a month. I’m such an idiot, it took me nearly two years to find out that toward the end of that time he had a string of other lovers while he was having sex with me.” Her disgust wasn’t lost on Luke. “After that I swore I would never ever let that happen again.” A grin spread across her face as she chuckled, her eyes twinkling back at him. “But maybe you’ve unlocked the prison door. Maybe I’ll be able to react to any man who propositions me now that I know sex can be so good.”

For some reason that thought didn’t please Luke.

Waking up in the same bed as a lover was pretty novel for Luke. He’d rarely spent a complete night with any of his previous lovers—his travel schedules usually meant an early start. Therefore, showering and getting started on the workday was difficult. In fact they couldn’t quite manage it without a very satisfying diversion that lasted quite a while.

Luke was surprised at how much he’d enjoyed cuddling Rhia into sleep around midnight, for although they made love again after going back up to bed, they also talked a lot, sharing personal information after their late dinner. They weren’t the kind of conversations he’d had with past lovers. The novelty of it was confusing but sort of… convivial.

Since she had no immediate family to factor into the equation, he was now aware of how simple it had been for Rhia to agree to a contract that would affect her life for a whole year. An only child, as he was himself, her divorced mother died just before she had gone to university at eighteen. Her father had largely been out of the picture since her early teens. From her nonchalant attitude Luke could tell she didn't hate or dislike her father: she just had nothing in common with him.

Rhia had a bunch of friends, but most were still in the London area, so their contact was sporadic. Again not a factor she needed to accommodate.

After an initial brief meeting at nine o'clock at Greywood Hall, Luke spent the remainder of the morning on other business needs in Rhia's spare room, constantly on the phone, manning several computer monitors concurrently.

Rhia did most of her work downstairs at her computer station, or on the dining table that doubled as an additional work desk. Super aware that she was downstairs, he paced about, finding it difficult to compartmentalize his desire and his work. That wasn't normal. A woman he was currently bedding never encroached on his workday! He rationalized it was just the sheer proximity—nothing else.

At twelve-thirty he was gratified when Rhia brought him coffee and sandwiches but he was also thanking his lucky stars for he'd been determined not to seek her out himself—determined that his control would prevail.

Sod it! Control was overplayed. Breaking his phone call short he reached for the plate and mug, put them down on his desk and took her into his arms, grinding his mouth down on hers in a punishing kiss of welcome.

"*Madre di Dio*!" he shuddered, "I'm starved." His words were punctuated with tiny kisses under her chin and down to the V between her breasts. He ignored the ringing of phones and other machines.

"That's why I brought you food." Rhia gasped as his hands reached down for the hem of her shirt and peeled it up and off. Then he dragged her into her bedroom and proceeded to divest her of her other clothes. He effortlessly lifted her and threw her onto the bed. He followed moments later, already protected, his frenzied body mating with hers, leaving them both shattered and panting.

Wiping the sweat off his brow with his fingers he declared, "You're the thing I was starved for." Grasping her hand he laid it over his pounding heart. "Do you realize I've been thinking about you all morning, knowing you were just a stone's throw away?"

The telephones next door rang relentlessly. Luke snagged Rhia's gaze, his smile matching hers for their thoughts were akin.

"Bugger the phones!" Luke's lips teased her breasts, licking them to a proud stance once more. "At this rate I'll never get any work done."

"Me neither." She reached for him again, running her slick hands up and down, just the way he'd taught her to do.

"Woman, you're going to kill me," he groaned, enjoying her caresses, wanting her to finish what she'd started. "You are such a quick study," he gasped collapsing onto the bedcover as her clever little fingers released him.

Rolling off the bed before he could catch her again she teased, "You can owe me one, Luke. Rain check until tonight?" Her wagging finger clinched the deal as she turned to gather up her discarded clothes and hit the shower.

Luke leaped off the bed to follow before she had a chance to lock the bathroom door. He joined her behind the glazed shower door just as the spray hit the ceramic base. The rain check didn't last very long, not long at all, for he hoisted her onto his newly sheathed permanent erection before they were barely wet from the showerhead. Supporting her against the shower tiles he thrust into her as though it had been years and not minutes since he'd been in her body.

The phones continued to ring.

Rhia fled downstairs after getting dressed, poured him a new mug of coffee and called up to him. No way was she venturing upstairs again.

"I'm coming for it," he shouted as he loped down the stairs and caught her fleeing out the back door.

Fending off his marauding hands, she chuckled. "No more, you insatiable creature! I'm taking Thor for a very, very long walk. You need to get on with your work. And when I'm back…" Luke's leering grin accompanied her groaning exit. "…so do I!"

Rhia and Thor stayed out for ages. They walked through the wood at Grcywood Hall on their return, curious to know what was happening there. The estate teemed with workmen. Some were conspicuous clambering on the rooftops; other groups examined the exterior of the building. Ladders and scaffolding were everywhere, the men assessing woodwork and stonework independently of each other. She was so desperate to get her hands on all the Greywood treasures she almost breached their barricades!

Over on the main drive, she hailed a couple who were discussing the plantings. "Hello! Are you here to assess the garden by any chance?"

The woman stared at Rhia before answering as though reticent to reply before knowing her identity.

"My name's Rhia Ashton." She held her hand out in welcome.

The couple still looked undecided. After all, Rhia could have been anyone at all, especially wandering around dog walking.

"I'm going to be Mrs. Luke Salieri in a few days, and just wondered how much of the garden you've seen already."

The word Salieri was the magic key. After that there was no holding the couple back. Bob and June Renton lived locally and were joint owners of a garden design service, with a team of gardeners at their beck and call. It was far too easy to spend the next couple of hours talking horticulture as they wandered around the grounds before the Rentons declared they'd have to get back to their work base.

Thor was confused. It was fine when he'd been in the wood where he could scurry around, but witnessing the workmen in action seriously dented his territorial rights. Rhia kept him very close to heel, curbing his tendency to bark when they got close to any of the workers. It was weird seeing so many people milling around what had been such a lonely and neglected old place. Only last week? It was so hard to credit it.

It was all happening so quickly; Luke had only known about Greywood Hall for five days. Though impressed by what a massive cash injection could do to change the state of affairs on the property, Rhia was astounded at how he could have all the relevant personnel on site so swiftly. How rich was this man she'd got entangled with? She wasn't interested in the amount of his wealth, she was just overwhelmed by his bountiful financial flexibility…not withstanding, his sexual prowess.

Back at the cottage he paced around above her, his footfalls accompanied by the murmur of his voice. It wasn't any good. Rhia knew she couldn't possibly get any work done in the sitting room. Resolutely taking her laptop, knowing already that her internet router was efficient enough for outside coverage, she worked at her garden table, shading it as much as possible by lowering her parasol to the lowest level.

Thankfully, the summer weather was still behaving, and it was pleasant to be outside. For the next couple of hours she tried to complete some work. Unfortunately, the least distraction broke her concentration, her thoughts gravitating to the magnetic man in her upstairs bedroom. The man whose voice she could hear through the open window answering one phone call after another. How could Luke be immersed in his work when she could hardly string two sentences together? Sighing she entered in another computer search and worked on it till Luke appeared at the back door.

"So this is where you are," he said, his expression indicating delight, and—she couldn't be sure—maybe some relief? "When I saw the sitting room was empty, I thought you'd abandoned me."

"Just avoiding your pacing feet, Luke," she countered, her cynical smile drawing his gaze. "Thought my ceiling was going to collapse under your pounding treatment."

"Don't, woman!" Luke groaned melodramatically covering his ears. "I'm going to pretend your never said that P word!"

Her perceptive laughter peeled out as she pressed on, "What could be wrong with 'pounding' Luke? Pounding is descriptive of what you do so well."

Luke's face was a picture of mock agony as he gripped the doorframe, his eyes rolling, his head mimicking a throbbing beat against the wood.

"You're going to kill me! I am not coming near you, you sexy sprite!" Holding up his hands in a gesture of surrender he backed away, grinning wide. "I'm resisting. I'm resisting..."

"Why?" Rhia was enjoying teasing him. "Pounding is a good—"

"Not taking the bait!" he laughed again. "I'm going along to Greywood right now for some briefings that I'm already late for, but we'll eat out tonight. Be ready to leave just before eight."

Rhia was glad he'd stayed at the door because she'd not have been able to resist him had he come nearer.

After selecting one of her best outfits she put on a minimum of makeup and was ready just before eight. Luke removed her lip-gloss about five minutes after she put it on.

"*Formidabile.*"

She'd already worked out that he resorted to Italian when he was angered and equally when he was aroused.

"You look absolutely wonderful. But we must get out of here before I eat you, *cara.*"

It took a lot of self-control to walk out to the car for the short drive to the restaurant. Later that night they lay entwined, both of them drifting off to sleep, exhausted but for the moment sated.

"Is it always like this for you, Luke?"

"What?" He was shattered by their arduous sex.

"Sex. Is it always as..." She searched for the correct word but decided on the truth. "Desperate...as this, once you've started an affair with a woman?"

"Sometimes, I guess." His voice was fading. "Till the initial lust wears off."

"Luke?"

Rhia whispered into the silence for he'd fallen asleep. She was gutted, disappointed beyond measure by his truthful answer. Lust. That was all he was feeling for her, and it always wore off. She was just his current woman. She was in no doubt there had been many before her.

For all that she was almost crying with the revelation she determined she'd take the sex for the time she was with him. She was hooked on lust and sex just as much as he was, and if that was all he could give her, then she'd continue to use him like he was using her. She couldn't, and wouldn't, stop herself, for she might never ever in her life feel this way again.

The next morning at an early breakfast Rhia made a suggestion, knowing she'd succumb to temptation if they both worked in the cottage at the same time. She had to do something about the almost compulsive need to be with Luke: she had to create some distance and concentrate on the professional aspects of their contract. They'd already delayed their showering by at least a good half hour after Luke's watch alarm rang off.

"I only have one small investigation to do to finish the current project I'm working on. It will only take about an hour. I've nothing pending that's in any way urgent so..." She determined to sound businesslike as she gathered their used cereal bowls and dumped them in the sink. "How would you feel about me using my spare time at Greywood Hall? I could do something like cataloguing the paperwork discovered or...start making an inventory."

Awkwardly sitting opposite him again, she couldn't quite maintain eye contact because just one look from his gorgeous eyes would send her lust rip-roaring free again.

Luke was slow to answer. "Not being in the same building might be a good idea, Rhia. Maybe we'll both get more work done."

He'd picked up on her tension and slight withdrawal, his guarded answer indicating he was being careful about his response though his slight grin defused the tension.

"Running away from me already? Had your fill of me and want to be elsewhere?"

Peeved that he'd seen right through her, Rhia

retaliated in the only way she could, by bandying a false statement. "What if I said yes? What if you've taught me all I need to get me started on a sexual foray?"

"I wouldn't believe a word of it."

His hands reached for hers across the breakfast table, his fingers twining with hers. The tingling response from her body was automatic when it came in contact with his. He was teasing, but she couldn't tell if he was bothered by her feelings or not.

"If you want to do something up at Greywood, I wouldn't say no to you using your research skills right away." He pulled her to her feet and locked one arm around her, lifting her mouth for a gentle kiss with the other. "But before that, you're officially going onto the workforce."

"Oh no! That's not what I meant at all," Rhia protested against his searching lips, aghast at the thought she sounded grasping for the money he'd promised as a salary. She squirmed around in his hold.

"No. Please listen." Luke gentled her struggles, his earnest gaze searching for her compliance. "If you're officially at Greywood it means you can be factored into the safety record of the building," he explained. "My safety officer, Mike, always needs to know which personnel are present in the building, where they're working, so that any messy repairs or even demolition can be done with everyone accounted for and wearing any necessary equipment."

"Oh, sorry. I didn't realize. Forget I asked." Rhia backed off from her suggestion, backed off from Luke too as he released her stiff torso.

"It's just normal business practice." His tone was professional. "Your idea's magic, but I'd want you to be safe at all times, and I can arrange to bring you on board. I'll only need a few national insurance details and your signature in a few places after we're done eating."

"If you're sure."

"Of course I'm sure. I haven't asked you to sign on yet since I thought you still had other clients' work to finish. But if you're free now, then there's no need to delay." His earlier grin reappeared, his eyes a soulful plea. "You know how keen I am to get you started on the search for why Amelia chose me."

Without giving feed to their sexual urges they bypassed her bedroom and went into the makeshift office. After signing the few documents Luke had printed she was giving him the last of the information he needed when the doorbell pealed. Rhia looked at her watch, her face beaming as she blithely informed him, "Oh, that has to be Gus."

The thump Luke felt in the solar plexus felt real. Gus? No way was he letting her go down to resume her...relationship with Gus. Or anyone else, for that matter.

He loped after her.

Near the foot of the stairs he watched her being bear-hugged by the caller. This was Gus? A dull flush of embarrassment whomped him in the chest. Feeling stupid or feeling used wasn't his norm. Resentment clawed at him realizing Rhia had led him on. Days before she'd allowed him to believe Gus could be her lover.

Gus was seventy, if he was a day, and was barely bigger than her. The happy, dwarf-like grin that spread across the man's face told Luke way more than he wanted to know about Gus and Rhia's relationship. He was her postman. *Madre di Dio*! He'd been green over a neighborly seventy-year old.

Turning back he crept upstairs hoping he'd not been detected, and vowing he wouldn't be duped or so stupid ever again. In the office he paced around before resuming his phone calls, needing to settle his pulse. His Italian nannies would have been shocked at the lovely expressive Italian words that poured from him.

What was there to be mad about anyway? He didn't do jealousy. Jealousy was for serious relationships—and that wasn't what he had with Rhia. She just happened to be his current lover; he'd be tired of her soon enough. Not serious at all—give or take the official piece of paper that would shackle them for a year. *Dannazione*! A whole year!

He sat at his desk and pulled up his e-mail. A nice, inanimate interaction. This was the kind of mail he could relate to. He didn't want to talk to anyone—no one at all.

Ten minutes later, with a lot of local gossip updated, Gus left. Down in the sitting room Rhia could hear Luke pacing, his voice a muffle, immersed in work once again. The last research needed to complete her own current project was done after which she organized a new time schedule for completion of the two small client orders that still needed to be researched. A couple of hours during each of the next three mornings should be sufficient, allowing her to clear the rest of her time to investigate the contents of Greywood.

She itched to start, for the thought that something important could slip through her grasp was taking on nightmare proportions. Luke needed to know why Amelia bequeathed him the property, but the way his team swooped in to do their initial assessments didn't make her feel at all secure about the amount of time she had to investigate the contents of Greywood.

What if they boxed everything up and carted it off? That thought horrified her! She didn't want one single thing moved, not even the broken bits in the attics. Nothing must be missed.

Pulling out two digital cameras and a small

video camera she checked them all. Not good. None had been used for quite a while. Their battery power was too low, especially the video camera. Popping them into the chargers she prepared to wait the short time necessary. The rest of her camera equipment, the zoom lenses and portable tripod, were checked and set in the camera bag.

Mentally cataloguing, she needed new notepads from the storage boxes in the spare bedroom upstairs, but the volume of Luke's voice wasn't in the least inspiring as she bypassed the temporary office.

"I don't bloody care what you have to do or say, Jeremy! I've told you before. Don't ever pass over any more calls to me, do you understand, no calls at all."

Rhia was glad to zoom back downstairs for if that was Luke in a temper she never ever wanted to be at that end of his tongue. The pads and pencils were popped into her camera bag. Ready. Now all she had to do was make sure what she planned would be agreed by her new employer.

"Luke?" she called up the stairs at lunchtime, not daring to make the mistake of taking it up to him. "I've lunch ready down here if you want something to eat."

A few minutes later Luke entered the kitchen, plonked himself at the small table, avoiding eye contact and fiddling with the cutlery she'd set out.

She didn't know if his cool entrance was because she hadn't taken the food up to him, or if his phone calls had blackened his mood.

"I wasn't expecting you to feed me lunch," he stated, looking out of the window, his fingers tapping the edge of the table.

Rhia wasn't quite sure how to handle his chilly tone but it rattled her composure. "It's nothing fancy. Just lasagna I made last week and put in the freezer. All I had to do was warm it and toss some salad." Her nippy tone matched his fairly evenly. "You don't have to eat it if you'd rather go elsewhere!" The local caterer was already supplying to Luke's workers at the site.

"Salad and lasagna would be just fine, please," he grunted so slowly she could almost hear the gritting of his teeth as he continued to avoid her eyes.

His answer didn't make her any happier. Was it sarcastic? Did he hate lasagna? Was he annoyed at having to come downstairs? She found she didn't care. She needed lunch to be over so they could part company.

There were no flirtatious looks or attempts to touch her; Luke's mind was still elsewhere. Rhia was both pleased and contrarily irked. She wanted his sexual attention. But contrarily she also wanted to prove she could exist without his habit-forming lovemaking. She was becoming obsessed by the fact that being in the same room, and breathing the same air as him, fired off all her sexual receptors. It was like she'd thought the night before: for Luke it was only sex, at a time that suited him, when it didn't interrupt his work schedule!

And it seemed right that moment the last thing on his mind was having sex with her. Metaphorically biting her lip she served their lunch. A few awkward nibbles in to their meal he swore vehemently in both Italian and English then slammed down his cutlery. He reached for her fingers and crushed them in his own, not enough to hurt but enough for her to realize he was straining for a physical connection again.

"Rhia, I'm sorry!" He stroked her palms. "Something came up this morning that put me in a bad mood, but that's no excuse for taking it out on you."

"Apology accepted." Rhia's tone was still brittle,

but she did relent sufficiently to add, “Forget it and eat your lunch please.”

Afterward, they managed to converse better, but underneath, tension simmered a merry tune as Luke related some new developments. His tone was friendly enough, yet he was still in the grip of some pressure he wasn’t talking about. Although he was a man of many moods, she hadn’t yet seen all of them—not by a long chalk. Would a year be long enough for that? She wasn’t at all sure, for Luke played lots of cards close to his chest. She would just mark up the present one to experience and act as though it didn’t bother her.

“I’m heading for Greywood now,” she informed him as he dried up the dishes she’d just washed, not expecting his help but pleased when he’d automatically done his share. “Is there any particular place you’d prefer me to start the investigations?” she asked.

“Not really.” Luke stacked the clean plates in her small cupboard. “What were you thinking of tackling?”

“I’m no professional photographer, but what I’d like to do first is take a good photographic record of what the place looks like right now. For historical purposes,” Rhia informed him, adding as an afterthought, “though maybe you’ve had someone do that.”

“No. Nothing like that yet. My usual inventory team will be busy elsewhere for the next few days,” Luke explained giving her some of his company’s normal procedural background. “Cataloguing for historical purposes, for future use, has never been a necessary part of my job. The properties I buy over don’t need anything like Greywood will need.”

“Don’t any of your sites ever retain original artifacts?”

Rhia was eager to know that answer because

Luke had mentioned that in his past dealings some furniture and artifacts had been part of his original purchases. Her pulse spiked in alarm. What was he going to do with the contents of Greywood? All she knew at the moment was that with her co-operation regarding the marriage, he would end up as the owner of Greywood and its contents. She didn't know what would happen to it at the end of the all-important year of occupation. The speed at which Luke implemented repairs to the roofs told her that major changes would happen to the interior before too long.

She didn't want to think of Greywood becoming a luxury hotel. She didn't want it to become a centre for team-building or corporate functions. Having only seen the inside once she could hardly bear the thought that it might not rise like a phoenix and become a happy family home.

"Occasionally an artifact is used in one of the re-designed rooms," Luke told her as he completed putting the dishes away.

Rhia forced her concentration back to his answer.

"My inventory team does a sweep in case any previous owner has made an oversight and might perhaps want to reclaim an item. They're usually accompanied by my interior decorators who decide whether an object might be suitable for a re-designed room either in the original property or in another that we're developing."

As Luke explained, he trapped Rhia against the work surface, detachment and control not effective for him any longer. She wasn't complaining. His earlier anger seemed to have faded, and her lust had never gone away.

Luke stole a lingering kiss before continuing, showing just how he could segue from being cool, to lover, then to businessman. He added, "Till I get all the permits for internal renovations at Greywood—they're being speeded through, by the way—we'll concentrate on the roof repairs and replacing damaged woodwork in the attics and third floor to make the building sound. Any other internal restructuring, or decorative work, will come later."

"Am I safe to wander around everywhere today then?" Rhia asked, stunned by the intensity of his kiss after their awkward meal.

"It should be fine today, but make sure you check in with Mike when you arrive. He's in charge of safety. He'll issue your safety gear and tell you of any new developments as they occur." Another tiny nibble at her neck made her knees weak before he detached himself and stood back from her.

"Where will I find Mike?"

"He'll find you. I'll call to let him know you're arriving." Luke snatched another kiss before he headed back upstairs, still talking as he mounted the stairs two at a time. "Make Thor bark when you arrive. Mike's bound to hear him and come down to meet you!"

"That's no problem, Rhia. You've arrived just in time," Mike said, having greeted her at the first level doorway. Mike, a rounded mid-to-late-forties guy, smiled as he handed her a hard hat and a reflective jacket and showed her how to adjust them to size. "Luke phoned about your plans. You're lucky we're not quite ready yet to start with the removal and renewing of the roof trusses on the damaged side. We'll need to clear the floor space before that happens..." Mike stopped on hearing Rhia's gasp of dismay.

"Oh, my God! Has anything been moved yet?" She was scared to ask for she didn't want a positive answer.

"Don't panic!" Mike grinned back, amused by her distress, his pale blue eyes twinkling. "Nothing's been moved yet. You'll be able to take all the photos you want, so long as it's today. Tomorrow's another story though, for we do want to get into demolition mode on the roof tiles at the damaged end from first light."

"So you're saying I should start at the top of the house?"

"Good plan. Although you should be aware that some of the roofing guys will be wandering around assessing the inside woodwork more thoroughly in the attics, but they know you'll be in the house and will work around you."

"Don't they need a clear space for that?"

"Not to inspect the woodwork itself." His deep voice was reassuring. "But when you've finished photographing the whole attic floor we'll get everything transferred to the non-damaged side. We'll use the empty attic bedrooms for storing the items and the two big areas on the better side if we need to. And if that's still not enough we'll move it down to the third floor."

Rhia's heart flutter settled to a steadier rhythm. So long as she had a good photographic record she'd feel better about items being displaced…even temporarily.

Her digital cameras and video clicked constantly for the next few hours though she acknowledged the basic emergency lighting that had been installed by Luke's team for inspection reasons was inadequate for good photographic quality, but it was sufficient for what she needed as she moved from area to area in the attics. Finished there she worked her way down to the lower levels with Thor at her heels, still mystified by the comings and goings of workmen around the place.

Her video recording skills were pretty basic, but she made sure to methodically still-capture with her digital cameras. Though she had never undertaken anything like this job before, she had a historian's instinct for recording prime sources. She was meticulous in recording the order of the photographs, room by room, in her brand new notebooks.

The hours passed in a blur.

Though it was obvious that some expensive pieces of artwork had been removed from their hanging spaces, there were still many very old paintings and lithographs both on walls and set in frames that decorated tables and cabinets. They were a fascinating and time-consuming study in themselves. Everything was, and Rhia was itching to start investigating.

The permanent grin that accompanied her, she couldn't prevent. She was so excited about the whole project, so honored to be given the responsibility. In her current euphoric mood she was also glad to be legitimately wandering around Greywood Hall!

What if her affair with Luke ran an early course? If he decided he'd had enough of her body? Then she'd still have plenty of exciting work to do at Greywood Hall.

Somehow, only some parts of that reasoning pleased her.

As she toured, she noted the rooms that would require the bulk of her research time. The library in particular heaved with books and other paperwork. What had been Amelia Greywood's bedroom suite had a small dressing room attached, which groaned with information. Inside a walk-in closet in the dressing room, Rhia found boxes packed with facts relating to Amelia's activities, letters from friends and details relating to charity work and local organizations she'd been involved with. There was a wealth of local history contained there—months of study in them alone.

When she'd photographed every floor, she had

just enough time to venture back up to the attics. They were a veritable treasure trove, and like a child in a sweet shop, she was desperate to investigate everything. There were cartons and boxes of paperwork, larger chests holding artifacts and clothing, discarded furniture and toys strewn about.

Some portable cupboards and boxes could be investigated in situ, since they contained larger items but others would be best moved downstairs for further analysis. A particularly large cabin trunk looked so enticing she couldn't wait to find out what it contained. The ornate metal padlock dangled open, though the dust on the lid indicated it hadn't been touched for many a year. The top was just groaning free when strong muscled arms reached around her and helped her lift it up.

Chapter Fourteen

"Let me help." Luke's lips nuzzled Rhia's ear.

He pulled her into his arms and kissed her, elated when Rhia slipped into his embrace as naturally as breathing. His ardor had to be banked though for much as he might want to take their lovemaking further, his teams of workers didn't need to be witness to his weakness for her.

"I'm meeting with the project leaders in the dining room in a few minutes. We'll no doubt run on till around seven thirty or eight." His voice was matter of fact but the twinkle in his gaze and his rueful smile indicated he'd rather be doing other things.

"I'll make dinner for eight thirty then?"

Luke settled his hands on her bottom, his strong fingers easing her closer to the erection that was again stretching his jeans. "We could go out for dinner," he muttered, nibbling at her neck.

"I don't need to be taken out every night," Rhia informed him, giving him all the access he needed. "I'm happy to cook for us."

"Okay." He stole more kisses from the lips he couldn't resist. "If you're sure."

Very domestic. Eating in was a conjugal thing to do; he'd best get used to it. But it was something he had always been rigorous about. Eating at the best restaurants gave very different signals to the women he'd dated in the past. He had to concede though; the present situation was anything but normal. And if he played house with Rhia for a year then they would have to do all these very domestic things a lot more often. It was quite amazing that one week ago the concept would have been farcical.

As he walked downstairs to his meeting Luke asked himself some very pertinent questions. Would he be prepared to be so domestic if he didn't find Rhia so compulsively attractive? What if he'd only engaged her services in a paper marriage because she was a historian, to help him fulfill the conditions of the will and find out the historical mystery that dogged his heels? The thought of doing even basic domestic things with someone he wasn't attracted to now seemed a complete travesty.

When Luke returned to the cottage around eight fifteen, delicious smells wafting around the kitchen made his stomach gurgle. Rhia had planned their dinner very well. The table was set; the chicken and rice dishes were in the oven, keeping warm. It was a meal that usually could survive a delay, which was good because Luke couldn't wait any longer to sample Rhia.

The chicken was a tiny bit dried up but they ate it anyway.

The next morning Rhia was stacking away their breakfast dishes when Luke loped back downstairs, having only been up there for a matter of minutes. His face was like thunder. "I'm off to London to oversee meetings for other ongoing projects." His words were clipped; his manner distracted as though traveling was the last thing he wanted to do.

"Now? It's Saturday!"

Rhia was amazed at the speed of his decision-making though she shouldn't be, everything went at warp speed with Luke every day of the week...except maybe during some of their more lingering late-night lovemaking. That made her smile—he could spend a lot of time at that.

"The helicopter is on its way so I'm off to Greywood to check on a couple of things first." He left soon after saying his return would be late that night.

Realizing their so-called wedding day was looming Rhia took advantage of his absence. Though Luke had offered to buy anything she needed, she shopped for something suitable to wear. A couple of hours later, having visited a number of boutiques and department stores in the nearest large city, she returned home, thrilled with the embroidered full-length sheath dress in white silk. Its vaguely Grecian design that bared one shoulder, was perfect. She couldn't resist new lingerie that included a garter belt and white silk stockings. Her new shoes were high strappy heels that looked great. It wasn't in the least a traditional wedding outfit but it was within her budget, clung to her curves and made her feel sexy. She didn't have a clue what Luke would wear but guessed it would be a formal suit of some kind.

Back at the cottage she stored the items away and settled down to process a digital record of Greywood Hall till Luke returned. Unfortunately it didn't quite work as planned.

By six that evening he called to say he wasn't quite finished and that he'd have to continue the following day but would be back as soon as he could.

Rhia was lonely in her little cottage in a way she'd never been before. Thor, although just as enthusiastic in his adoration, was no substitute.

After lunchtime the next day Luke returned and found Rhia surrounded by an array of diaries and boxes of paperwork in Amelia's walk-in closet. Their reunion had to be circumspect again because the house was thronged with workers even though it was Sunday. After brief but heated kisses, Luke went off to the cottage to resume his work.

From the upstairs bedroom window Luke watched Rhia enter the garden about six o'clock. He waited just long enough for her to feed and water Thor before he dashed down the stairs and intercepted her, hauling her unresisting body close, his desire for her palpable as his forehead made a soft touchdown with hers.

"Good God, woman!" he panted right in her face, his arms a loving imprisonment. "I've missed your body so much!" His lips covered Rhia's as he proceeded to seduce the life out of her. Minutes later she struggled away from his too arousing grip.

"Let me breathe, Luke!" she protested to his deaf ears, a half-hearted remonstration for her huge smile remained in place.

His hands were already roaming as he drew her in the back door, excluding a poor whining Thor as he kicked it closed. In seconds they were making love on the kitchen table as though it was their first time together. Luke was astonished that he still craved her with the same burning intensity.

Later, their lust slaked for the time being, they headed upstairs for a quick shower, Luke insisting on going out for dinner, again to an expensive local restaurant.

Rhia pulled out a classy outfit saying it was an item she'd worn often during her London days. Luke wore a light grey suit and formal button-down shirt and tie that Rhia claimed made him look like every woman's dream.

Dinner was extremely succulent but took too long. Tangling of feet under the table was no substitute for the passion Luke craved. Passing up on desert and coffee he hurried them back to the cottage with undue haste.

The next few days passed quickly. Rhia couldn't prevent herself from tempting Luke at every opportunity and found he was rarely able to resist her. Yet, at other times, she was reluctantly impressed that he dredged up the necessary restraint to remain disengaged and businesslike.

"I've decided to renovate Greywood as a domestic facility," Luke informed her as they ate dinner in the cottage.

"No corporate re-styling at all?"

"None." Luke's answer was curt as he looked out of the small kitchen window. Rhia couldn't gauge how he felt about the decision but he seemed tense, maybe even a little irritated about it. "I've researched the housing market in Northern England and it will be easier to sell off as a luxury domestic property when the year is up."

"Okay…" The thought of it being sold made Rhia cringe but all she added was, "So…should I still carry on with the researching?"

"Of course."

Rhia couldn't talk to him after that. She took refuge in clanking their plates into the sudsy water. She did want Greywood to be restored to its beautiful best, but the thought of some unknown family living in it was gut wrenching. That part of the deal wasn't up to her though. Her aggressive attack on the dishes was more than they needed and her refusal of Luke's offer to help was resolute.

"Since it's a lovely evening, I'm taking Thor out again when I'm finished here." Her statement brooked no compromise, making it sound like she didn't welcome company, but when Luke declared he still had plenty of work that evening, he didn't seem to notice her mood.

She was more subdued in bed that night than she'd been, still responding to his lovemaking but a tiny part of her remained detached. She'd launched herself into their frantic affair refusing to think of its end, but that wasn't a realistic way to tackle the inevitable.

His fingers feathered through her hair as he curved her body into his before they settled for sleep.

"Is there anything wrong, Rhia?"

"No," she lied, making her voice sleepier than she felt, "why should there be anything wrong?" Curled there in the dark, surrounded by his gorgeous body heat, Rhia convinced herself to just enjoy the time she had with him and learn to disregard mention of the future beyond this year.

Rhia focused on her researching, but there was nothing perceptible pointing toward why Luke was the one who had inherited. None of the portraits indicated any likeness to previous Greywood males.

The library research would be a huge undertaking and needed a lot of time. The diaries she'd found in the library and attics spanned a couple of centuries and would also take a long time to evaluate.

She decided her best bet would be to focus on Amelia's personal correspondence and paperwork and work backward from there.

Mere hours later, Rhia bounded up the stairs to the makeshift office clutching a few small photographs. "Luke! I've found it."

"Already?" Luke completed his call, a huge grin on his face. He snatched her up and whirled her around the small space in the centre of the bedroom floor. "Why me then?"

"Oh no!" Rhia's chagrin was unmistakable. "Oh God, Luke! I'm sorry…so sorry. I haven't found out why she named you. It's just that I was so excited at finding these photographs of her that I wanted to show you."

Rhia detected Luke's disappointment and rushed to make things better. "You can now put a face to her. This one here?" Rhia flashed a very small black and white Box Brownie type photo first. "This one is dated 1956 on the back. Read."

Luke read the spidery faded pencil writing. Left to right. Me, my mother Bethany and Julie

Borthwick (her best friend) at Brighton Pier.

"This is what she looked like when she was 38."

"Thank you, Rhia. You're the greatest!" Luke gave her a sound kiss as he held the photograph. "I just knew you were the woman for the job. I've wanted to know what the damned woman looked like since I heard of her peculiar bequest."

Rhia was pleased as he devoured the details in the photograph. Amelia's strong boned face wasn't smiling, but she didn't look unhappy either. Her dark hair was clipped back from her face, a small pair of fancy winged glasses perched on her nose.

"Now look at these two!" Rhia was beside herself with excitement as she handed over more evidence. "These are even better; taken in 1988." Again there was writing on the back of the larger color photographs. To Amelia. These are the best two photographs of the three of us at the Skipton County Fair, 1988. Best regards from Sophia and John Somerston."

Amelia's face looked remarkably similar to the earlier one. Though the hairstyle was the same, her hair was a steel grey. The glasses were a different style, but she still had quite a strong set to her jaw. Rhia reckoned she'd been a forceful woman. Luke agreed.

Amelia had certainly been forceful enough to embroil Luke in their ongoing saga. Rhia slipped him all three photos. At least now he could rant and rave at her photograph when he got fed up of Amelia's little mystery that seemed impossible to solve.

"Make me copies!" He handed them back. "If she keeps me in the dark too much longer I might get frustrated and tear them up."

Rhia continued to immerse herself in cataloguing Amelia Greywood's personal memorabilia. It was fascinating to see how much had survived the decades. She'd found earlier photographs she suspected were of Amelia as a younger woman, but couldn't authenticate them.

In the attics and cupboards, Rhia unearthed priceless items of clothing dating back more than 50 years. After very extensive searching of rooms she found jewelry and ornaments which, though not valuable, were an indication of the lady's style. Rhia's camera clicked constantly, cataloguing everything. Her notebooks and computer spreadsheets loaded up.

However, nothing in those searches pointed to why Luke had inherited.

At dinner a few nights later she brought up the subject of the bequest again. "What exactly did the lawyer tell you about it?"

"What do you mean?"

Luke probably wasn't following her trail of thought, because he was sidetracked by her lips. "You want a copy of the details of the will?" he murmured after a long perusal.

"No." Rhia was quite sure about them for they'd pored over those details before. "When we looked at them, did you take note, for example, of when you were made the beneficiary?"

"She made the will about a year before she died but stipulated I shouldn't be informed of it till after she was buried."

"Mmm..." Rhia was puzzled. It was still quite a touchy subject for Luke, but she couldn't help thinking it a bit late to make your will when you were around ninety! Then again maybe a previous will had indicated something like a charity...or the state. She made it a point to discover why there was that very odd bit about leaving the place to rot.

"I'm going to go the local church tomorrow to look at their records, though I don't imagine they'll go back as far as the earliest inhabitants of the house," she told him.

"Sounds like a good plan," Luke agreed, playing with her fingers.

The simple contact distracted her. His touch kick-started a flutter deep down, his one single kiss to her fingertips increasing it to a whole body tingle. To keep on track she concentrated hard, trying to ignore his obvious signals. Sexually speaking, Luke was in fact a very obvious guy. "After the church, I'll go on to the library. It might give me good insight into some of the forebears more quickly than poring over the library records here at Greywood."

"Sounds good too," Luke chuckled as he raised her up from her chair and led her upstairs, even though she was still giving her update. At the top of the stairs he ravaged her lips, then lifted her into his arms…something she could get used to.

"That huge family bible in the library has given me a lot of names to start with. The family recorded births and deaths in it," she gasped as he dumped her unceremoniously onto the bed.

"Am I in it?" Luke asked as he slipped off her top and snuggled up close.

Rhia squirmed out of her skirt. "You know you're not in it or I'd have… Oh God, Luke…" she groaned as his mouth suckled her. "You're so good at that!"

"Finish your sentence, woman." Luke shrugged out of his clothes and into a condom in a second. "I need to stop that gorgeous mouth with kisses."

"Haven't a clue what I was saying," Rhia grunted as he covered her with his body.

"Family bible…" Luke nibbled his way from her neck to her navel.

Her reply gushed out, "No. Not your mother Elizabeth either. Elizabeth's not a handed down Greywood family…name. Oh yes…Luke!"

No more full words ensued—that was if she

didn't count the Italian mutterings that always accompanied Luke's lovemaking.

"We need to stay here at the cottage for a bit longer than I first imagined, Rhia," Luke said when she returned from Greywood the following evening. "The whole house is going to be rewired during the next few days to match up to current specifications, and it will be pretty messy."

"Okay. I'll check in with Mike about where to avoid. He's a nice guy." Seeing the light in his eye that meant he was bent on seduction, she stepped away from Luke's questing fingers.

"Nice guy?" Luke grabbed her around the waist and brought her close in to his body, his again interminably aroused body. "Nicer than me?"

"Not going there, Luke!" She giggled as he tickled and chased her around the kitchen table. "Stop! Stop! No tickling." She held up her hands in submission. "I saw some plumbing materials being delivered today," she ventured getting her breath back but allowing him to caress her instead. "Are the new bathrooms going in soon as well?"

"Not quite that soon," Luke laughed. "I got the planning permission today for the creation of the new rooms needed for en-suite bathrooms…and the permits for the plasterwork, but they'll take a little longer to create." His tone became a teasing chuckle. "As you once told me the architectural changes need to be sensitive!"

Rhia remembered how she'd challenged his integrity that day. "I'm sorry about that." She grinned. "I was pissed at you that day. Okay! Now you've had my bit of groveling."

"I knew you were." His sparkling green eyes drew her into a long and satisfying kiss. She nuzzled into his neck and stroked his back till he broke off the kiss and sought her concentration. "I want you to attend my meeting tomorrow morning with my interior decorator." He locked his arms around her and trapped her at the sink.

"Why? I'm not an interior decorator," she mumbled into his questing mouth. "What...do you expect...from me?"

Chapter Fifteen

"Just your gorgeous body."

Rhia's clothes were off a few kisses later. Luke's jeans and boxer shorts were at his knees and protection was in place. Desperation was her middle name as she used the door for leverage and wrapped her legs around his waist to encourage his thrusts.

Luke groaned. "Look what you do to me, Rhia!"

His mouth latched onto one nipple; his fingers teasing the other as Rhia panted, "Well, I need you too." A few frantic plunges later she raced to a fast climax, the pulsations of her orgasm barely ceased when she felt the heat of Luke's release.

"*Madre di Dio*. Just give me a minute."

Before he let her slide down his body to the floor, his whole weight slumped against her until he regained his breath.

It was a while later during dinner that the topic of the next morning's meeting with the decorator was brought up again. Rhia was delighted when he said, "I want you there to ensure the decorative touches are going to be correct for a private family home."

"What makes you think I can do that?"

"This little cottage has a homely feel about it. Your personal touches are everywhere I look."

Rhia glowed; glad that he liked her home. They discussed the decorative style he envisioned for Greywood—he wanted some of the rooms to retain the grandeur but still be a home people could be comfortable in, with modern comforts and contemporary accessories.

In turn Rhia was pleased to update him with her day's work in town. "I think I've got sufficient information to put together a family tree from the first Alexander Greywood who built the house in the late sixteen hundreds. His gravestone is still in the churchyard, although the detail is difficult to read. There's a sectioned off area in the graveyard for the Greywood family, including the more expected mausoleum building for the Victorian era."

The meeting the following morning was a revelation to Rhia. It shouldn't have been for she knew what a dynamic person Luke was, but the energy and verve he instilled in his employees was a measurable thing. His teams of workers enjoyed what they did and were energized by his work ethic. It was exciting being part of the decorative planning, and she was happy to make her own observations where relevant. Luke's interior designer wasn't averse to having ideas put forward.

They left the dining room where the meeting had been held. Luke dragged Rhia into the large room next to the library. She hadn't been in that part of the house for a couple of days and was astonished to see it was laid out as a fully functioning office.

"The electrical wiring is completed, so it's ready for me to move into." He wrapped his arms over her shoulders and rested his chin on her head. "Until I moved into your little bedroom I never realized my normal *modus operandi* was to march around so much." His Adam's apple bobbled against her nape as he chortled. "It's tried my patience no end being unable to pace more than three steps in any direction."

"So your office is moving today?"

"Yep! Jeremy's arriving soon. He'll be using this desk here." He nuzzled her neck as he indicated the one nearest the door. "Mine is that one over there.

I'll be bringing my personal belongings right away. By tomorrow your spare room will be restored to an empty room again. The office furniture that's currently in there will be moved to a smaller room on the ground floor here at Greywood as an office for Mike."

"You don't hang around much, do you?" Rhia laughed, deliberately making his whole body respond as she nudged him.

"You've no idea how much hanging around I'm doing." His reply was cryptic. He drew her close for a lingering kiss regardless of who might walk in on them.

Rhia was puzzled later that evening, and during the next few days, when Luke insisted they dine out at the end of each very long and tiring shift. "I don't need to be wined and dined every night, Luke." She repeated the same argument as before, sparking off one of their mild disagreements.

"I want to sample everything the area has to offer." His answer was urbane—so they ate out.

"Ready for my latest update?" she asked as their main courses were delivered. They'd segued into the habit of her giving him any major historical updates during dinner.

"Fire away."

"Okay, get your handkerchief ready. It's all a bit sad."

Luke's answer was wry as he tackled his food, "Isn't history peppered with sad happenings?"

"You're right." Rhia nodded. "So far you know there have been Alexander Greywoods at Greywood Hall for centuries, as some of the portraits bear out."

Luke nodded back, his attention focused. Rhia loved how alert he could be, although she wasn't duped—she knew his thoughts were still predominantly sexually charged.

"Well, to cut to the chase. I've found out that

your Amelia Greywood was the granddaughter of Alexander Greywood the umpteenth."

Luke grinned at her expression. "The umpteenth? Is this a new erudite historical term?"

"I'll get you for that later, Luke Salieri!" Rhia threatened, waving her fork at him. "Listen up, boy!"

Her mock tutor voice went unchallenged as he tucked into his succulent steak.

"I've not quite authenticated how many Alexanders there have been because a few infant mortalities cloud the process." She cut a bit of fish and put it in her mouth. "Anyway, Amelia's great-grandfather continued to make money around 1840 from the Greywood Thread Mill that was started in 1804—a good time for manufacturers as they were producing clothing for the navy and for the regiments." She stopped for a breath and to pop a piece of artichoke into her mouth. "Following me?"

Luke answered around a mouthful of salad. "Trafalgar?"

"Wow! You're good, boss." She grinned at him. "For an Aussie, I'm impressed."

"Remember I was educated at private English schools."

"Right!" Rhia shrugged as she tackled more of her succulent fish. "Slipped my mind for a moment."

"Continue please."

"Okay. They also had a string of Greywood Drapers shops here in northern England, which for a while brought in a tidy profit. Till Amelia's own dear granddaddy—also an Alexander, born 1852—seemed to put the scuppers on that. As far as I can tell he was a wastrel and worked his way through quite a fortune. Most of the shops were sold and the mill closed down by 1889, though I've yet to peruse the estate records which should authenticate that."

"So you're thinking that by the time Amelia came along, the funds were already drying up?"

"Most certainly, but it's far more complicated than that. Her grandfather Alexander had three daughters but no surviving sons, which in the way of things probably pissed him off quite a lot. The old inheritance thing—and no poor new little Alexander who survived infancy."

"Rhia Ashton! I'm shocked that as an historian you can be so glib." From Luke's wide smile and twinkling green eyes she knew how serious he was, though it was also clear he knew she was kidding.

She ignored the slight on her professionalism and finished off her main course before continuing, "The eldest of these three daughters, Lucinda, married in 1902 and went to live in Cornwall. According to one diary, her visits to Greywood Hall were rare."

Luke signaled the waiter to top off their wine glasses as their dessert was delivered.

"The middle daughter, Jocasta, born 1888, lived at Greywood till she was approximately 22. The trail for her mysteriously stops around 1910."

"The Jo-Jo of the broken leg?"

Rhia chortled around her sorbet. "The very one!"

"So her broken limb didn't kill her then?"

"No. But there remains some mystery about what happened to her around 1910."

"And the youngest of the three?"

"I've found evidence that Bethany, born 1892, eventually inherited Greywood in 1920—long after her father died in February 1911."

"Bethany, as the youngest, inherited?"

Rhia slipped cool mango sorbet between her lips. Though she was small and slender she knew Luke liked the fact that she loved her food and shoveled it in. He might be preoccupied with her story but she knew he also wanted to sample her delicious dessert. Without stopping her conversation, she held out a forkful for sampling. He caught hold of her fingers and held the spoon suspended, hovering at his own lips before allowing it to glide inside.

"Mmm...delicious," he replied, "just like you."

They shared a moment of searing heat.

"Want to hear the rest?" she asked.

"I want everything you give me, Rhia," Luke's reply was triply loaded.

Rhia was enjoying this man's company far too much and not just when the entertainment was sexual. "Well, Bethany was the youngest but somehow the estate worked its way to her by 1920."

"Sounds like this is where the handkerchief is needed?"

"Yep!" Rhia's enthusiasm was infectious. "The process of Bethany's inheritance was slow because the eldest, Lucinda, as first daughter, became heir when their father Alexander died. Unfortunately Lucinda also died two weeks later in March 1911 during the confinement of a stillborn daughter. According to one of the diaries, the poor woman only had one surviving, but sickly, daughter named Melanie, who was born in 1904. Lucinda had had a string of miscarriages over the years and was never in great health. Melanie then became the official heir."

Luke complimented her on her sleuthing but needed something clarified. "Wouldn't the estate have passed on to some distant male heir when Alexander the howevermuch died?"

Rhia's burst of laughter startled the diners at the nearest table, causing her to blush and then make her apologies. "I love the howevermuch! I must use that one again." she chuckled before resuming. "The answer is no, because as far as I can tell there was no problem about a female being the heir. Victorian Society was riddled with newfangled ideas and lots of innovative practices, so I'm guessing Alexander wanted to keep the estate for his own children and changed his will accordingly."

"Or maybe because it isn't such a large estate in the scheme of English estates?" Luke was speculating too.

"Probably." Rhia agreed because there were no aristocratic rules in place. "Remember, their money came from trade so the male heir thing would maybe never have been a problem. Trade families never quite had the same hang-ups about women inheriting. The problem was sometimes about unmarried women being able to spend their inherited money."

"Poor fragile women, unable to manage their finances, always needed the firm hand of a strong man to help them survive and keep them happy…and fulfilled." Luke grinned at her, the seductive green of his eyes darkening. "Just like you, Rhia?"

"Don't go there if you value something you hold dear below your belt, Luke Salieri!" Rhia flashed messages back to him with her eyes, more aroused than she wanted to be by his sexually loaded conversation in a public place.

"After the deaths of both Alexander and Lucinda," she continued, "the estate officially belonged to the ailing seven-year-old Melanie. Bethany's diary indicates that because of the health of the child her father, John Trevanyan, never brought her from Cornwall to visit Greywood Hall. As Melanie's executor Trevanyan was quite happy for Bethany to remain at Greywood and continue to run the place. Any disposable money, whatever was left after Alexander's profligate lifestyle decimated it, remained in the hands of Trevanyan after the death of Melanie in December 1912."

"Okay. So, Melanie inherited after her mother died?"

Rhia nodded.

Luke continued, "The estate and some money that was left from Alexander?"

"Yes." Rhia finished her dessert and laid down the cutlery. "Bethany's diary indicates that Alexander left £10,000 pounds to Jocasta and £10,000 to herself. The rest went to Lucinda but I haven't found the exact amount yet."

"I'm guessing that was still quite a tidy sum for Jocasta in 1911?"

"Sure, if you considered it as sort of pin money...but not enough for Bethany to run the estate as you'll hear if you let me finish!"

She sipped the last of her wine as her coffee was poured. "This is where it gets complicated. Melanie was, of course, a minor. Her father, as her next of kin, was deemed to be the recipient of anything that belonged to her."

"Was that usual?"

"I think it was, yes."

Luke sipped his coffee. "So why did Bethany inherit—if it went to Trevanyan after his daughter's death?"

"I've no official documentation to back this up yet, but from Bethany's diary and the internet searches I've done, John Trevanyan was well set up himself and had a sizeable estate in Cornwall. He didn't want anything to do with Greywood Hall. Bethany's diary states that Trevanyan officially got the ownership of Greywood transferred back to Jocasta about two months after Melanie died."

"But he kept any cash Lucinda then Melanie inherited?"

"It seems so."

Luke rubbed his chin, fingering the light stubble. "So the estate became Jocasta's but no money to run it?"

"Yes. Except..." Rhia drew out the suspense... "she was missing. From well before her father died.

She went off on a visit with friends, to Naples, in July 1910 and never returned to Greywood Hall."

"Never?" Luke's ears perked up at that one. "What about the friends? Didn't they know where she was?"

"No. It appears they parted company when Jocasta went on to Florence, and they returned home. Her trail ends at that point. Again, from what I can track from other sources, and according to the diaries, but as you know I've only dipped a toe in the water regarding them."

"So, Greywood Hall and £10,000 belongs to Jocasta but she doesn't know about any of these deaths. Or about her portion?"

"I've no reason, or evidence yet, to believe she knew," Rhia clarified as they left the restaurant. They climbed into the waiting taxi—Luke preferred not to drive when they ate out.

They continued the conversation in the back of the taxi, Rhia's hand in Luke's light grasp as he played with her fingers.

"At times in the diary, Bethany is quite distraught. It's hard to read some of the heartrending entries that detail the lengths she and her lawyer went to, to locate her sister. They even paid a private detective to find Jocasta but it seems he drew a blank too, and Bethany's resources weren't sufficient for her to continue."

"Well you've certainly uncovered much more about the Greywood family than I would have been able to at this stage." He paid the taxi on their arrival back to the cottage. "That's it so far?" he asked.

"Nearly. Due to Jocasta's continued absence they ultimately had to assume something dire had happened to her. It took the stipulated period after that to officially declare Jocasta dead. By then it was 1920."

Luke led her into the sitting room and nestled her next to him on the couch, knowing her well enough to realize she needed to get all her news delivered before she would turn off her history trigger for the night and switch into sleep mode.

"The youngest daughter, Bethany, lived at Greywood all her life. She never married but her diaries divulge that she had a sweetheart during the First World War. The saddest thing is that he died without knowing he had made Bethany pregnant during one of his home visits."

Luke whispered massaging kisses to her fingers. "He was a local then?"

"Fairly local. He was from Skipton. He'd been shipped home to recuperate in late 1917. He spent six months recovering from a bayonet that pierced his lung, and of course the mustard gas he'd breathed in had done damage as well!" Her eyes opened as Luke maneuvered her into a more comfortable position.

"Guess his recovery was sufficient, if he got Bethany pregnant." Luke's eyes twinkled as he kissed the top of her head.

"You guess right! Unfortunately he was sent back to France in April 1918. His tragic death just one month later devastated Bethany. She gave birth to an illegitimate daughter, Amelia, in early December 1918 who was brought up here at Greywood, although to do so was a scandal at the time. Unmarried ladies palmed their illegitimate children off to an orphanage or to families who'd rear the child."

Rhia had by this time climbed onto Luke's lap so she could wriggle herself above his burgeoning erection.

"Of course by then Bethany had no elder relatives to dictate to her and I suppose at that time she had just sufficient monetary resources to fly in the face of convention. In the fullness of time, Bethany died leaving the property to Amelia."

"I'm guessing, since her name was still Greywood, poor Amelia never married?" Luke questioned.

"Correct, although she seems to have carved a niche for herself in local society even though she was illegitimate. I'm finding a lot to respect about Amelia Greywood. The sources of income dried up, and she had to make huge economies during her life, selling many of Greywood's treasures just to keep the wolf from the door."

But none of that explained why Luke was the one on the dotted line of her will.

On the fourth night out, they had a wonderful meal at one of the best establishments in the area.

"This place is magic, Luke," Rhia said after a beautifully presented meal.

Luke had been unaware of the ambience when he'd booked. The subdued lighting, tastefully low music from the live band, plus the excellent décor, added to the dreamy character and didn't help his crusade to disengage himself from her sexual allure.

"I've heard of this place before but never had an opportunity to come," Rhia told him, clutching his hand across the table and squeezing her appreciation, her fingers lingering to entwine themselves around his, a bit like her whole presence was welding itself around his libido-driven psyche. "Thanks for insisting we come. I wouldn't have wanted to miss this place."

By the time their coffee and liqueurs arrived, their conversation was strumming with sexual tension. Their tangled fingers across the table weren't enough for him.

"I'll just pop into the ladies before we head home," Rhia whispered.

She rejoined him at the taxi he'd ordered just as

he finished a call.

The moment he powered his phone back on, it rang. He cursed in Italian, reluctant to answer. Switching his cell-phone off during their meal was a habit he'd adopted, but he was now fuming as he slapped it shut and pocketed it before opening the taxi door for her. His jaw was rigid as he announced he needed another quick London visit in the morning.

He was so livid that he didn't risk speaking to Rhia in case he bit her nose off. She certainly didn't deserve his ire!

His anger had dissipated though by the time they reached her cottage.

Luke slipped away early the next morning, first dropping a light kiss on Rhia's lips, probably thinking she was still asleep. She wasn't quite but was too groggy to respond.

After lying in bed longer than usual, she shuffled into the shower to make a start on the day. The insistent ringing of a landline telephone accompanied her tuneless singing: not the one downstairs in her hall, the sound was too close by for that. It had to be the extension in Luke's temporary office. She let it ring knowing any business automatically transferred to the new number at Greywood Hall.

The summer weather seemed to have finally broken. Rain was sheeting her bedroom window as she toweled herself dry. Warmer clothes were needed as she rifled amongst her wardrobe contents for a pair of jeans and a jumper. As she brushed her hair into shape, the unrelenting buzzing of the same telephone grew very annoying. There was now no sophisticated answering machine to kick in so—and though she'd never invaded the privacy of Luke's provisional office before—she picked up the receiver.

"Luke!"

The strident word blasted Rhia's ear off. "I'm sorry, Luke's not here just now."

"I want to speak to Luke."

"Luke's not here just now," she repeated. "May I take a message for him?"

"Why are you answering the phone instead of Jeremy? Pass me on to Luke now!"

Rhia decided after only a few more words that she'd had enough of this extremely rude woman. "As I said already, Luke isn't available. Please tell me what I can do for you?"

"I'll get Luke to fire you, you moron!"

Moron? Rhia's blood boiled but she didn't want to cause any offence to a customer, or even a colleague of Luke's, so she forced herself to remain calm. "If you give me your name," she tried one last and final time, "I'll tell Luke you called."

"Fine! Tell him that his girlfriend Danielle called and that I can't make it for our dinner date this evening. He can come to my flat instead. I'll be home by ten thirty."

Chapter Sixteen

Girlfriend? Who was this woman?

Silence descended leaving Rhia with a dead phone and an even more dead lump where her heart had been.

Why was Luke meeting this Danielle person for dinner? And why did this Danielle assume it would be easy for Luke to go to her flat at ten-thirty? Rhia's stomach plunged to the carpet. Had Luke met up with this female the night he'd spent in London, last Saturday, and had he gone back to her today? More importantly did he have sex with her?

Rhia curled up on her bed, the bed she'd recently shared with Luke, the smell of their last bout of sex still lingering on the sheets.

"Bloody bitch, bitch, and bitch!" She didn't quite know who she was most angry with, but she wasn't happy with Luke.

No! She wouldn't be a victim like this. She might be new to the game of nearly-wife but she'd not concede like this. She ripped the sheets off the bed, lugged them downstairs and thrust them into the washing machine. Back upstairs she remade the bed with the ugliest sheets from her cupboard.

Later that afternoon Luke called. "Hello, gorgeous! Miss me?"

He had no idea how much his casual phrase and sexual undertones ripped the heart out of her. She'd had all day though to prepare for his call and knew she was acquitting herself pretty well under the circumstances. She felt as though she had no insides by then anyway.

"You had a call this morning on the cottage temporary office phone," Rhia informed him.

"I thought all calls were transferring to Greywood." His answer was blithe, unaware.

"Your girlfriend—Danielle I believe her name is—says to tell you she'll not make your dinner date tonight, but you can pop round to her flat after ten-thirty. It seems she'll be home by then," Rhia managed to inform him tonelessly.

The silence at the other end spoke volumes before she heard what she imagined was a tirade of creative Italian cursing. "It's not how it seems, Rhia."

"I don't want to know, Luke, how it seems, but if you've reneged on our signed agreement you can cancel our wedding. I refuse to share you with anyone, especially not with a bitch like Danielle." Rhia closed the phone with a thud.

Luke didn't try to contact her again but returned that night around nine-thirty, no overnight stay involved, but too late for dinner. She had given up on him anyway and had picked at her own food earlier, chucking most of it in the bin. The meal left for him was still warming in the oven and was probably like dried up birdcake. She didn't care if he ate it or not.

Their wedding was supposed to be the next day.

"Rhia!" His bellow would have wakened a great white bear in the North Pole as he thundered upstairs.

She was upstairs in bed, a book in her hands, when Luke erupted into the room. Striding close to the bed, he ignored her body language that screamed at him to keep the hell away.

"Rhia, you have to believe me!"

Luke was spitting angry but he couldn't possibly be as angry as her. She ignored him. He waited. She ignored him even more. Exasperated he stomped away.

The word uproar was a pretty good description of his volume. “I am not having an affair with Danielle. I don’t want to have sex with anyone but you, and I don’t intend to.”

More of the same followed, some English and some Italian, but try as he might Rhia refused to look at him, every thing about her furious as she pretended to read.

“We are getting married tomorrow, Rhia,” he persisted, lowering to a minor roar.

“There’s no damned way you’re welshing out on our deal Rhia. You said you’d marry me and you will!”

He ripped off his jacket and threw it across the room. Her ears rang like a clarion but she refused to acknowledge it as he ranted. “You’ve signed that bloody contract and Greywood needs you now. What you’ve started you have to finish!”

Bloody Hell! The way she was feeling she’d leave him high and dry…but Greywood?

She lifted her head. Luke’s natural olive skin tone was leached to a grayish white. Too bad! He deserved to feel as sick as she’d been feeling all day.

Her words were a whisper. “Who is Danielle?”

“Nobody important,” Luke answered into the dark, sinister cloud that enveloped them. His rage was under wraps for now, subdued by her example. At her unimpressed glare he added, “She’s a woman I was dating before I met you.”

Rhia exhaled, her chest heaving with the effort of replying, her eyes puffy from an earlier bout of crying. “Before you met me or…” her voice trembled on the last word “…while?”

“While?”

“Last weekend in London?” Her eyes were the sharpest darts, very pained darts, but she didn’t care now if Luke noticed or not. “Did you meet up with her then?" Her chin wobbled on the last, so difficult had it been to get the words out, but there was no way she was going to be palmed off with lies or platitudes.

"Sod it! I'm not going to lie to you."

Luke wrenched off his tie to the beat of some impressive Italian swearing. Plonking himself on the edge of the bed beside her he took a cautious breath before replying.

"Yes, I saw her in London last weekend."

Rhia couldn't stifle the sniff as she slid away from him.

"Danielle came, uninvited, to my office. But it was daytime."

"Daytime? What has daytime got to do with it Luke? You can perform whether it's full sunlight or full dark. So what does the time of day matter?"

She literally shook with anger, her fists primed as he trapped her hands between his cold-as-ice shaking ones. Her word 'perform' annoyed him, Rhia discerned that!

He was so close his words spat at her, his pallor even more marked than before. "I told Danielle ages ago that the relationship I'd had with her was long finished. And I told her last week too when she turned up like a bad penny. That's all I did last week."

A single tear slid down her cheek; she wrenched her hands free. "But she doesn't believe that, does she? She couldn't if she called again today."

"She may not have this morning but she damned well understands now," Luke answered. His temper was again only just under control as he plowed his fingers through his disheveled mop.

"She doesn't sound like someone who listens very well to you." Rhia intended her tone to stay flat as she swiped another tear away.

"She knows we're getting married tomorrow so

the message should get through her avaricious head." One long finger dared to reach forward catching the drip on her chin.

She whipped his finger away as quick as a fly swat. She wasn't done with him yet. She might not be sure of how to spell belligerent but she certainly felt it. "How can I trust she won't be replaced by someone similar next time you're away?"

Luke had a good solution. "We don't ever separate. If I need to be in London, you come with me, even if it's only for one night. I know you don't want to listen right now Rhia, but I will be faithful to you. I will honor my contract with you."

He needed to be sure she'd honor the agreement made for their year. She knew that. Although she was still incensed, she couldn't imagine not sharing his life like they'd been doing. And there was Greywood.

"You'd better not be lying to me, Luke Salieri! Not now and not ever."

"I do not tell lies, Rhia!"

She'd never seen pain in Luke's eyes before but she was seeing it now.

She accepted the olive branch for what it was. Luke had a sexual past she'd have to live with, even for a year, and the best way to live the year without this disgusting, gut-rotting doubt was either to trust him or to always be with him.

"I hate myself for saying this just now but I will marry you tomorrow."

The past day had been unbearable so always being with him had to be the closest to a workable solution. She was still angry with Luke, but she was also angry with herself, furious that she was always so bloody practical.

"Let me explain about Danielle."

His hands bracketed her shoulders to draw her in. She held herself rigid within his embrace, unable to give any more to him quite yet.

“No. You don’t need to tell me anything.”

“I do, you know I do...” He shook her shoulders to gain her full attention stopping only when the brown focus was deep enough for him to sink into. “...otherwise it’ll be a festering wound that will magnify at the worst possible time. I want to have no secrets between us.”

Shaking her head Rhia slipped out of his grip and lay down flat, still as stiff as a board, eyes fixed on the ceiling as she pulled up the cover tight to her chin. “No secrets.” Her voice wobbled again.

Luke crawled away and yanked off his clothes before sliding in alongside her, encouraging her to relinquish the cover for him to get underneath, for there was no way he wasn’t going to be plastered next to her. She shifted away from him; he followed. He took her hand in a light grasp and gently squeezed. Reassuring. Not in the least sexual.

Luke exhaled...and squeezed her fingers again. She relaxed, needing the comfort as much as he seemed to. Rhia felt the tension drain out of him as it drained out of her. She dared a look in his direction knowing he’d been silently begging her to do so. All his anger had fled, replaced with a tinge of sorrow and a whole heap of regret.

“Danielle is a lingerie model I dated five times. The last time I saw her was three weeks before I went on my last trip to Australia, which was five weeks before I met you. And I told her way back then that we’d not be seeing each other again.”

If what he was saying was true, Rhia had no answer for him. She was ashamed at her volatile reaction but also felt vindicated by his remorse for Danielle was still a bitch of the first order!

“Unfortunately, as you realized, she doesn’t take rejection well. She liked the idea of milking my money, loved being seen at the most popular high-class venues. She pestered me on my cell and kept ringing the London office even after I went to Australia. I instructed Jeremy, more than once, to never pass on her calls to me."

Rhia recalled hearing those very words instructed herself. And how!

"While Jeremy was up here on one of his quick visits someone else in the London office gave her the cottage number and she called numerous times after I set up office here."

"Bloody persistent bitch!"

"Yes, she is that. She tried my cell again last night, just before we came home, telling me she'd made a restaurant booking for this evening and expected me to be there. I realized I'd have to see her face to face to tell her officially to back off, so I arranged the impromptu visit to London."

"Were you at any business meetings at all today?" Rhia was miserable but had to know.

"Yes, one that had been scheduled even before I went to Australia, but an appointment I'd cancelled when I knew I needed to spend more time at Greywood. I rescheduled it for before lunch today, then I met Danielle at one o'clock in the little bistro near my office. I bought two coffees, not even any hint of the food she ranted about, then I spent a matter of minutes telling her in no uncertain terms that I was not ever going out with her again and that she was verging on entering the realms of being a stalker."

"What made her think you'd see her tonight? Is she the most stupid bitch in the world or what?" Rhia was now quite incensed at what Luke had been going through with the bloody woman and was now infuriated on his behalf.

"Her parting words at the bistro were that she would go to the press and give them details of our affair if I didn't relent."

"She's a bloody delusional bitch!" Hooked on using the word bitch as her new and most favorite form of swearing, Rhia shrugged out of his grasp and sat up. "Tell me you socked her in the jaw!"

"Violence, woman, will get you nowhere," Luke chuckled. "I had nothing to hide and I won't bow to anyone's blackmail."

They looked at each other and flew into a fit of giggles remembering their arrangement—what Amelia Greywood had done to them was a definite form of blackmail.

When they'd stopped laughing Rhia managed to add, "What will you do if she goes to the press?"

"What's she going to say? That we went out a few times? I never wrote any love poems or sent her lewd phone pictures. She'll have no record of anything remotely damaging on her voice mail—all I ever said was where we'd meet and when."

"So what on earth does she think she has on you that would be newsworthy?"

Luke shrugged saying he'd no idea. "Beats me. There was only sex involved between us three times, not even on every date, and I'm not proud to admit I felt lust only the first time...the other two times were..." His hands raked through his thick hair, his eyes were self-mocking as he sought Rhia's understanding. "She was all over me like a rash, I guess. Suffice to say sex happened and then I went home...as I'd also done on the first occasion too."

"Don't you think she might have a little something else if she's trying to bribe you like this?"

"No." Luke clutched her to his naked body, the ugly flannel pajamas she'd pulled on in her earlier fit of pique rumpling between them. "Unless it's because she wants to damage my self-esteem. She might say I can't perform in the sack...or that my equipment is sub standard..."

Rhia gasped and kissed him hard. "If the bitch

does that I'll send in a statement categorically refuting it! But I'd do it in such a way that would annihilate her."

Luke returned her kiss, deep and thorough till she sobered up and pulled herself out of his arms. She might be defending him now against the rapacious Danielle but she still hadn't forgiven him. No way was he making love to her…not yet.

"Go to sleep, Luke!"

He took the hint when she turned her back on him, curled into a fetus-like ball and closed her eyes. She allowed him small mercies when his toasty body arched around hers and his arms loosely cocooned her. Though she was still thrumming with tension it didn't take any time at all for her to slip into sleep, for she was drained.

Most unusually Rhia woke before Luke the next morning. Looking at his face in repose she knew she loved him more than life itself. She'd signed up for this marriage initially with a degree of coercion, but now it was unbearable to think of him with anyone else. She would marry him that afternoon, and she would make sure he never ever had cause to stray, but she wasn't letting him think she was a push-over either.

Sliding out from his light embrace, she showered and dressed. Unable to face speaking to him yet, she took the coward's way out and left a note beside the coffee she'd prepared, saying she was out walking Thor before going along to Greywood Hall.

They hadn't made love the previous night but Luke knew precisely when Rhia fell asleep, knew the second her muscles relaxed, but he had continued to think through the night.

Rhia would only be a temporary feature in his life, after which they'd say goodbye and go their own ways so why did it matter so much that she be happy? Dawn was breaking when he nodded off into a disturbed slumber with still no answer to his own question.

An hour later he dribbled himself downstairs, read her little note by the coffee machine and saw it for the cop-out it was. He got himself ready for what was going to be a momentous day. A short while later he tracked her down in the library. He couldn't start on any of his work till he'd at least seen her and knew how she was feeling. She must go ahead with the marriage later that afternoon without question—he wouldn't allow or contemplate any other result than that. He needed Rhia!

"What do you have planned for today?"

Her tone was cool, dispassionate. Usually she was bubbling full of optimism. It took seconds to realize she was avoiding eye contact again, and she'd returned to the stand-back-from-me-buddy body language.

"I'm amassing the paperwork I found upstairs. I intend to store it all in here for later investigation. Trips up and down will take the best part of the day, I should imagine."

Their meeting was brief and not at all private since members of Luke's usual team who took inventory were in the library with Rhia.

"If we head back to the cottage about four p.m. is that time enough for you?"

Luke's question was delicate, since he had no idea if in her present frame of mind she'd stand beside him and take her vows. And if she still planned to, was she wearing the jeans she was dressed in? Shocked at himself he found he didn't care a hoot what she wore, so long as she was there and said the right words and signed the damned bit of paper! No way was she copping out of it. He would put the pen in her hand if need be, but she would marry him.

"I'll make my own way over and see you just

before five at the cottage." Her tone continued, unforgiving.

That gave Luke a slight dilemma. The suit he planned to wear was hanging in Rhia's wardrobe so he needed access to the house for the time it would take him to shower, shave and dress.

At twenty to five Luke arrived at the cottage. Hearing Rhia talk to Thor in the garden meant he was able to nip upstairs and sort himself out. Back down in record time he greeted the registrar just before Jeremy and Roger, his London butler, arrived a few minutes before five o'clock.

In no time at all they stood in front of the registrar in Rhia's back garden using her garden table for the necessary signing of the documents. A simple vase of flowers freshly picked from the flowerbeds decorated the wooden surface.

Luke wore a dark suit with formal collar and tie, as did the witnesses. Rhia was stunning in a long white gown, Thor sitting at her side as her only attendant. Luke was unable to take his eyes off the vision she made. Not quite the fairy sprite of the woods he had originally imagined, but a sexy goddess, draped in body hugging silk.

Just before the ceremony started Rhia had been startled when Roger asked the registrar to pause for a few seconds. He'd dashed down the garden hastily breaking off flowering blooms and some matching foliage; he'd deftly wrapped some long grasses around the stems and then presented it as a simple spray to Rhia.

"A beautiful bride should have a bouquet," he'd stated formally, "and there's no doubt you deserve these, Miss Ashton."

Roger's kind statement brought tears to her eyes.

She would only be Miss Ashton for a few more seconds. She would have his name in mere moments.

Sweat trickled down Luke's back. Nothing could stop her being his wife now. No. Nothing! As well as the hint of fear, a good dose of chagrin oozed down there as well.

Though in his fantasies he'd given some consideration to what Rhia would wear, he hadn't given any thought to all the other traditional wedding trappings that somehow just happened. Bouquets. Cake. Venue. People. Photographs.

Roger's simple gesture tweaked Luke's conscience, but thrusting it aside, he consoled himself that their wedding wasn't supposed to be a normal one.

They said their vows.

The word love was a tiny part of the standard ceremony given by the registrar for they hadn't opted to write their own. Both parroted the words after the celebrant though neither made any mention of love. That wasn't what this marriage contract was about for either of them.

Luke clasped Rhia's hand as they were instructed to kiss at the end of the ceremony. He made sure the kiss was thorough, unwilling for her to pull back from him at such an eventful moment.

Jeremy and Roger signed the marriage certificate. It was all over in minutes.

After a celebratory glass of champagne, the registrar departed. Then, when the taxi arrived for the four of them, they went to a nearby restaurant for a quiet but convivial early meal—no frills and no wedding cake. If the circumstances of the marriage seemed unusual, neither of Luke's employees was crass enough to make it evident. After their meal Luke and Rhia took a taxi back to the cottage, and the other two went off to the hotel booked for them.

Thor barked like mad in the back enclosure on their arrival.

"I know he needs a walk, Rhia, but please, not

yet. Not just yet." Luke's words were a begged whisper as he led Rhia upstairs. He took her into his arms, his embrace cautious for he still wasn't sure of her disposition. "You look beautiful, but I want you out of that charming wisp of silk."

"You do?"

"Oh yes, my gorgeous, Rhia, I do!" He nibbled the bit behind her ears that always made her quiver. "Will you let me make love to you?" The request was muffled against her co-operative lips.

"I might…if you'll be good."

"*Cara*, I'm going to be good!"

The dress was beautiful but still, for some reason, he was disappointed in it. The ceremony they'd endured was very appropriate for the circumstances but it too, seemed lacking.

Peeling off her gown he uncovered the beauty beneath. The garter belt and stockings made the blood pound into his already straining erection.

"*Madre di Dio*!" he husked against her throat. "You must have known I pictured something like this…"

His words were muttered Italian endearments as he nibbled her lips. He'd not had sex with her since the night before last, and that was the longest they'd gone without intercourse during the short time they'd been together. Nine days of satisfying his sexual cravings followed by more than a whole day without had been complete torment. Luke didn't know how he'd survived the previous night just holding her but wanting her so badly.

His loving was slow. He suckled her through the material of her sheer bra and teased her into abandonment. Arousing her was easy. He knew exactly what she needed as he peeled away the gossamer thin white garment that gave tantalizing views of her nipples and caressed a pathway down to her navel.

"There… Absolutely… there. Ahh."

He knew now just where to kiss, and blow, and whisper against her skin to give her maximum pleasure and arouse her into a frenzy of squirming anticipation.

Her silken thong was next removed, thankfully worn on top of the garter belt. "The do-me shoes and stockings stay on…*cara mia*. You've cast a spell on me."

Soon Luke gave all his attention to pleasuring her. "Don't stop!" she cried. "I'm almost…"

"No chance. I'm not stopping."

Her pleasure was his pleasure. It made him feel better about the whole day that had just passed. She was now married to him. She was his. Her signature was now on that piece of paper.

Chapter Seventeen

"Tomorrow's the day, Rhia!"

Luke whirled her around and around sending the blood rushing to Rhia's head, spinning her so fast she could hardly breathe.

"What are you talking about?"

"I can't wait for us to be sleeping here in Greywood Hall!" Luke's enthusiastic verve was almost palpable. "The rooms we need are all ready. Nothing to keep us waiting."

Rhia beamed at him as he released her to the floor and hugged her tight. "You mean the still-to-be ready twenty or so rooms don't matter?"

"Nope!" Luke stole a kiss, something he still did all the time. "They'll get the place done but we have everything we need for now, Mrs. Salieri."

Rhia's eyes widened, but she refrained from saying anything. He'd never called her that in a playful tone, never really called her that at all. Every time so far, he made sure to introduce her to new people as my wife Rhia, but not Mrs. Salieri.

"So are you telling me in your devious way, Mr. Salieri, that you hate sleeping in my cottage?"

She pretended to be in a huff.

"How could I, *cara mia,* when I have you to hold every single night?"

It was true. They hadn't slept apart one single night since their marriage, Rhia accompanying him on his fleeting London or other site visits.

They'd been married five weeks, and although Luke expected to have moved into Greywood sooner, he'd had to deploy his man-resources at two of his other work sites, slowing the progress at Greywood. Business was business, and when all was said and done, it really didn't matter all that much because they only really slept at the cottage. Their days were occupied at Greywood, and with continual updates to the local lawyer, they still fulfilled the will conditions sufficiently well.

"How can we celebrate our moving into Greywood?" he asked.

He was in his favorite place, holding her from behind with her body welded to his own, a position where he could fondle her so responsive nipples, and where he could nuzzle and taste her neck and the erogenous areas behind her ears he knew she loved him to nibble.

"It's too soon for a champagne reception!" Rhia gasped as he rolled her nipple again. "Main rooms…not…all…ready."

Luke's question was almost forgotten as he got creative but her eventual reply pleased him.

"How about…" She turned around in his arms to kiss him properly. "We get in a case of really good champagne…" Another lingering kiss and a squeeze of body parts she knew Luke loved her to fondle. "And we have a private little party in every room possible…while we wait till the restoration is totally complete. And then we'll invite everybody for a very public spectacularly different kind of party." Struggling out of his tempting arms she twirled in circles, arms akimbo. "A restoration romp sounds just right to me…where we're all dressed in period costume, and…"

"I," Luke whipped her back against him and captured her lips, "love…your…thinking, woman!"

Rhia gasped into his mouth her heart literally thumping. For one wild, totally irrational moment she'd thought he was going to say "love you"…but with his body worshipping her it was easy enough to cast aside any disappointment.

The next day they moved their clothes and personal belongings from the cottage to Greywood. By then the main kitchen had been fabulously upgraded. All the historic kitchen utensils were either displayed somewhere, or stored carefully in the attics till decisions were made about where they should go. Rhia agreed easily that although she valued them as artifacts, she didn't actually want to cook with them—she loved her modern appliances. The kitchen décor was extremely suitable for a grand old house but it was still stuffed with state of the art equipment.

Eating out every night was not necessary. More often now Rhia got her own way and either she cooked for Luke, or together they rustled up something to eat, though he was still very much the novice in the kitchen. On many of those nights, dinner literally waited on the back burner: their case of champagne gradually emptying.

They had a lot of fun not even getting as far as their bedroom: the hallway staircase was spectacular; the dining room table beautifully restored and re-waxed offered endless possibilities; the new sofas in the drawing room just had to be tried out.

Luke curtailed sexual explorations one evening till after she'd delivered her latest bit of news. "I can't make head nor tail of it, Luke." Rhia flashed a small piece of faded white lined paper, and an even more fragile piece of blue airmail paper at him. "As far as I have found out so far, Amelia wasn't inclined to go gallivanting. Not enough money most of the time!"

He had already learned to let her emotions vent before he could slake his lust if she was in her "terrier mode." "But surely even poor Amelia was due the occasional holiday?" he said.

Rhia's research had uncovered that Amelia had gone to university, gaining an English Literature degree but she'd only ever worked part time with a local children's charity. This had earned her lots of kudos but little money. Very much required money.

"Of course she was!" Rhia paced around their den—one of her favorite rooms. "But this trip was in the late 1970s, Luke. Back then, any trip to Australia was incredibly expensive. Airfares were astronomical. People saved for years to pay for them."

"But somehow she managed the occasional trips to Europe."

"Well, yes." Rhia exhaled loudly. "And we know too well she sacrificed quite a few paintings to do that!"

"So what did she sell to finance the trip to Australia?" Luke was curious now.

"Her bank account was credited with money from the sale of some Victorian jewelry." His eyebrows rose appropriately at her sleuthing. "I found receipts for considerable sums for a diamond necklace and a Victorian pearl choker."

That information didn't seem to bother Luke but Rhia's agitation obviously did so he tried to trap her. "Why does this particular trip annoy you so much?"

"She financed the trip by selling off probably the last of her valuable jewelry. After all, the trip lasted only six days!"

Luke often journeyed back to Australia to sort out business, trips that had not been much longer than that. He told her about them but still couldn't appreciate why she was getting so uptight.

Rhia slumped onto the couch clutching the pieces of paper like a lifeline. The white one she flashed in front of his nose. "This is an itinerary, Luke. It details her flight from Heathrow to Brisbane with three stops at airports along the way.

No hotels or cushy layovers, as far as I can tell, just boring long delays for refueling and necessities."

"She's noted the hotel she stayed at in Brisbane for three whole nights then she repeated the journey back to England." Luke still couldn't see that as being a problem. "All that expense for three nights in Australia? In the 1970s?" Rhia continued.

He waited.

"Who would have gone to Australia at vast expense to stay for only three days? As far as I can tell, she saw virtually nothing of Australia. She traveled for longer than she set foot on Australian soil!"

"The airmail letter?" He patiently indicated the blue paper.

"This," Rhia's voice grew subdued as she held it aloft. "This is merely an acknowledgement from someone in Brisbane, who confirms that it was very pleasant to meet her and thanked her for doing business with him."

"That's it?"

"That's it." Rhia sank into gloom.

"Well, at least she had one trip to my place of birth Rhia," he chuckled. "That's surely the best connection to me yet."

"Luke, the trip was made when you were exactly two months old."

"Luke?" Rhia was unsure as she stood at the open door of his office a couple of weeks later. The news she had for Luke was a surprise but she hoped it would be a good one. "Can you spare a minute?"

He was alone since Jeremy had whisked himself off in the helicopter to sort out something at one of the other work sites.

Luke beckoned her in with a smile as he finished a call, "I'll call you back after I've read the details of the offer."

Approaching Luke's desk, Rhia was extremely

nervous; her palms were sweating as she searched for the perfect words. She dreaded he'd think she didn't trust him when she gave him this particular bit of news.

"Um..." She couldn't prevent the blush from spreading as she fiddled with her hair. "Bloody hell! I'd best just come out with it."

"Uh-oh! Sounds serious. Who have you fallen out with now?" Luke's widely amused chuckle broke the tension for there had been quite a few times Rhia's temper had gotten the better of her. "Do I need to grovel to anybody in particular?" Sparkling green eyes asked many questions of her.

"I haven't fallen out with anyone for days, Luke Salieri!" she retorted, her wince wryly embarrassed. She had it out the other day with the interior designers over paint colors that didn't suit the period room they were intended for. "And hopefully this news won't make you fall out with me."

"I never fall out with you, *cara*!" Luke ignored the bleep of the telephones, his eyes curious.

"Okay, here goes! I just came to tell you that, as of today, I'm officially starting my second course of oral contraceptive pills."

Luke stared at her his expression almost totally blank.

"I didn't tell you before," she faltered at his continuing silence. "I wanted it to be a surprise for when..." her eyes implored but she found no reassuring response, "we don't need to use condoms any longer... Now that I'm sure I'm safe."

Good God! His non-expression was unsettling. Why was it so difficult to say something? Why wasn't he responding?

Since he wasn't saying anything she stuttered on, "Well anyway. We don't need to have the bother of condoms, if you don't want to." Rhia couldn't believe Luke could sit there and say nothing, but that's exactly what he did. For ages. A stone monolith sat on his chair. Then Rhia saw a tiny twitch pulse at his neck.

"Okay. Thanks for telling me."

His words were spoken so quietly into the incredibly tense silence that enveloped them. Then his eyes dropped from hers as he focused his gaze on his monitor and lifted the still-ringing telephone.

"Sorry, I need to answer this," he mumbled into the wood of his desk.

Dismissed.

Rhia backtracked out of his office and made her way along to the library. She wasn't sure if the okay meant it was okay that she'd taken that bit of initiative, or okay he would still use condoms anyway. From his lack of expression and pathetically poor positive response, she didn't think he seemed particularly bothered either way.

But it made Rhia feel safer, more in control of her own life beyond their contract year that was now already more than two months gone.

Later that night, Luke made love to her in their massive canopy bed in the master bedroom. After bringing her to fulfillment with his expert mouth and proficient fingers, he pulled her to the edge of the bed, spread her wide and hesitated before plunging into her—minus a condom. He held himself rigidly in place, motionless for so long that Rhia wondered if something was wrong. When he eventually moved he slid himself almost fully out, leaned down to her and groaned into her receptive mouth, "Rhia, look! Look down at us!" He waited till she could see where they were joined.

Craning her neck she watched him slide out completely so that she could see him re-insert his penis, glistening with her own juices.

"I want you so much, Rhia; you can't know what this feels like with no barrier between us." His eyes closed shutting her out.

But she did! She really did.

After a few long languid strokes he pulled out yet again, whipped Rhia's body over, set her onto her knees, and slid in again with a satisfied grunt. "*Formidabile*! Rhia, you are so gorgeous!"

After that it was fast and furious, leaving them both grinning and gasping with mind-blowing climaxes. The second time they made love that night Luke made sure it was slow and delicious, his eyes never leaving hers once as he slowly thrust and thrust and thrust till she could stand it no longer and cried for him to come with her, "Luke! Now!"

When they were both fully spent he slipped out and cradled her spoon-wise—no awkward break where he had to deal with a messy condom—his arms secure and content around her midriff.

"*Madre di Dio*! That was so fantastic!"

His deep chuckle whiffed up her hair as he snuggled in even more, drifting off into exhausted slumber.

Rhia accepted that Luke liked not having the additional fuss of using condoms and it meant they could give in to lust anytime and anywhere...not that that had bothered them before since Luke's pockets had always been crammed full.

The next months of life at Greywood Hall continued to be a busy time for both of them. Rhia had thought her routine would consist of daytime research and nighttime loving in Luke's arms, but it was a little more varied than that.

She quickly realized that improvements to Greywood Hall were pretty standard fare to Luke and his teams. By that time there were, in fact, five other sites being currently remodeled in England. The squads of workmen Luke employed were a well oiled machine, rotating from site to site, coming to Greywood Hall when it was most suitable for their particular work schedules.

"I can't believe these other venues can remain unique," she said skeptically, thinking that the renovated places would be clones of each other.

"We'll visit them all, you doubting Thomas, and then you can tell me just how distinctive we've made them." His winning smile said he obviously wasn't offended by her cynicism.

And Rhia found that each venue had retained its original character. She was fascinated by the expertise involved in getting the sites ready for corporate hire, but also seriously impressed by the speed at which it was all happening.

After that she was fully cognizant of the fact that it only happened because Luke delegated many decisions to his very competent management team; though the final decisions always rested with him. Luke leased a small fleet of helicopters that whizzed between the venues, transporting personnel more efficiently than by road. Rhia found herself climbing into one of them as often as she stepped into her car.

Renovations at Greywood Hall continued at a furious pace, money piled into it where necessary. Luke seemingly had a bottomless pit of the stuff. Solar heating systems and other devices to reduce the carbon footprint had been put in place, and since the window frames all required replacing, special glass had been installed to reduce heat loss in winter and address the need for rooms to be cooler in summer—all naturally in keeping with the original style of the building.

"The stonemasons have done a superb job," Rhia said when the final exterior work was completed. "The new curving staircases are fabulously grand—just like they must have been when the house was newly built. And the terrace is perfect to walk on now."

They'd been entering Greywood from the back

kitchen doorway for weeks while the front of the house was being worked on. The stone facade of the building was now blasted clean, the timber of the new window frames gleamed and the roof slates had been replaced. She wasn't joking; it really did look tremendous. "You asked me ages ago what we should do to celebrate moving into Greywood…"

Luke grabbed her and kissed her before she could even finish the sentence.

"That's not what I mean. You're insatiable, Mr. Salieri!"

"Only because you make it so."

"Stop!" she protested. "I'm trying to have a serious conversation here."

"Okay. Spill quickly, and then I can make a serious attack on your gorgeous body." Luke released her long enough for her to continue.

"Right. I'm not butting in here, I hope, but if you want to make any kind of memorable event for the completion of the renovations, why not have something like a Masked Ball, or a Period Dress event, like I mentioned a while ago?"

Luke nodded and his lips did that little twitching thing that meant he was considering the idea, but she also knew his mind was on other things too—like their frantic lovemaking.

"Remind me of that when we get closer to the end of renovations," he declared, snuggling into her neck and kissing her senseless.

The front curves of steps were a magnificent way to ascend to the impressive hallway now sparklingly illuminated by the cleaned and renovated chandelier. Rhia was doubly impressed knowing all the electric lighting was of the most effective and eco friendly low energy adaptation. The interior decorating team, using local painters and decorators, had made fabulous inroads. All were changes Rhia was pleased to have been involved in, even if it was only a tiny bit.

The gardens were also looking impressive. She'd had a hand in those decisions too, at times disagreeing with Bob and June Renton but they'd always come to some kind of compromise, which pleased her no end.

It became a stately and grand house anyone would be proud to live in; despite the new changes it retained a homely feel. Like Rhia's little cottage along the road, Greywood Hall now had lots of bright touches in fabrics, cushions and wall decorations and was filled with beautiful flower arrangements. At present the flowers were brought in but the grand plan was that in the next few years a huge selection of flowers and vegetables could be harvested from the fabulously renovated and newly planted walled garden and re-glazed greenhouses.

Weeks passed by in a blur but there was still nothing conclusive on why Luke had inherited.

Meanwhile, Luke conducted his business from his office at Greywood with consummate ease. It was very convenient for both of them. They touched base with each other at lunchtime, and sometimes in between, if Luke couldn't quell his libido. It was very…sexually exciting, but also very domestic.

"London tomorrow, Rhia," Luke informed her yet again. Sometimes twice a week they flew by helicopter first, then jetted to London when Luke went for meetings or business related social events.

On those occasions she acquiesced and allowed Luke to add to her wardrobe so she was decked in the finest and most appropriate style for the occasion. It was easy to fall into the luxury of flying off from the back field then being picked up by chauffeured car, living in supreme comfort in Luke's London apartment. Rhia didn't allow herself to think about how she'd miss it when the year was over. She had acquitted herself well at the social events, charity functions and business dinners they attended. She was pretty sure Luke had been proud of her. People they met readily accepted her as his wife, not knowing anything about their accommodation but short of telling her she looked beautiful—and he did that often—she had to guess at whether he was happy with her as his companion. He never actually said he liked having her with him.

Chapter Eighteen

"I'm really pissed off, Luke."

Rhia's mood was obviously not good. After more than six months living together Luke knew the best thing to do was let her blow, listen, and then maybe…make some suitable comment.

"You've had no update on my researches regarding your inheritance for ages. I purposely held back till I had something concrete, but all I've got is still a puddle of mush!"

Her disgusted tone left Luke in no doubt of just how frustrated and exasperated she was feeling. Settled into the comfortable couch in the modest sized room they had decorated as a family den, he cradled his wine glass. Rhia strode around the room having set her glass on the nearest table when they retreated there after their dinner. Luke had sensed something was bothering her during their meal preparations but realized she wasn't ready to tell him at that point.

After months of extensive research at Greywood Hall, Rhia had yet to make the final connection between himself and his benefactress…and that lack of success really bugged her.

From Luke's perspective he didn't really care what she'd uncover, although he still admitted to curiosity about it. His initial drive to use Rhia's considerable skills for that task had dissipated. He loved that she was still so motivated to find out, but he hadn't found parting with his own money to restore Greywood Hall a chore. For the first time ever he was feeling he had a proper home taking shape, a place he was settling into comfortably like an old shoe—absolutely nothing like the cold and emotionless mansion his mother and father called home.

"Everything I've found leads to the assumption that your great-grandmother was Amelia Greywood's disappearing aunt Jocasta. It's the only thing that makes any sense, any sense at all."

Rhia had hinted at this a number of times before but he'd rejected the possibility. She continued to pace about, dragging her hands through her hair, fanning it out from her ears, a cute habit he loved to watch.

"Are you sure your mother's name really was Elizabeth Low?"

"Definitely!" Luke was positive. "When she married my father she double-barreled her name and called herself Elizabeth Low-Salieri. She always claimed it made good business sense; she deemed it was easier to keep at the helm of her father's engineering business when her name was almost the same as it had been pre-marriage."

"But you don't think that was why she did it?"

"I've told you already how much my mother revered her English origins. She really didn't want to take my father's name at all but in those days it was unheard of for a married woman to retain her maiden name."

"Why wouldn't she have wanted your father's name?" Her question was cautious for she knew how prickly he was when discussing his mother.

"My mother was a snob. Probably the biggest snob in Brisbane." He laughed, but it was a hollow one. "In her estimation, Italian immigrants in Australia didn't quite have the same kudos, unlike anyone with a hint of upper echelon English background."

"Why on earth did she marry your father then?"

"I've never had a friggin' clue!" Luke got up and also stomped around the room. "I never, in my twenty plus years with them, ever saw them kiss or hug. I don't even remember them ever laughing or smiling at each other. They didn't exactly hate each other but they lived a sterile, extremely formal existence."

"Where did you fit in with that?"

"Me? Fit in? You must be joking!" Again Luke's derisory laugh was hollow to the point of pain. "I was trotted out occasionally to prove they had a son, but I can assure you, not that often. And not especially after I was sent to school in England at the age of seven."

"Luke, I'm so sorry they were mean to you." Rhia stopped his pacing and hugged him tight, aware that he was itching to metaphorically free himself from the loneliness of his youth.

He intensified his grip on her, his lips hissing against her forehead as he denied her words. "No. Believe me. They were never actually physically mean to me, Rhia. It was just that for long periods of time I was out of sight, out of mind. Their separate business needs always came first for them. They employed the best nannies so they knew I was being well cared for."

"Materially looked after, Luke. It's not the same as love and care from your own parents."

"You've not exactly had it easy either," he said, remembering her parents' divorce and the aftermath of it. "You're not exactly hunky dory with your father."

"No, don't ever think that! My upbringing was a picnic compared to yours." Rhia pulled his head down and kissed him thoroughly, desperately, and with a passion he felt right down to his toes. "My mother loved me unconditionally till the day she died. And my father? In his own way he did what he could."

He cradled her gently.

"After my parents' separation my father did try his best to keep contact with me, even though he'd relocated to Belgium. He did love me and I knew it. I was the one who couldn't handle his very quick remarriage to a much younger Belgian woman. I was the one who rejected his second family."

"You felt he betrayed your mother?" Luke was trying to understand.

"A shrink would probably say yes. But really and truly?" Luke watched the hurt and embarrassment fly across her features. "I was just a spoiled little girl who didn't want to share. I couldn't handle him having other children that weren't my mother's."

"*Madre di Dio*. With our backgrounds, Rhia," Luke groaned his pain into her ear, "neither of us have a real clue about being a long term parent. That's why I never want to inflict the hurt and loneliness on offspring of mine. I never want children who could be tainted with the problems our parents have inflicted on us."

"Okay, I get that, Luke!" Rhia's voice was as pained as her expression; and Luke loved her empathy. "Back to the Australian connection that isn't," she repeated. "Then if Elizabeth Low was definitely your mother's name, are you sure your maternal grandfather was called Alexander Low?"

"Again, definitely." Luke sat on the couch, relinquishing the pacing to Rhia. "The engineering business was named after his father: Low Engineering."

"I know Alexander was quite a popular name, but doesn't it make you wonder if it was somehow a passed down name?"

"You mean as in Alexander 'the howevermuch' of Greywood?"

"Maybe." Rhia grinned at his 'howevermuch' but they both knew just how many British families named a son Alexander, and knew just how spurious the conclusion might be.

Luke was increasingly worried about Rhia's preoccupation with her lack of success. At times he felt she was becoming obsessed with finding the answers and was working herself to the bone.

"Is there anyone in Australia who can verify your mother and grandfather's origins?" Rhia asked.

"What do you mean verify?"

Rhia explained what she needed beyond the internet information she had already accessed. Unfortunately Luke was sure there wasn't anyone left alive in Australia who might have more information on his grandfather's origins.

"Okay," Rhia stressed, urging him to pay attention. "You know the story so far. Listen and maybe you'll detect something I've failed to pick up."

Luke stifled a smile for when Rhia was perturbed and intent over things like this she was like a wriggly little terrier with a particularly recalcitrant bone. He didn't dare laugh though for she was in full flow. He was entranced by her dedication to the job she'd undertaken since she wouldn't allow him to pay her more than her usual fee rates for what she was doing at Greywood Hall, not the double salary he'd originally stipulated. It had caused friction between them, but Rhia had been adamant. She wasn't paying for rent or food, and she accepted that he was buying the special clothes she needed, so there was no way she would take double salary for a job she loved doing.

"Okay, back to poor Bethany. And she was getting really poor, by the way!"

Luke nodded his agreement for he knew only too well what the upkeep of an estate like this would have been like.

"I've managed to go through the estate records I found in the library..."

Luke caught her by the waist and pinned her onto the sofa for her wanderings were making him seasick. "Sit at peace for a while, woman, and tell me your story before I throw up or need a neck brace."

Rhia playfully punched his arm. "Cheeky bugger that you are! Do you know just how much you pace?"

His answer was a quick kiss; just enough to tide him over till her update was done.

"By the way, did you know the current estate records are held by the local solicitor?"

"Sure," Luke answered. "The lawyer has been outsourcing the estate finances to a land management firm for years. They deal with the monies involved in the leasing of the Home Farm and the rented properties like your cottage. That stays the same till I become the official legal owner. I've told you that before, haven't I?"

"Probably." Rhia cuddled into him as she marshaled her thoughts.

"Right, back to Bethany. Her sources of income dried up quickly, especially since I've noticed that during the late 1920s, during the depression years, the estate rents were waived. You might think, in the grand scheme of things, rents from a few cottages wouldn't make any great difference, but you'd be wrong. The rents from the Home Farm, and the other more outlying farms and smallholdings that at that time still belonged to the estate, had the same payment-suspended deal. For three whole years!"

"That would have been a huge loss of income," Luke agreed, finding that quite a piece of information for it certainly made no business sense to have done it. "The farm rents formed the bulk of the estate finances."

"I know. But remember, the depression years

were horrendous. It seems to have been Bethany's way of keeping people on the estate. Remember she still needed lots of manual labor from them."

"Did their wages dry up too?"

"No. She seems to have managed to keep paying that, no rises of course, but the same payment as in the early 1920s."

"So that's when the treasures started to be sold?" Luke guessed.

"Absolutely. Selling Greywood's treasures was her way to keep the wolf from the door."

"How do you know this?"

Rhia's soft doe brown eyes filled with a sudden rush of tears, tears that hovered but didn't fall. There was no way Luke could miss the emotion that surged through her. She gripped him tightly as she continued. "She must have been the loneliest woman in the universe, Luke. Her diaries for those years are unbelievably heartbreaking; except of course when she mentioned your Amelia who was a very, very well loved little girl."

She'd taken to emphasizing the words your Amelia and Luke found he actually looked forward to it peppering her conversation. It gave him a sense of...place. A sense of real ownership, which was stupid because he still wasn't the clear and outright owner of the property.

"But your findings still don't explain why I was made the beneficiary."

"No, so far I can't unravel that last detail. I'm beginning to think you need to get a private detective on the case."

Rhia didn't know Luke had long considered that himself but, although curious about being willed Greywood Hall, he hadn't quite wanted to stir up skeletons in his own family closets. He was astute enough to realize that the indications were that something was amiss.

Rhia continued, "Did Amelia Greywood's lawyer ever hint at all why you were the beneficiary?"

"Not at all. But remember at the time I found out about the will the local lawyer was out of the country on holiday and his work was in the hands of one of his juniors."

"So, maybe if I contacted the older lawyer he might have something we've yet to know?"

Luke took her hands between his own and squeezed comfortingly. "No problem with trying but don't get your hopes up." He kissed her, not a compensatory kiss, but just because he still needed to whenever she was close by. "I admit that once I got onto the whole bandwagon of persuading you to board, and what with our wedding to arrange, and moving up the business office to this area, I never thought to ask for an appointment with the older lawyer."

Luke distracted her from her task when he lifted her onto his knees and proceeded to do what he did oh so well—seduce her! No more talk of his inheritance surfaced that night.

However the next morning, Rhia did pop into the nearest town having made an emergency appointment with the lawyer. The answers he gave Rhia were intriguing. Luke had not suddenly become the beneficiary of a new will—for years he had been named as prime recipient in earlier versions of Amelia's will.

An earlier will had been substantially revised, when she'd turned ninety, the year before Amelia's death. Adjustments were made to the small bequests for her caregivers since there was almost no capital left in the bank. The expenses of living at Beechlee Nursing Home had eaten well into Amelia's remaining cash resources, the rents from the leased land only barely covering her medical costs and basic repairs to the leased properties. She'd apparently, and extremely reluctantly, had to go to Beechlee because she was wheelchair bound and the cost of her care and general living at home in Greywood Hall was astronomical, but her mind, it seemed, had been sharp right till she died.

There was one particular clause concerning Luke that had been altered the year before Amelia died.

"I'm not sure how to tell you," Rhia's voice faltered when she updated him at lunchtime. "I can hardly believe it but the lawyer's information clarifies that Amelia always knew you were living in Australia." Luke's face blanched at that piece of new information so she hurried on, "She had you added as the main beneficiary nine weeks after your birth...so somehow, she always knew of your existence."

Luke was just as astounded as she had been. "What was the thing that concerned me then? That she changed a year ago?"

"She changed the condition of you residing in Greywood Hall with your spouse but the lawyer won't reveal any more to me. He might give you more though if you contact him."

Incensed was not too strong a word for how Luke was acting when he ended the call. He looked to be a hairsbreadth away from punching something. "Amelia's lawyer tells me that until a year ago, the original bequest had no mention of me living here with a spouse. This was apparently because, about five years ago, she hired a private investigator to check my marital and financial status. For the following four years she had a yearly update on that."

Luke stomped about the room exasperated by the information he'd just learned. "The friggin'...woman knew exactly how I was fixed, financially speaking, and that I obviously had no intention of getting married. The gall of her. What right did she have to dictate my marital status?"

Rhia was gutted by his vehement affirmation about avoiding marriage but she determined not to let her feelings show. "We have irrefutable evidence that she knew about you, but we still have to prove how she knew. I've searched everything I can find here. The answers definitely lie in Australia, Luke."

Rhia was like Thor when he had a doggie treat to sharpen his teeth on.

Blisteringly angry with Amelia Greywood's interference in his personal affairs Luke decreed that they'd pick up his Australian connections next time he ventured into the antipodes, but heatedly declared that wouldn't be for quite a while since he had no business reasons to go there at that moment. He refused to consider a trip immediately, telling Rhia it didn't really matter about the legacy now that he knew Amelia really always intended for him to inherit.

He insisted she should continue to enjoy the local historical details about Amelia that she was constantly enthusing over. She was only mollified to a certain degree but acquiesced, knowing she'd traced as much as she could through English and Australian internet connections and couldn't do more without actually visiting. She still had plenty of other things to research: in fact she was finding enough to write a book about Amelia Greywood and the house itself.

Before the inheritance mystery reared its ugly head, Luke had happily visited Brisbane every couple of months to check up on his Australian businesses but now he found plenty of solutions to steer clear of visiting the country.

He constantly told himself he was keeping faith with the terms of Amelia's will about residence in Yorkshire, reluctant to admit that he just liked living at Greywood with Rhia. Everything was centering very efficiently round residing there. He couldn't picture a day without her companionship, amazed he still hungered after her body...and her camaraderie. Hell! He even liked their occasional disagreements, and there had been plenty of those because Rhia could be quite dogmatic if she thought herself in the right. Making up after their conflicts of opinion was a joy.

He resolutely refused to consider, at that point, what he would do with the property when it became legally his. Greywood was creeping into his heart; it was becoming a home that, for the first time in his life, he actually enjoyed living in.

He really loved the notion that Rhia was always somewhere around and he could intercept her when he needed to make contact with her, or snatch some quick caresses during the work day. Although a confirmed workaholic, and he continued to be that, he squeezed in opportunities several times a day just to touch base with her. The drug that was Rhia was definitely well anchored in his system.

Chapter Nineteen

More than seven months into their co-habitation things began to unravel. Much as he didn't want to Luke had to spend a night in London without Rhia. She'd picked up a disgusting cold followed by a persistent chest infection and wasn't well enough to travel.

On his return the following evening he swept her into his arms and kissed her cheek soundly-because she turned her cracked lips away just in time. He was distressed to find she was still under the weather, her cough rattling like mad, but he had the very thing tucked away in his pocket. After a theatrical flourish, he presented her with a beautiful white gold amethyst pendant with matching bracelet and earrings.

"To cheer you up."

"I don't need jewelry, Luke!" Rhia croaked, handing the set back to him.

It was grossly unfair of her to take her mood out on him, but he could see how miserable she was feeling. Any amusement vanished though when her next retort blasted out.

"Take them all back and get a refund!"

An attempt to soften her nasty comment failed, even though she told him she was touched he'd thought about her and had taken time out of his work-filled schedule to buy the gift. She was shrewish over the incredible expense, and even cast doubt on his purpose. "It makes me feel like your mistress-waiting at home for your return—someone who has to be thrown a bone to keep her happy,

Luke. I don't want them!"

In her present mood he couldn't persuade her otherwise, her vehement reaction to the gift creating tension between them.

"I wanted to cheer you up, Rhia," Luke protested. "My first proper gift and you throw it back in my face. I wish I'd never bothered."

A week later they went to an awards function in central London. The ceremony was graced by the wealthy and worthy. Luke was delighted with how Rhia coped at the events he sometimes felt were a necessary chore, but her natural humor and candor endeared her to his colleagues and contacts. Her natural beauty meant she looked spectacular when gowned and glittered like she was that night.

She'd come back from a brief shopping trip the day before enthused that she'd bagged a tremendous bargain: a gorgeous gown she'd got at half price! Her delight and enthusiasm was infectious. He was still amazed that she always thought so carefully about spending his money. She was unique.

She looked stunning in the simply styled deep purple sheath, a piece of heavy silk that hugged her curves lovingly, the cowl neckline revealing enough cleavage to be enticing and not brash. Luke went to the wall safe and withdrew the amethysts that had caused such dissention the previous week. The jewelry set he'd purposely brought with him to London: still undecided exactly what to do with it.

"This will match your gown perfectly, Rhia." His eyes begged her to agree. "Please? I'd love to see you wear these tonight. Will you? For me?"

Rhia gave in.

After he'd fastened the clasp of the pendant his hands curved around her. His lips nibbled her neck as he whispered, "*Incantevole, bella.*" Italian endearments dripped off his tongue.

"I want you, my lovely Rhia. You look stunning

in that gown; I want to rip it off you right now." He turned her in his arms for a long and lingering kiss that turned into two and then three.

Reluctantly Rhia reminded him they were late, so late they had to hotfoot it out of the London apartment. Luke was being given an award for a reconstruction project he'd done a couple of years previously on a derelict estate, and he had to attend.

Resplendent in their finery, they mingled with Luke's friends and acquaintances till quite late in the evening when a strident female voice interrupted their conversation, making them turn.

"Good evening, Luke. Isn't the time passing rapidly my darling?"

Luke cringed, silently cursing a blue streak as the glamorous redhead leaned in with both hands at his cheeks, not to give a typical air kiss, but to place her lips deliberately on his for a lingering kiss. Luke was stunned at her audacity and was slow to disengage from her. He'd never wanted to meet up with Danielle ever again, but here she was as bold as brass and stirring her mischief as only she could do.

As he removed Danielle's hands from his face, her eyes flicked condescendingly over Rhia for a fraction of a second before she returned her heated gaze to him. The bitching tone that followed was one he'd never expected to hear again.

"You know that amethyst trifle does look a bit better on her, my darling. But then, you were also correct that diamonds were much better suited to me."

Danielle performed an insolent bow in front of Rhia before drifting off, her heavy perfume lingering long after her slender high-couture-clad body had gone. Luke could swear Rhia's feet were welded to the floor, her legs so rigid with tension she seemed petrified into stone. Her instant white alarmed him.

No…more than that, it terrified him.

He excused them from their companions and dragged Rhia to a quiet side of the room. “Are you feeling all right?” He could barely speak he was so angry.

“Danielle?” Rhia numbly asked, her eyes pools of misery as she strove for composure, composure he could see was hard won. “How could I mistake that voice?”

“Yes, that’s Danielle,” Luke answered but ventured no further explanation. “If you’re feeling unwell we’d better just leave!” He yanked out his cell phone out and tersely summoned his chauffeur.

“No!” Rhia stopped his call, her hand over the phone. “I’m fine. It’s far too early to go. The awards haven’t even started yet. You have to be here for that.”

So they stayed.

For the next hour Rhia tried to appear happy by Luke’s side, but her insecurity ate away at her confidence and made her unusually silent and less responsive. What could Danielle’s cryptic words mean? Time passing rapidly? Her diamonds? What was that all about?

Rhia could tell Luke was displeased with her withdrawal, and his persistent concern for her wellbeing was beginning to grate. Though she was desperately in love with him, he’d never said he loved her. And though she was sure Luke got pleasure from her as a companion, and a temporary lover, she couldn’t be sure he liked her any more than that. For the second time in their relationship she felt used.

In the ladies cloakroom, just before they left, that vicious voice intruded again. Danielle’s image towered over her own in the mirror as Rhia washed her hands, far too close for comfort.

“I hope you like Luke’s choice of jewelry,”

Danielle said. "He wanted me to have that set at first because they're such distinctive designer originals, but I much prefer diamonds." Her hands fluttered to her neck and fingered the huge solitaire that sparkled there. "They suit my coloring so much better. But I hope every time you wear those paltry amethysts you'll think of me wearing these!" Her laugh trilled out again sending ice cool drafts down Rhia's spine. "But it doesn't worry me overmuch that you have that little trinket. Luke will buy me much more expensive jewelry in the future—after he's got shot of you."

Her exit was too swift for Rhia to summon any retaliation. She removed the jewelry and jammed them into her clutch bag before donning her serape and walking out to join Luke.

"What the hell happened in there?" Luke demanded when she reached him.

"Nothing that matters," Rhia replied woodenly, desperate to get back to their Mayfair apartment.

"From the way Danielle stalked off it's obvious there was some mud slinging. What did she say to you?" His face was thunderous. When she refused to answer he bellowed, "Let's get out of here!"

Rhia was far too depleted to give any comeback. The ride back was in total, crushingly awful silence.

In the bedroom of the luxurious apartment in Mayfair, she got ready for bed, her heart heavy, her mind numb. Luke's anger had abated a bit but his earlier solicitous concern had returned and Rhia felt smothered.

"I'm fine, Luke, can't you get that!" she murmured through grated teeth, "I'm exhausted. I just need to sleep."

For the first time she had difficulty responding to him. She had never said no to sex before. Well, maybe just the once. She turned her back on him and told him to go to sleep.

The jealousy and insecurity was crippling her. Her heart had cracked open: the gaping fissure burned and bled raw. Her brain couldn't wipe out the fact that just one week had passed since Luke returned with the now-detested amethysts that Danielle claimed were intended for her. Had she and Luke spent that evening together? And more importantly what did she still mean to him? Would Luke and Danielle resume their relationship after he took possession of Greywood Hall as Danielle hinted at?

Rhia woke with the dawn light creeping in through the drapes. She was snuggled into Luke's embrace, a typical morning erection prodding into her spine.

"Mmm..." he murmured only just surfacing himself. "You're so warm and gorgeous."

Rhia hadn't forgotten last night's discord, but she'd had enough time to make up her mind. She wanted Luke! She wanted Luke to make love to her. She locked her lips onto his and initiated a thorough exploration of him with her fingertips.

Fast and furious lovemaking ensued, each yearning to satisfy their desperate need for a climax.

They spent three days in London. Three very cool days, since she still wasn't quite relaxed around him, followed by three very hot nights. Rhia initiated the lovemaking, spurring Luke on to inventive positions and arousal techniques but for all her fervor it lacked their earlier spontaneous camaraderie.

Afterward, she was ashamed of her behavior for she'd deliberately and purposely used him to satisfy her sexual needs in a callous way. Contrarily she persuaded herself her conduct was justified. If Luke had been consorting with Danielle behind her back...

But she'd signed on the dotted line for the whole duration. No way would someone as reptilian as

Danielle compel her to renege on her word! If staying with Luke for the year would destroy her sanity then that's what would happen. Danielle was not undermining her integrity. No. She would use Luke for sex for as long as she chose.

Their relationship suffered over the next weeks. Though part of the time Rhia was drawing back, Luke on occasion felt the intercourse was even more intense, more passionate. Yet somewhere they'd lost the fun. Something wasn't right, but he ignored it in the assumption that it would blow over. How could she not want him as before? He wanted her just as much as he had that very first time. And now not just for the sex they shared. He'd even stopped reminding himself he'd get tired of her soon.

In his previous life this would have been a turning point. No fun, no point! But there was no way Rhia would slide out of his life. He'd get back their in-sync relationship or die trying. She meant much more to him than any woman ever before. He couldn't imagine one single day without her beside him. It was just a matter of how to approach the issue.

He stared at his computer monitor, his concentration shot to pieces as he worked out strategies to get them back to where they were before the now-detested awards event.

Also, there was another problem that needed to be addressed: Rhia was working herself into exhaustion. She pored over diaries and paperwork all day long: the negative results frustrating her for there were still no definitive facts pointing to why Amelia chose him. Rhia's eagerness was waning, she often appeared unable to summon up enough energy or enthusiasm, but doggedly plowed on. She was sometimes moody for no good reason; mood swings that couldn't be put down to attacks of hormones gone wrong because it had continued for weeks. Her pallor was increasing day by day.

She'd even stopped insisting the answer to his legacy riddle would only be solved in Australia. In fact, the bequest question hadn't been discussed for weeks. Guilt swamped him because he'd caused her mental condition.

He reluctantly concluded that only a visit to Australia would banish her depression. If Amelia had some kind of proof he was related to her through Jocasta, would those implications be devastating? Was he some kind of cuckoo in his parent's nest? Had he inherited both his father's and his mother's separate fortunes somehow illegally, if he wasn't their son?

Thinking about his inflexible attitude over visiting Australia he realized he'd been an arrogant shit about many things during their months together, for apart from business trips to London, all they'd had for months was a lot of work, their co-habitation...and fabulous sex.

No days off or holidays.

He'd never properly wooed Rhia, or done any of the courtship rituals he'd entered into with previous lovers. Normal courting hadn't been part of their contract. Since she never seemed to need any of that, it hadn't occurred to him that it could be an element in their relationship that was lacking. She'd always filled the cottage with flowers from her garden so he'd never bought any. Nor had he bought her chocolates. They'd been far too busy restoring Greywood Hall and partaking in the extra jaunts necessary to his business.

Apart from the fiasco of the amethyst pendant set, he'd never bought her any gifts. In his defense, she'd made it clear she wasn't interested in material things.

All she seemed to want from him was sex. She'd been the initiator of some frantic coupling during the last couple of months. Now he wondered if that was all he meant to her. A stud for a year?

But where did that leave him if she was now turning away?

"I've postponed the schedule for the new property in Cornwall," he declared that evening as they prepared dinner. "Instead of Bissoe, you're going to have a holiday in Brisbane."

"I don't want a holiday!" She fiddled with the spoon as she swirled the pasta in the boiling pot. "Go yourself if you need to check out the Brisbane office." Verbalizing all sorts of reasons why he should go himself she carried on with their meal preparations, avoiding eye contact. "You can ask all the necessary questions just as well as me." Her voice was of the no-holds-barred variety that Luke knew meant business. "I'll make you a list before you go."

"We'll only be away for ten days, Rhia." Luke's patience was getting thinner as he set the table.

"Too long, and you know it!" Rhia set the bowls of penne marinara on the table with a determined thud. "You know what the stipulations are."

"The lawyers have agreed." Luke still couldn't get her to make decent eye contact. "I wouldn't be telling you about it if they hadn't."

His deadly patient tone was creating as much tension as Rhia's reticence. Neither enjoyed the dish they'd created a few times and had thoroughly enjoyed. Rhia twiddled her fork one more time before, with a disgusted grimace, she pushed her plate away as though the very sight of it made her gag.

"This isn't a good time for me to be away so long. I'm almost finished cataloguing the library; it's not good to discontinue the flow."

He dropped the subject when she wouldn't back down, and because he couldn't deal with the friction it caused between them.

Their life continued at Greywood Hall for another month with intermittent day-long work jaunts, but Rhia was looking even more exhausted by the time she declared she'd completed the library cataloguing. By then Luke reasoned that taking her somewhere closer than Australia might do the trick so he arranged for them to have a surprise weekend trip to Rome.

"Rome?"

This time he was so glad to see Rhia's eyes were a picture of delight.

"I need to discuss the shares I inherited from my father in the Salieri import-export business. I'm considering selling but I want to speak to my uncle Stefano first. It's easier to meet with him in Rome than it is for him to come to London. He doesn't travel as well as he used to. Ever been to Rome?"

"Me?" she squeaked, "I've only been outside the UK when I visited my father in Brussels. And one other time when I went on a school trip to ski in Austria."

The following day they were in Italy. Greeting his aunt and uncle was poignant for Luke; he hadn't visited for some years, and their welcome was effusive. He was used to their lingering hugs and kisses but Rhia wasn't—her high color evidence of her discomfort. His uncle spoke excellent English. His elderly aunt less well, but Luke was aware of her efforts to make Rhia feel comfortable for he explained that Rhia had only studied French at school.

They dined at a fabulous restaurant that evening. His other uncle and aunt came, along with several cousins and their spouses, and as many other extended family as could join them at such short notice.

Luke knew it was quite daunting for Rhia to cope with his boisterous Italian relatives. The older adults were very formal in their approach to her but the ones of contemporary age were eager to learn details of how and when Luke had met her. Most of them spoke pretty good English.

Luke was impressed when Rhia gave them a credible version of the truth; entertaining them with the true story of her having him arrested by the police at Greywood Hall. He was surprised by her creativity—it sounded so plausible as she explained it: it had been love at first sight for both of them when they'd shared the back of the police patrol car. Their love spiraled from that first day; their marriage a scant two weeks after. He'd happily gone along with Rhia's version for his relatives' sakes, wondering just how possible her tale could be.

Could she have fallen in love with him that first day?

He still wasn't sure what love was, but he did know he lusted after Rhia just as much as he had that first day. And he honestly admitted to himself that he didn't think that was ever going to change. He was very fond of her, liked daily living with her, sharing Greywood and all its trials and tribulations, and he was very concerned over her welfare.

Did that mean he was in love with her?

Luke happily translated when needed, but that wasn't too often. The younger women were chatty and friendly: some of the men were flirty, Luke jealously fended off a few unattached male cousins whose attentions to Rhia were just a little too assiduous for his liking.

The evening passed in a blur of conversation peppered with invitations to join in other planned family occasions in the future. Rhia was struggling to answer; her delicate coloring alerted Luke to her discomfiture. He replied for both of them.

Seven and a half weeks? Was that all? After that Rhia would no longer be bound to him. She'd be able to leave Greywood and...do what? Live alone in the cottage? With him living alone at Greywood? Till he sold it and moved on?

Could he sell Greywood now that he'd done so much there?

Seven and a half weeks? No wonder Rhia was flustered about accepting the invitations from his family. The fact hung heavy on his heart. He'd put Rhia into an unbearable situation yet again, but she endured it with her silent fortitude. It hit home that, over recent weeks, she'd also tactfully sidestepped invitations issued by colleagues and friends back in England. She always used their hectic work schedules as an excuse.

His family's total acceptance of her as his wife sat heavily on his conscience, for in normal circumstances she'd fit in extremely well with them. Hell's Bells! She did fit in.

Nobody else would fit in the same way.

"Your uncles and other family are lovely people, Luke," Rhia said once they were back in their guest suite and getting ready for bed. "Was your father like your uncles?"

Luke yanked off his tie and threw it onto the back of a chair before giving a curt answer. "Not at all. He was nothing like them." He was aware of Rhia's eyes tracking him as he unhurriedly drew his belt through the loops of his trousers then she flinched as he summarily slapped it down on the floor. "He favored my uncle Roberto in looks, but his personality was nothing like any of my Italian relatives. They're lovely warm people. He wasn't."

He was more than aware that his last statement said a lot about his relationship with his father, but Rhia knew better than to intervene when he recalled unhappy childhood memories, knew just how much talking about his parents always put him in a bad mood.

"My father had none of their charm or warmth." He slumped down on the bed to remove his shoes and socks. "Well, at least not for me." Luke knew his laugh was full of bitter undertones but he was at pains to prevent it. "My esteemed father could be very charming to women in his company, but he never ever wanted to be shackled to a growing boy. If I didn't favor my Italian relatives in looks, especially my father, for I'm said to be his clone, I'd be thinking the sperm came from someone else."

Rhia was silent as she lay on the bed. But how could he expect her to respond when he'd just disclosed such a revelation?

"But if I say my father was cold, he was like the blazing sun compared to my darling mother, who barely tolerated me. Oh yes, she trotted me out for her women friends to admire, then patted my head and sent me back to the nursery."

His naked body hit the sheets where he lay rigid as a board. "I've told you that at aged seven going on eight, I was shipped off to England to begin my education in the best prep schools. After that I was sent to Cambridge."

He reached for Rhia's hand as he continued in fits and starts—drowning in past memories. "During those years in exile..." His terminology earned him a tighter grip from Rhia's fingers. "My mother always managed to make sure I spent lots of holiday time in England...or in Europe with parents of boys who were at school with me. Or they came to our house in Australia to be supervised by my current nanny—a nanny engaged for that time only—for why on earth would she employ the same one all year while I was away?"

He was so wrapped up in his lonely recollections that at first he scarcely felt Rhia's gentle stroking. Then her little fingers soothed his temples and massaged his chest where his heart thumped beneath her fingers.

"Sometimes she shipped me off to my uncles here in Italy to improve my Italian, which was unnecessary because my father insisted some of the nannies be Italian, so I was as fluent as I could be." Luke grunted and shifted onto his side, taking her in his arms. "I always knew my mother resented having to arrange for me. I was a reminder of the biggest mistake of her life." His arms squeezed her into a tighter embrace his head buried into her neck.

"I have to ask, but you don't have to answer, Luke." Rhia's whisper was tentative. "Were you born soon after your parents married?"

A grim laugh echoed in the room and Luke relaxed a little for the first time in minutes. "Strangely enough, the answer is no. I was born a couple of years after they married."

There was a tense silence for a few seconds, then Luke opened the floodgates and let the fetid acid flush out of his system. He'd never divulged so much about his parents to anyone ever before.

"My father strayed a lot, although he was always discreet. My mother turned a blind eye." The exhalation of his breath fluttered Rhia's hair as he clutched her even more tightly. Confident she knew it for what it was, his search for solace. "To my knowledge my mother never had any extra marital sexual liaisons, but she was so efficient I guess it was possible and I never found out."

"Were your parents never close at all?"

"Not so far as I could ever tell but remember I was hardly at home." Luke idly stroked her hair with loving touches. "They had separate bedrooms in the huge mansion where we lived. They weren't even adjoining. In actual fact they existed in separate wings of the house." Luke's lips caressed her brow. "I lived in a third wing with whatever nanny was on duty at the time.

His hands absently stroked her back and down to her buttocks where he kneaded her softness. "The fourth wing was strictly for guests. Mother had a lot of those, mainly women of her acquaintance. Father rarely had guests. At least while I was home."

Rhia's arms crept around him, her lips seeking his in a kiss of succor, no heavy demand, just pure, reassuring tenderness. He stroked her breasts with his palms as the kiss lengthened.

Dio Santo! Was she squirming away from him? Withdrawing, disgusted by his pathetically feeble disclosures. She was wriggling away from his touch. *Dannazione*!

Angry at her rejection he removed his hands and loosened his grasp, slipping onto his back where he drew in deep breaths.

"People should never have children if they are not going to love them. I never want any!" He pulled up the bedcover and turned his back on Rhia, angry with himself for offloading his family grief on Rhia. She was the only person in the world he could ever talk to in this way. Rhia, who was moving back even further from his touch. He needed her badly, just to hold. But she'd shied from his embrace.

Resolutely remaining on his side, he bid her good night. Tonight he just wanted her...comfort. Her...love?

Sleep was long in coming for both of them.

They were both good at pretence the next morning as though the revelations had never happened.

Playing tour guide, Luke led her on a whirlwind tour of sights around Rome before they flew back to England that evening, but by late morning Luke had made up his mind about something. He would make Rhia want him again. He would make her want his touch again; he couldn't contemplate the alternative.

At every opportunity he held her hand, stroked

her back if they were queuing, casually slung his arm across her shoulders, keeping her close. All gestures Rhia seemed to love and happily reciprocated but which confused him even more. Why could she allow his touch in public but not in the confines of their bed?

Luke couldn't decide whether the visit to his relatives had been a success or not. He'd never introduced any other woman to them before, nor had he ever wanted to.

He did want to include Rhia in all aspects of his family life, which included information about his less than salubrious time with his parents. Rhia was a first for so many things!

She'd loved visiting the tourist spots. A spark of her natural enthusiasm returned for those all too-short hours. Her genuine smiles warming him to the core. He was certain she'd enjoyed meeting his family, but there was a sadness he still couldn't quite explain. On balance though he decided he'd been right to drag her to Rome.

However, the issue of her rejection of his touch devastated him. On their return journey he dwelled on the fact that before she'd met him Rhia had been averse to the touch of many other men. Was that what he'd been relegated to? Had she had enough of his loving and wanted no more from him? Had it become more of a contracted status that she knew she was tied into for a few more weeks but wished it were over?

Madre di Dio! He couldn't contemplate that!

He realized when his troubled thoughts tortured him he was using the word love all the time. Love? *Madre di Dio*? He did love this temporary wife of his, but it seemed she might only be continuing to honor their stupid contract.

Till their year was over.

Chapter Twenty

Rhia's problem had nothing to do with finding Luke boring. She wasn't just going through the motions of honoring their contract. She wasn't disinterested in visiting Italy or Australia or in pursuing his family history.

It had eventually become clear why she'd felt off-color for some weeks. Since the persistent cough lingered for ages, she'd thought the lingering tiredness and nausea were a legacy of the chest infection she'd had. It was only when the light-to-almost-non-existent bleeding she'd had in February was followed by nothing at all in March that her concern was jump-started.

"Nothing to worry about, Mrs. Salieri," the doctor beamed at her after asking a few initial questions. He took blood and urine samples. "You'll be right as rain soon. Lots of women feel tired and out of sorts in their first stages of pregnancy. Some vitamins and folic acid will address that."

"But I've been taking contraceptive pills," Rhia spluttered.

"You were recently given a course of antibiotic for a chest infection?" he'd muttered as he read her notes on screen.

"Yes, and I took them right to the end of the ten day course..."

"Sometimes the efficacy of oral contraceptives is affected by an antibiotic. Weren't you informed of that at the time?" the doctor questioned.

Rhia had to be honest. "Er...yes, I was warned to be more vigilant."

"I'm sure your husband will be delighted with your news, Mrs. Salieri, but I have to say that you can come back and discuss your situation with us at the health centre, so long as it's soon..."

Rhia had stumbled out on autopilot, a prescription for the necessary vitamins crushed in her hand. Pregnancy was not part of their bargain. How on earth could she tell Luke?

The time clock on their agreement was ticking to a close: they only had mere weeks left of their contract.

Yet it took no time at all for Rhia to make up her mind about the pregnancy. She would have this child, regardless of how Luke felt about being a father.

Guilt lay heavily on her shoulders for she was the main one who'd started most of their love making sessions during those vulnerable days. She couldn't tell him, but she couldn't run out on him either!

In her eyes Luke had always—apart from the little jealous problem of Danielle—been the sexual partner she'd signed up for in her mind, and the contractual partner she'd signed up for with her pen. If she went away before the year was up, without telling him about her pregnancy, then he'd not own Greywood.

"Greywood!" she cried to no one in particular when she was out walking Thor in the woods that afternoon. "How can I sabotage your future?" She'd no earthly idea what would happen to the estate if she, and Luke, didn't fulfill their residence terms.

For another whole week Rhia worried herself sick over the problem but found no immediate solution. She couldn't possibly go on till the end of the contracted year and keep the secret either. Luke was far too in-tune to her emotions. At times he made love to her so tenderly she wanted to weep. At others he was the quintessential strong lover of the historical romances she read when she made time. He muttered Italian sweet nothings all the time when he gently aroused her, sweet nothings whose meanings she still hadn't a clue of, but she never asked him for she didn't want platitudes.

He knew she was taking vitamins and supplements; he'd seen them in her toilet bag when he'd gone looking to borrow her nail clippers. At first Rhia had been horrified when he'd noticed them but he said he was delighted to see she'd sought help to improve her health, assuring her she'd feel the effects of them soon and that her energy would perk up. She abhorred lying to him…not telling the truth seemed just the same.

The issue of a trip to Australia caused problems again. Luke declared a visit to sort out business concerns was essential.

"I told you before; you can ask all the questions yourself, Luke." Tension was so great Rhia felt she'd probably lost some enamel from her teeth. "I don't need to go and I don't want to go."

"I have to," he insisted. "Where I go…you go! You know the rules." The postscript he added was the clincher. "Anyway, you know too bloody well this stupid problem of my inheritance must be resolved before it kills you. We're leaving on Saturday."

In two days.

Petulance was one thing but practicality was another. Although reluctant to take a long trip because at times she still felt queasy Rhia knew she'd have to capitulate. She had been lucky that although bone tired, and often nauseous, she hadn't had morning sickness as such. She had learned a few techniques to keep vomiting at bay and continued to employ them during their travels.

On arrival in Brisbane they went to his mother's house.

"Why did you just mothball this place, Luke?" Rhia asked as Luke drove a hired car to the expensive Brisbane suburb. "What made you keep it all this time?"

He took a few moments to answer; nothing to do with the light traffic he was dealing with. "Not for any sentimental reasons, Rhia." His tone was indifferent. "I guess I just never wanted to spend the time it would take to get the real estate people on board." His answer sounded lame, and Rhia knew him well enough to realize that wasn't the full answer.

As they drove up a very impressive curving driveway, Rhia whispered, "No use me guessing. I suppose that this is prime, hugely expensive property and a great addition to your investment portfolio?"

"You could say that!" He chuckled and then added, "It was easiest to keep it in the care of mother's housekeeper and her husband, who is the general handyman. They'd been with mother all my life. I suppose I've kept it on for them more than for any other reason."

Rhia smiled as she nudged his arm. "So it was for sentimental reasons, you big jerk!"

"Rhia." He brought the car to a halt and parked. "Meg and Andy were the grandparents I never had. They were the most constant things in my life. I always came home at holiday time to a new nanny, but it was Meg's arms that hugged me at the door."

It was a handsome old property. As a student of history and architecture, Rhia could appreciate its design, and the ornate styles of interior decorating his mother had established; very quaint English touches; but it was formally ornamented and was characterless for a family home.

"It's lovely Luke," she mumbled after a warm greeting from Meg and Andy, who, as Luke predicted, warmly welcomed them both at the front door. The couple had then left them to it after Luke asked for coffee in the library as soon as possible.

"Liar!" he grinned, "It's the most uncomfortable place you can imagine. But no worries, Meg won't be offended. If she shows you their little house in the grounds you'll see the cozy retreat I escaped to whenever I could."

It wasn't a place Rhia could imagine a child growing up in. Not like Greywood Hall now was…and probably had been centuries before.

Once they deposited their suitcases and Luke gave her a very dispassionate whistle-stop tour of the whole house—all four wings built around a central patio courtyard—they settled in for coffee in the library. It was a grandiose room with an extensive mahogany desk and two high walls of books. The other two walls were crammed with photographs of people and places. Browsing around the framed photographic collection Rhia gasped as she made a more than interesting discovery.

"Luke!" She ran toward him, excitement moving her feet as she groped for his hand to drag him back to where she'd just been. "I can't credit this!"

Rhia was equally excited when Luke jumped up and twirled her around, crushing her close, showing his own thrill as he shouted, "*Incantevole… Bella*! My old Rhia's back!" His eager kiss told her just how pleased he was, but she pulled out of his clutches and dragged him to the photographs she'd been looking at.

"Have you ever looked at these, Luke?" she asked, tripping over her words she was so animated by her findings.

"According to my mother, they're family, friends, and business acquaintances," Luke's smile showed his delight in her enthusiasm.

"Is there some kind of record of who they might

be?" Rhia asked, wondering if he would think her question odd.

"Darn right there is!" Her answer was interrupted by a few more kisses: kisses Rhia responded to with mounting excitement. "My mother was a stickler for that sort of thing."

The twinkle in his eyes and his quirky smile meant he was dead set on teasing her. Rhia had seen that look plenty of times over the past almost-year! But she played his game, a little, for she needed answers. She allowed one more kiss then pulled away again.

"You're no fun, Rhia," Luke complained though she knew he wasn't serious. She held herself back from his questing lips and marauding fingers. "Okay." He smiled. "You win. For now."

He looked at the rows of photographs as though he needed to remind himself of the information she sought, then caught her unexpectedly around the waist and twirled her in circles. "The names, my darling dogged little terrier, are likely to all be on the back."

"On the back?" Rhia pointed to one particular photograph, blinking hard at his use of 'darling.' Usually endearments were in Italian. Quelling the flutter of hope his word stirred she made herself sound excited by her question. "Would you mind if we opened up this one to see who this woman is?" She indicated the Edwardian era sepia photograph.

When Luke removed the back clips of the expensive frame and extracted the picture he inhaled sharply. Jocasta Greywood.

"How on earth did you know?" he asked, "We've barely been in this room for ten minutes."

"Can't you see the likeness?" Rhia giggled at his amazement. "She looks like the woman on the horse in the dining room painting at Greywood Hall." Rhia chuckled again, amazed that a connection with

Greywood was so out in the open.

Luke slumped into a chair beside her, reverently holding the photograph.

"But my mother redecorated this whole library less than a year before she died. She had everything reframed, at vast expense, according to my father, who grumbled about the inconvenience at the time. The money for matching reframing was peanuts, but this room was always his sanctuary, his personal retreat. He hated anyone even in here to dust it when his paperwork was strewn all over that very desk."

"Is this your mother's writing or someone else's?" Rhia displayed the back of the photograph.

"Definitely my mother's," Luke confirmed, getting angrier as he worked through the implications. "But that would mean she was familiar with the name Jocasta Greywood. She must have known the Greywood Hall connection and never ever breathed a word of it."

Although Luke's mother had been an extremely organized person, on searching her personal domain in the mansion they found no trace of any important documents. There was no trace of her Birth Certificate or her Marriage Certificate. That seemed strange, even to Luke.

"My mother's lawyer must have had the originals, or at the very least, copies," he reasoned, "I never had anything to do with them when my mother's will was read."

"And your father's?"

"By the time my father died he'd removed all his personal documentation to Italy," Luke told her but together over the following two days they searched every wing of the house just in case.

Rhia set in motion an even more thorough search through the Australian Records system, much more detailed than she'd been able to access from England. She paged through local Church Parish registers, and other official sources, and had more success. It took three days of extensive searching to find the details of his mother's connections to Jocasta Greywood, during which time Luke went to the Brisbane office and caught up with business. Although she was again working herself to the bone, she was energized by the excitement of her findings. Her verve was back: Luke commented that he couldn't be more delighted.

Eventually what she found explained the mystery of Greywood Hall. "On arrival in Australia Jocasta Greywood was pregnant—father unknown—but she'd conceived during her sojourn in Italy," Rhia explained to Luke, showing him the evidence she'd printed.

"Why would she come to Australia?" Luke wanted to know.

Rhia's answer, she told him, was conjectural. "Maybe she was too embarrassed to return to Greywood Hall as an unmarried mother. Or perhaps the father was an Australian national and she'd followed him here."

Purely speculative reasons, with not a shred of evidence to confirm it.

"But look at this, Luke!" Rhia was once again beside herself, so excited with her sleuthing. He took the slip of paper she held out. "This is the Australian Records Department copy of the birth."

Luke was confused as he read it. "But this is for Alexander Low."

Rhia laughed at Luke's puzzled expression. "Yes, it is. And this is why I couldn't make the connection back in England, Luke. But don't worry, there's more to tell you—this isn't Alexander's original birth record."

Still an unmarried mother, Jocasta gave birth to an illegitimate son she named Alexander Grey

Wood, registering the name Wood for a surname.

"Why would she do that?" Luke asked.

"I'm guessing she was still mortified about giving an illegitimate son her proper name. Or, maybe it was a genuine mistake, as sometimes happened when registering births. Or, maybe because she was in a different country, she thought it might be easier to conceal it."

Archived local newspaper sources of the time confirmed that before her son Alexander was two years old Jocasta married a much older man named David Low. David Low was a manufacturing giant in Brisbane at the time; articles featured him and the family for many years after their marriage.

Rhia's searches had revealed that Alexander had been officially adopted after Jocasta's marriage to David Low, and his surname changed. She had uncovered those details from adoption records in Brisbane: records not available from England. A completely new birth certificate subsequently registered Low as his surname, the old one having been expunged from the official records.

Normal practice in the UK would have been to amend an original birth record with changed circumstances. Rhia had been, during her earliest searches at Greywood, working on the assumption that Australian documentation would have been similarly altered. Months before all she had been able to authenticate had been a birth record for an Alexander Low—not Greywood. Why a totally new certificate had been created and the first destroyed seemed highly irregular: but it answered the mystery.

Chapter Twenty-One

"This is why I couldn't work out the connections from England, Luke!" Rhia sounded both chuffed that she'd found the irrefutable proof and annoyed she'd not been able to access the details from Greywood Hall.

Since Jocasta and David had no other children, Alexander became the heir to David Low's engineering firm.

They could find nothing to prove David Low might, in fact, have been Alexander's biological father, but he certainly had brought the boy up as his own son.

In due time Alexander married. His wife gave birth to Luke's mother in 1935, their only child. They had called her Elizabeth Lucy Low.

"Lucy? I didn't know she had a middle name," Luke said. "Do you think that might have been a diminutive of Lucinda?"

"And Luke a sort of Greywood name?" Rhia added.

"No, I don't think so. Remember that my recorded birth name is the Italian Lucca, not Luke."

"But what's to say your mother didn't influence that choice? Maybe she wanted the closest Italian to a Greywood name."

It was good reasoning but unfortunately they'd never know.

Luke realized his mother must always have known the Greywood family history but chose not to tell him. But why? Maybe because Brisbane society did not tolerate infringements to normal patterns of behavior, and she had been such a stickler for social acceptance.

From another thorough search of his mother's wing of the mansion, they eventually found a letter that gave their theories credence. Tucked into a novel in the little bookcase in his mother's bedroom—it had remained unopened all these years—a lawyer's letter addressed to Lucca Salieri had been sent on behalf of Amelia Greywood of Greywood Hall in Yorkshire. It confirmed that Luke would inherit Greywood Hall when Amelia died. It was dated twelve years ago, just before he turned twenty-one.

"How could my mother not have told me about this, Rhia?"

She comforted him, her empathy unrestrained. It was only when Rhia asked Meg, the housekeeper, if she could add any details that other surprising revelations were made.

"It isn't good to speak ill of the dead," Meg reluctantly told her, "but I was the woman's housekeeper for twenty-five years before she dropped like a stone!"

Rhia related to Luke that Meg was disinclined to spill the beans but there were quite a few to spill.

It transpired that his mother died of a massive heart attack one week before Luke's twenty-first birthday. Elizabeth told neither Luke nor his father, that she'd had heart problems for some time before that. Meg had known but had been sworn to secrecy. On Elizabeth's death, his father discovered from the family doctor that she'd been taking medication for years, but against her doctor's advice had not eased her working day. The stress of running the engineering company she'd inherited from her father, and the construction company she'd established herself, had eventually killed her.

It was possible the lawyer's letter arrived just

before she died, and had been secreted among her possessions. Meg had no ideas as to why it was tucked inside the book, saying that all she'd done at the time was tidy away any items that had been lying around his mother's rooms. The letter certainly hadn't been opened. Maybe Elizabeth planned to tell him but never got the chance? Luke would never know.

"I'm wondering why your father never went through her things and found this?" Rhia ventured, very carefully.

"He didn't do anything at all with any of her things." Luke's tone was as flat as a pancake. "Remember they lived in their different wings of the house and the saying never the twain shall meet was the daily norm."

"Surely he must have done something with her things."

Luke's sarcastic laugh hurt Rhia, though he didn't mean to. "You must be joking! After my mother's death he couldn't sell up his Australian based Import and Export business quick enough. Within five weeks he went back to Italy to stay with his brother Stefano before he bought a house for himself. He never returned to Australia; he died later that same year in a freak alpine avalanche while skiing."

Rhia seemed astounded. "He just up and left you in Australia?"

"At twenty-one I was old enough to make my own way in the world, Rhia," was his cynical reply. "I had inherited my mother's businesses and was rolling in money. It would have been far too late for him to have been any kind of father to me."

Luke had never needed Rhia more. Uncovering the illegitimate skeleton in his family cupboard had been more devastating than he bargained for. He now knew he wasn't the illegitimate one but the repercussions had still affected him down the line.

Rhia talked him through the issues confronting him.

"If I'd known, ten years ago I could have done something for Amelia Greywood!" Luke ranted in his anger and sorrow. "I could have visited her, got to know her. Hell, I could even have started renovations on Greywood Hall at that time. The only business I retained in Australia was mother's construction company. The increased revenues were skyrocketing at that time."

"Maybe your mother was waiting till you reached twenty-one to tell you, but by then it was too late. Maybe she didn't think you were ready to handle the issue of Greywood properly before then."

"Before then?" Luke laughed, a harsh, bitter uncompromising laugh. "In her eyes I would never be ready."

Rhia tightened her grip on him, soothing his back with loving touches.

He said his mother had given him an ultimatum when he was only seventeen. Elizabeth declared that to date she'd provided him with the very best English education he could ever have, and it was her intention to continue that through to university level, but that he'd also need to learn what it was to be a part of her business. What followed had been the most difficult years of his life. Having been brought up with the expectations of a privileged background, his mother then made him start from grass roots in her construction business. During every vacation he worked at the most menial of manual labor before moving up to managerial tasks.

"She was right in her own way." Luke's laugh was sardonic. "By the age of twenty-one I knew what a day's work meant. And that work ethic has remained in me."

"Surely that was a good thing, Luke?" Rhia

reasoned, knowing his memories were still bitter.

"You'd think so!" A harsh snort accompanied the rake of his fingers though his hair as he paced about. "Yet in my mother's eyes I still never made the grade."

Rhia had the temerity to intervene at one point to ask, "Did your father ever have a say in what you were doing?"

Luke's grunt was sarcastic. "Not so much as I noticed. He was never interested in what I did, and never seemed inclined to interfere if it meant challenging my mother's plans. He never ever rocked her boat."

Luke then recalled his twenty-first birthday gift from his parents. "They sent me to America for two months before that. No construction work was expected overseas, just a jaunt so I could become familiar with some US cities like New York, San Francisco, and what comes in between. I was in San Francisco when my father's message reached me to say my mother had had a heart attack."

He clutched Rhia while he struggled with his emotions. "The heart attack was massive, so naturally she was long dead before I could get back to Brisbane. She was such a cold-hearted bitch. Not loving like you," Luke wailed. "Things like illegitimacy mattered to her but this with Amelia Greywood was beyond the pale. Why did she leave an old lady without the relatives she needed in her old age? Amelia was in the nursing home. My mother and father were cold people, Rhia."

"Luke you're so easy to love, they must have loved you."

"No. They never should have had a child. I was a mistake."

Rhia was so shocked…and troubled. He felt her shivering in his arms.

"They tolerated me. They did their duty, raising

me. Then went their own ways. It was an effort for them to even be at home for Christmas dinner." Luke was on a roll. "Look at this magnificent house, Rhia. What do you honestly see here?"

He knew it was difficult for Rhia to answer truthfully.

"It's a beautiful place Luke, but I wouldn't have wanted to live here as a child."

"It's a cold monument to gracious living. That's all my mother was interested in. She spent as little time here as necessary yet do you realize this was her own parents' home? This mausoleum was also where she was brought up!"

What could Rhia add to something that was testimony in itself? He didn't expect any answer, he just loved the empathy she radiated, as she listened to his rants.

"I will never ever do that to a child. And that's why I'll never have one." Luke stomped out of the room.

Much later that night Luke found Rhia fast asleep in one of the guest rooms. She'd chosen the one wing never occupied by anyone in the family. She was curled up, clutching a pillow to her chest, the streaks of tears still visible on her cheeks. Luke was devastated. How could he have done this to the one person who mattered most to him in his entire life? She did. He understood then that no one in his past had ever mattered like Rhia.

She stirred, aware of his presence coming into the room. Before she could utter a word, Luke gathered her to him in a crushing embrace.

"Rhia, please forgive me." His voice broke on the last word, as his lips sought the comfort and solace of hers. "I never meant you to cry over me. I love you," he whispered, his voice breaking with remorse, "I'm sorry if I hurt you. You are everything to me. I can't wait any longer to tell you I love you. I don't want the year to end. I want you to be my wife well beyond the year."

"I can't, Luke," she whimpered, her still-sleepy eyes brimming with even more tears, her voice ragged with despair. "I can't be the wife you want."

Luke was devastated. She didn't want him?

"I'm not going to let you go. I won't give you a divorce at the end of the year." Luke was adamant, grasping her close to him.

Rhia struggled out of his embrace and wriggled off the bed, her cries hysterical. "No. No, Luke! You have to divorce me." Her eyes were wretched, huge brown eyes full of agony, her lips quivering and her hands pushing him away from her. "I won't trap you into marriage. You'll hate our child and then you'll hate me too." Rhia was inconsolable as she ran from the room.

Luke sprinted after her into the hallway and halted her frantic flight. "Our child?" he gasped. "What do you mean, our child?"

"I'm pregnant and…you don't want any children, but I won't give up our baby." Rhia's words were nearly indistinguishable among her sobs. "I don't care how you feel, but I'm keeping this tiny part of you after our agreement is over."

Luke pulled her down to the carpet and cradled her in his arms.

"You're having my baby?" His voice was a whispered incredulity.

Rhia sobbed even harder. "I know how you feel about being a father, about what your parent's did to you Luke, but this child will be something to remind me of you after our contract is over. I will give it all the love it needs because it will remind me of how loving you can be. You can't take it from me, but I can't have it and be your wife too. Although I love you more than life itself. You have to divorce me!"

Luke scooped Rhia into his lap. "I'll be damned

if I'll divorce you!" He peppered her tear-drenched eyes. "I'm going to tell you something that will probably shock you." His ear-to-ear smile was all for her. "Do you remember the first time we made love without a condom?"

Rhia nodded as her sobs lessened.

"When I slid into you and couldn't move?" Luke trapped her lips between his, capturing her in a kiss of sheer longing, eventually breaking off to continue, "In my mind I was consciously spilling my seed into a woman for the first time. I wanted to make you pregnant. Only you. Never ever had that feeling occurred before. I wanted to impregnate you, to have a child that was a part of both of us."

"You did?"

"It shocked the hell out of me." Luke kissed Rhia tenderly again. "I froze when it struck me that although it was the first time I'd not purposely used protection it was a futile gesture because you were on the pill. I loved the thought of making love to you, knowing I could give you a child, for you're nothing like my mother."

"And you're nothing like your father," Rhia added.

"I want to have my child with you, Rhia. I love living at Greywood Hall with you, and I've proved I can make it my main base."

Luke drew them both up onto their knees, and holding her hands in his he kissed her knuckles, one after the other. "Rhia, will you marry me?"

"But we are married."

"Forget that. Will you marry me for real? I want you to be my wife forever, the real wife of my heart, and not a stupid contract. I want us to have a proper wedding and show you off to the world as the wife of my soul."

Some time later, Rhia managed to persuade Luke that most other people thought they were a loving couple and that they'd be confused by another wedding.

"Luke?" Rhia asked as they lay satiated. Her voice was still troubled as were her eyes. "I can't go on with any of these wonderful future plans without telling you what Meg also said. Your mother had a miscarriage…around four months after she and your father got married."

"And?" Luke knew what came next would be shocking.

"The fetus was about seven months old…a female child." Rhia's breath hitched before she continued. "I've found a hospital reference to back this up."

"So you're thinking that my father got my mother pregnant and felt he had to marry her?"

That made their whole, cold marriage a more realistic possibility.

"Yes," Rhia answered. "But that's not the most difficult thing to tell you. Meg was really at pains to tell me she honestly wasn't gossiping and that she doesn't ever want to hurt you."

"But…" Luke smoothed his fingertips across Rhia's tense brow.

"Meg was distraught when she told me these things, Luke. She hated keeping them secret for so long and she's desperate that you don't ever think badly of her!"

"How can she ever think that?" Luke cried. "She was always my rock."

Rhia's eyes sought his before she continued, "Meg's words were…Elizabeth preferred the company of women. It seems it wasn't possible for Meg not to know that some of your mother's female guests were also your mother's…lovers!"

"*Dio*!" Luke shot out of the bed so fast he dragged the sheet with him and left Rhia bare.

"I'm so sorry!" Rhia cried following him and

throwing her arms around his waist. "I don't mean to hurt you, but it might explain why she didn't seem to love you, Luke."

"Good God! I must have been a mistake then!"

Rhia continued, stroking his back. "Meg thinks your mother tried to sublimate her sexuality and forced herself into a relationship with a man. It seems she got pregnant almost immediately. They got married but later on Elizabeth miscarried. According to Meg, they always had separate bedrooms, even right after the wedding. She doesn't think they ever slept together till they conceived you…again a time when Meg thinks your mother deliberately seduced your father into going along with her plan of trying for another child."

"So you're saying I wasn't quite a mistake?"

"I don't think so…" Rhia still sounded hesitant.

"Not a mistake then but, knowing my mother, I was the thing that would have gained her credibility in Brisbane society, for having done her duty she could then have lesbian affairs as much as she liked!"

What had his father been thinking?

"Meg reckons that your father did love your mother at first, or at least the woman he thought she was. Meg thinks he eventually realized Elizabeth couldn't love him as a woman should, but he wouldn't divorce her after your birth, since you were his legitimate son."

"And Italians didn't do divorce!" Luke laughed a tense, hurt laugh. "But he couldn't love me?"

Anguish flit across Rhia's face as she answered, "No. It seems he just couldn't quite manage to love you. Or at least he couldn't show it."

"And my mother?"

Again Rhia's face clouded. "Meg thinks if you'd been a girl, like her first baby, Elizabeth might have loved you—or at least liked you."

"But I was the wrong sex!"

The letter from Amelia Greywood's lawyer arrived the day after their year of cohabitation was completed. It confirmed that Greywood Hall had officially passed into Luke's ownership. It was accompanied by another letter from Amelia herself, written after her latest will revisions, less than a year before her death. In it she explained that her expectation was that Luke would love living in a restored Greywood Hall with the woman of his dreams. Luke slowly read out the letter to Rhia.

"I also apologize, Luke, for any serious inconvenience I caused when you made your decision. I knew from my very clever private detective that your finances were in good shape. Perfectly sound enough for you to restore Greywood to the splendor it used to be. You were at liberty to walk away, of course, and leave Greywood to rot…but I hoped you wouldn't do that.

"My greatest wish was that you didn't sell the property without having had the opportunity to experience the pleasures that could be had from it. I knew you'd had many women friends over the years but had not yet settled on one particular woman. If you're reading this letter after the property is legally yours I do hope the woman you married is the perfect woman, with whom you want to be for the rest of your life. I have never personally been able to fill Greywood with my own spouse and children but it would please me greatly to know that you will."

They read on that in including the matrimony clause, her intention was meant to be a nudge in the direction of him settling down and staying in one place, specifically at her beloved Greywood. She also wrote that she couldn't ever countenance selling it because she couldn't bear to have it go out of the family connection, even though Luke was the one and only very remote link.

Amelia finished the letter more tentatively. Luke read, "My sources showed me that your parents' marriage was perhaps not particularly successful, and I wept for the lonely boy I know you must have been, Luke. But when you were younger it was not my place to intervene. It was your mother who chose not to continue contact with me."

They both gasped a little at that before Luke read on. "You may be surprised to know I met you once when you were only weeks old, but your mother decided at that time that she didn't want any further communication with me. I think she was ashamed that Greywood Hall had sunk to such low depths and that the coffers were bare. She was also extremely upset when I informed her that her father had been born illegitimate, as was I myself. She wanted no one to ever know about those social infringements."

"Oh, my God, Luke!" Rhia cried, "Poor Amelia. I think your mother must have hurt her very badly."

Luke paced around, the letter crumpled in his hand. "I know how hurtful my mother would have been. She rarely minced her words and I'm sure Amelia heard a virulent mouthful."

He gathered Rhia in his arms and rested their foreheads together, a place he always found comforting. "She was such a cold-hearted bitch!"

A few moments later they resumed reading the letter. Amelia had written that she'd had irregular communication with her aunt Jocasta when she was in her twenties, her aunt having re-established the link. But she'd had virtually no communication with Alexander, who had wanted to sever all connections with his English heritage. Amelia had one hurtful letter from Alexander, who'd been made aware of the lack of money at Greywood Hall and wrote back to her one time only, saying there was no way he would be shackled with that "white elephant back in

England."

Amelia finished her letter with a heartfelt plea. "Please forgive me for meddling in your life and accept my sincerest wishes for your future."

"Oh, Luke! That is so sad." Rhia cried on Luke's shoulder.

On the trip back to England they'd made excited plans for the celebratory party Rhia had outlined so many months before. Although it was short notice for such a spectacular event, Greywood Hall was completed. All they had to do was make it happen—not such a problem as Rhia, in her enthusiasm way back then, had sketched out the planning details for a grand period dress reception.

It happened one month after Luke became the official owner of Greywood Hall.

In the end, Rhia compromised on the new wedding by having a ceremony in the restored gardens at Greywood Hall, where they retook their vows in earnest—having written their own and recited a short time before the bulk of the guests arrived. Those attending the ceremony were the most important of their friends and acquaintances. Luke was prepared to swallow his earlier jealousy when Rhia was given away by her good friend Gus. Her father and family attended as important guests.

Rhia wore a frothy white confection that made her look like his nymph of the woods. They'd chosen it together just like he'd envisioned so many months before. It matched Luke's idea of what his bride should wear, albeit she was much fatter around the waist. Rhia was happy to compromise since his delight was all the reward she needed!

When the throng eventually departed, Luke whisked an exhausted Rhia back to their bedroom where he made a farcical event out of removing her clothes.

"You are so gorgeous, my darling wife, but I

have to take off that spectacular costume." In between lust filled kisses he explained, "A very long, long time ago, *cara mia*, I imagined my bride—you—in a dress like this one, and I imagined even more what you had underneath it…to remove kiss by kiss."

Luke was delighted to find that although Rhia's pregnancy was advancing very healthily she had worn the garter belt, the gossamer sheer white stockings, and the white silky lingerie—the removal of which he negotiated with dramatic panache. Unfortunately the sexy spiky heels had been replaced by ones more suited to a pregnant lady.

Some time later, and having found yet another method of overcoming Rhia's advancing bulk, Luke kissed her soundly and declared, "I love you, Rhia. I love everything about you."

Rhia gurgled into his neck, "You liar! I'm a big fat flab now!"

"Yes!" Luke agreed, grinning like a Cheshire cat, "But you're my big fat flab. And with you by my side we'll put the life back into Greywood that Amelia craved." His promise was followed by actions. He kissed Rhia senseless.

Rhia's replies were muffled under his loving lips. "Along with our children."

"Children?" Luke mumbled, backing Rhia down onto the bed again, "I like the sound of that. When can we start on number two?"

A word about the author...

Nancy Jardine writes contemporary and historical romances and is also currently writing fiction for children. Nancy has always loved words. Reading them, writing them—and even handling them. Coincidentally jobs over the years have always had something to do with words. A vacation job in a publishing firm dispatching orders to bookstores was often sheer torture because there was no time to read the books. That ten-minute coffee break was not nearly long enough! Clerking in a bookstore gave her the opportunity to sell some heavier tomes, but her main career has been teaching 7th graders for many years. Now Nancy only teaches part-time to give her lots more hours to devote to writing.

When not reading or writing Nancy loves to try out exciting experiences she's never tried before, especially enjoying them when they become extended family fun weekends. Her two grownup daughters (and sons-in-law) are great at egging her on!

Thank you for purchasing
this Wild Rose Press publication.
For other wonderful stories of romance,
please visit our on-line bookstore at
www.thewildrosepress.com.

For questions or more information
contact us at
info@thewildrosepress.com.

The Wild Rose Press
www.TheWildRosePress.com

To visit with authors of The Wild Rose Press
join our yahoo loop at
http://groups.yahoo.com/group/thewildrosepress/

Lightning Source UK Ltd.
Milton Keynes UK

177896UK00001B/1/P

9 781601 549655